SHADOWS OF EDEN

SHADOWS
OF EDEN

TIMOTHY F. BONE

Bonneville
Springville, Utah

© 2009 Timothy F. Bone

The views expressed within this work are the sole responsibility of the author and do not necessarily reflect the position of Cedar Fort, Inc., or any other entity.

This is a work of fiction. The characters, names, incidents, places, and dialogue are products of the author's imagination, and are not to be construed as real.

ISBN 13: 978-1-59955-268-2

Published by Bonneville, an imprint of Cedar Fort, Inc., 2373 W. 700 S., Springville, UT 84663
Distributed by Cedar Fort, Inc., www.cedarfort.com

LIBRARY OF CONGRESS CATALOGING-IN-PUBLICATION DATA

Bone, Timothy.
  In the shadows of Eden / Timothy Bone.
    p. cm.
  ISBN 978-1-59955-268-2 (acid-free paper)
  1. College teachers--Fiction. 2. Missing persons--Fiction. 3.
Motels--Fiction. 4. Private investigators--Fiction. 5. Fathers and
daughters--Fiction. I. Title.
  PS3602.O6571515 2009
  813'.6--dc22

                        2009009887

Cover design by Angela D. Olsen
Cover design © 2009 by Lyle Mortimer
Edited and typeset by Melissa J. Caldwell

Printed in the United States of America

10 9 8 7 6 5 4 3 2 1

Printed on acid-free paper

To my wonderful wife, LeeAnn,
who moved a dreamer to action

This is not the traditional benign universe of conventional religiosity in the West, constructed for the benefit of living and especially of human beings. Indeed, the very scale of the universe—more than a million billion galaxies, each containing more than a million billion stars—speaks to us of the inconsequentiality of human events in the cosmic context.

— Carl Sagan, *Broca's Brain*

Are not two sparrows sold for a farthing? and one of them shall not fall on the ground without your Father [knowing]. But the very hairs of your head are [all] numbered.

— Matthew 10:29–30

preface

Like a steel needle in the back of his brain.

Not disarmingly painful but persistent, pricking his every thought. Anxiety? Apprehension? Surely not fear! It was tough to put a name to, impossible to locate an immediate cause. But something was out there, beyond his vision, a dark planet pulling at him.

It was true that things had not ended well. He could admit it. He could be honest, when it paid him to be. But you can't foresee everything. Brigitte, for instance. Where had she found the strength? The woman had been practically embalmed, for heaven's sake.

So he had had to tidy up after her, too. Only a short time before that it had been the mess left by Ulrich. Ulrich—there was another one for you. They wouldn't even be in this jam had Ulrich controlled himself. Ulrich and his women and ever an eye peeled for a new one. What had it gotten him?

No matter. He had mopped up after Ulrich (and was out of pocket a pretty penny for it) and he had mopped up after Brigitte. He'd made only one mistake, one uncharacteristic for him, but he had been distracted. So now one final clean-up job that should have been taken care of but had to be tackled now.

He smiled; lately he was as much janitor as he was scientist. Good to have something to fall back on!

And it was all so unnecessary. The Project had been a success. Not likely to be written up for peer review but an achievement nonetheless. All each of them had to do was keep quiet, keep his head. There was no evidence—well, only the one thing, but it would take them all down and so, like a warhead, couldn't be used—and there were no leads, at least none he could think of, and he was confident he had thought of everything. Even if caught up in an exploratory net with others—and it would have to be a pretty big net—they would not stand out and so be returned to the sea. What could be proved?

He could control Karol. The other one wanted watching, but surely self-preservation would win out. If not, well, the bucket and mop. Fortunately, he was a man who was prepared to do whatever it takes.

And yet, the needle.

one

Boston Harbor had once been seawater, but the liquid that now slurped at the rocks below us was a fraction slower than brine, and it fought the tides. The collection basin for two rivers that flush past homes, cheating industries, and the esoteric experiments of five universities, the Harbor has become a stewpot for every element on the Periodic Table. Commercial fisherman have adapted and now pull forth the *frutti di mari* with powerful magnets. Anywhere else, an environmental perversion of this magnitude would elicit civic embarrassment, but this is Boston and Boston defends its own, the just and the unjust, to the death.

An appropriate setting, then, for a meeting of two men who have chosen, or perhaps were called, to peer into murky lives.

It was a week after Thanksgiving and a month away from the new millennium, its secular manifestation at any rate. Frank and I were downtown, standing at the end of Long Wharf. He was hunched over the railing, gazing across an undulating fun-house mirror to East Boston and a skyline of cranes and rubble, the perpetual construction project that is Logan Airport. I had my back to the rail, facing into the heart of the city and the gray piles of progress thrown up on this side by the Big Dig, a decade-long Pharaoh's dream designed to bury the three miles of I-93 along the waterfront. The sky was a hard gray as well and though it hadn't begun raining everything had already given up, already looked wet.

In blue slacks, blue shirt and tie, and black leather jacket, I had fought the chill to a draw. Frank was contesting the end of autumn with dark brown slacks, a navy blazer, blue shirt, and a solid brown necktie.

Frank is Lieutenant Detective Francis Connor Kilcannon, a homicide cop out of District D-14, the western frontier of Boston comprising Allston and Brighton, decaying neighborhoods lying between Boston University and Boston College and densely packed with college students and immigrants.

His call had come shortly after the Del Price Agency had shooed away its only petitioner for the day. Jerome was a nervous little guy from Revere with a fleeing hairline, pinched face, and a rehearsed tale of woe and betrayal that had all the traction of new soles on wet cobblestones. He was oblique about it, but what he wanted was someone to break into an ex-girlfriend's apartment and retrieve a painting he claimed was his. In his late twenties, five-seven, and maybe one-sixty, he was a couple of years younger, a half-foot shorter, and fifty pounds lighter than me. He had dressed to impress—khaki chinos, an alligator belt, blue-striped Oxford and navy club tie, lacking only a monocle—but remained a tough sell as either a collector of art or a collector of women who collect art. I had, in any event, consulted my lists of Things I Do and Things I Don't and eventually located art heists on the latter. So out the door he went with my opinion (free of charge) that breaking into people's apartments to take things was both wrong and illegal and that his problem was best given over to an attorney, concepts as incomprehensible to him as the Nicene Creed.

Kilcannon is in his early fifties and a solid five-foot-ten with a nice head of hair, coarse and wavy. What sets Frank apart is his face. Not the eyes. He has the eyes of a cop—knowing, skeptical though not unsympathetic—eyes that see everything and behind them a brain to store it all away and retrieve it at will. I've seen Frank come up with the name and address of someone he had questioned fifteen years before, a guy he'd run across only that one time. If that cadre of white lab coats and clipboards from a leading university wants to research brain function, it's cops they should wire up.

Not the eyes, then, but the face they're plugged into. Sharp lines, sharp features, high forehead, a prominent nose, full but clearly defined lips, slightly crooked teeth. A softening of his gaze and what you'd have is Father Kilcannon, a prince in the City of God rather than its mortal subversion. After I'd known him a while, he told me he had once considered taking Holy Orders but didn't say what had dissuaded him. He had married, but that apparently happened after he joined the force. He still attends Mass weekly. Perhaps, like me, he is perplexed by the attraction of self-destruction. There are those who, facing a hundred and fifteen opportunities to choose right over wrong, go zero for one-fifteen.

Why?

It was noon but he had nothing with him, so had either finished lunch or hadn't started. Maybe gum was lunch. He may have smoked once and so exchanged habits—I don't know—but he was always chewing gum, rotating between the different mint flavors.

"Thanks for coming down," he said.

Kilcannon speaks with a Boston accent but doesn't affect an Irish brogue. I like to imagine him, though, pushing up the brim of a police hat and saying things like, "*It's off to the hoosegow with you, me boy!*"

"You're lucky I was able to squeeze you in," I replied.

Kilcannon looked down, shook his head, and grunted. He grunts once in place of laughter. I'm not sure what sound he makes when he just wants to grunt.

"Tell me again why you keep an office?" he asked.

"Classic Marxist theory requires me to own property on which I can oppress workers." He knows I have only one full-time employee, and she oppresses me.

More head shaking. "The funny Mormon. You must really have it socked away."

"Enough and to spare," I replied. We'd been over this.

"Yeah, the gentleman detective."

He fell silent for a few moments and then turned towards me.

"My cousin's husband seems to have taken a breeze."

"Do you know them very well?"

"Not really. Weddings and wakes, that sort of thing. Lorraine is my second cousin once removed."

Being Irish, precision in genealogy is important to Frank. I could probably call someone in Salt Lake and get a five-generation family tree to him inside ten days. Perhaps as a Christmas present then.

He was back out on the horizon. "Kooyman. Larry and Lorraine Kooyman." He pronounced it *Coyman*, but explained it was spelled in the Dutch manner. "Larry is a professor at Harvard. Genetics. Does cancer research. Lorraine is his second wife. He has a daughter from the first marriage. Lorraine called me this morning. She thinks something's happened to Larry. Hasn't seen or heard from him since he left for the lab yesterday. When he wasn't home by nine o'clock last night, she drove up to Longwood and found his car still parked there. Didn't find *him*, though."

He faced me again. "Here's the thing—when the department office manager opened the store this morning, no car. Gone. No one in his lab or the department has seen him since lunch time yesterday. That was it. Poof. Except for the car, which went poof later. Lorraine called me after she found out about the car, and I stopped by her house. She's not the panicky type, but she's on edge."

"I can imagine."

"I went through the usual stuff when someone hasn't been gone long. Lorraine had already called the hospitals, but nothing. I told her I'd call around as well and check accident reports. Maybe he got knocked out during a mugging and was left without ID. Who knows? Also homicides, but I didn't mention that. I put the car and plate out there. It all comes up blank so far. I also told her I knew someone who could help out."

He didn't have to explain that this was well under the radar for the police. Already overburdened with teenaged runaways who, if found, could be leveraged about as minors, adults were presumed, justifiably in most cases, to have taken off under their own steam and with no legal way to force a return. Except with proof of kidnapping, the police aren't ordinarily going to direct much firepower at adult disappearances. Having an in with the police would help but only to a point. The good news was that in these cases the police were generally happy to share whatever they had with private detectives because we wouldn't be stepping on their toes.

"I'll go talk to her," I said. "At least the trail isn't cold. What are your feelings about this?"

He shrugged. "I don't know. I don't know what to think. He seems like a real decent sort. I have no reason to think that the marriage is on the rocks. Lorraine doesn't think he was especially worried about anything. As far as she can tell, his stuff is still at home, but I'm not sure how many drawers she's pulled open or whether anything less obvious is gone. Like money."

"Where do they live?"

"West Roxbury."

A neighborhood of shade trees and well-groomed homes to the southwest. I would have to return to my office for my car. In a city where a handful of wet spaghetti thrown against a wall describes the downtown traffic pattern, you park at the periphery and work your way in on public transport, rickshaw, elephant, whatever you can find.

"Okay," I said. "Let me have the address and phone number. I'll call Marjorie and get the ball rolling."

We shook hands.

"Thanks, Del," he said.

Poof—and a husband vanishes. No clues, no leads.

Well, I had the time. I had already chased off one guy. No insurance claims to investigate, no subpoenas to serve, no runaways or parent-kidnapped kids to track down. I don't provide muscle or, I was gratified to learn, steal art treasures. In fact, I'm well set up with inherited money, so I don't have to do a lot of anything.

So what *do* I do?

Like Frank, I study the mortal moment but from a different angle and with less public oversight. I investigate the lives of people in trouble, helping where I can but finding too often that what's obvious to me is a tough sell to them. I want to know why, when the freight train to misery rolls by, so many come running, throwing themselves into a boxcar—spiritual hobos. I consider the only thing people take away from this life and the beads for which too many trade it away.

Del Price, detective of the soul.

I investigate sin.

two

My office is in a corner building on Beacon, about halfway between Kenmore Square and St. Mary's Street. I got off the T at the latter, choosing a slightly more (95 percent urban blight vs. 96) inspiring walk. This is not the Beacon Street of the Brahmins, downtown in the heart of history, but its final, tired limp out of Boston and into the city of Brookline. Each side of the street mirrors the other: faded red brick, four-story apartment buildings that scream asbestos, each flush against the next. No black shutters and white trim here; the knee-high balustrades along the roofline and other grudging architectural afterthoughts are cement, as are the stairways spaced every fifteen feet along the block. The only relief from this urban solemnitude comes spring and summer from spindly curbside maples that now stood as splayed gray skeletons.

My minions barely reacted as I stepped through the office door. To the right and angled to face the door was the desk of my office czar, Internet seer, and a former stay-at-home mom, Marjorie Green. She doesn't like to be called Margie. Marge is also out; I have never heard anyone even attempt it. Sister Green is fifty, a neat, sharp-edged fifty with dark, perky hair and perfect vision. An audience of family photos faced her on the desktop. Of four children, the three oldest are married. The youngest, nineteen-year old Naomi, has thrown in her lot with Nihilist Youth and with it the body piercings, tattoos, and black uniform with its needless steel buckles, loops, and chains, as well as headphones that dispense a round-the-clock volume 10 sonic lobotomy. She is angry because her mother works for a private detective who can always find her and even angrier at the guilt that sticks like tar at the edges of her mind. It was the Church's fault, of course. We were waiting for Naomi to come to herself or hit bottom, praying for the former. One half of Marjorie's brain is wholly given over to her daughter; the other half is for everything else. *"Any news of Naomi?"* I'd ask. *"No change,"* her mother would say, as though reporting on a coma patient.

Marjorie harvests the staff of modern life—information. I do fine on the Internet, but Marjorie goes at it like she's running a child molester to ground. If you were to put your hand between the monitor and her face you'd pull back seared flesh. Right now, though, she was reading *People*. I suspected that it had been ready at hand, awaiting my arrival.

"Thanks for helping to maintain our professional office image, Marjorie."

"In the unlikely event of another client, I'll throw it across the room and sit up straight," she replied. With this job Marjorie had discovered and then liberated a dormant sassy self and was feeding it vitamins. I was hoping she was working up to this sort of patter at Sunday school.

On the other side of the room, on our unusually comfortable sofa, sat Karen O'Donnell, who showed no interest in intercepting magazines in flight. She was doing cross-stitch, likely for an expected grandchild. Karen is one of several part-timers I employ, whose job it is to sit on the unusually comfortable sofa and build up Social Security credit. I do this not because Marjorie and I are likely to blow a gasket but because as Mormons we seek to increase decorum in a lax world and so avoid even the appearance of impropriety. As another benefit to me, my assistants often bring cookies.

"This is where I shout, *'Report, staff!'*" I announced.

No one jumped. Marjorie slowly straightened her chair, put down the magazine, and picked up a neat stack of papers from her desk.

"Well," she began, "this whole genetics thing is pretty complicated."

"I bet."

"No, I mean the organizational part of it. There are all these interconnected departments and institutes. It's going to take a while to fit them together. There's a Department of Molecular and Cellular Biology as well as a Department of—uh, I've got to say this carefully"—Karen laughed—"Organismic and Evolutionary Biology."

"*Organismic?*" I asked. "You've gotta be kidding. There *is* such a word?"

"There is at Harvard."

Not wholly authoritative, but I shook my head and let it pass. It sounded like Resume English. Why not just call it the Department of Evolutionary Biology?

"Okay," I said, "so Larry Kooyman is in there somewhere?"

"No, I'm just giving you an overview. Both of these departments are part of the Graduate School of Arts and Sciences at the campus in Cambridge. Dr. Kooyman is at the Medical School, in the Department of Genetics."

"Over here at Longwood?"

"Yep."

That's what Frank had said. It was good news for me; the Longwood Medical Center, a densely packed triangle of hospitals and labs that included the Harvard Medical School, was less than a mile away. Like the airport it was a never-ending building project and, as such, another traffic and parking purgatory.

"Now the medical school," Marjorie continued, "is also divided into all kinds of sub-units. There's a Department of Genetics but also a Department of Microbiology and *Molecular* Genetics. Then there's a Howard Hughes Medical Institute that does genetic research and an interdepartmental Biological and Biomedical Sciences Program. There's also a new thing, the Institute of Human Genetics, which looks like an attempt to put an umbrella over all of this."

"You through?" I asked.

"Nope." She had paced herself for dramatic effect. "There's *also* something called the Bauer Center for Genomics Research. I haven't figured out yet how it fits in."

"No wonder the guy's missing—he's lost in an org chart. I'll have to go in wearing a pith helmet."

Karen and Marjorie laughed.

A thought struck me. "I suppose all these organizations have acronyms as well." The thorns of language.

"Oh, yes," Marjorie cheerfully confirmed. "The HHMI, the BBS, the HMS, you name it. The Harvard website even has a glossary of all its acronyms."

"Beautiful." World language is reverting to Hebrew.

"Here's a photo and faculty bio of Dr. Kooyman,"

She handed me two prints from the website. I regarded the pleasant countenance of Lawrence Kooyman, MD, PhD. He appeared to be in his sixties, round face, thinning hair. He looked like the help you'd find at a garden center. Kooyman had gotten an MD at Boston University and then a doctorate in genetics from Harvard. When had Watson and Crick done their double helix stuff, I wondered? Back there sometime. Perhaps he had been inspired, there at the dawn of a new age. In any event, he now headed a little kingdom called the Kooyman Lab.

"Thanks, Marjorie," I said. "I'm heading down to West Roxbury to see Mrs. Kooyman. Can you stay here in the office until four or so? Depending on what I find I may need more information about his work. I want to drop by Longwood, too, before everyone there leaves. Karen, you may leave whenever you like; I don't plan on coming back today."

I went into my private office and exchanged the leather jacket for a navy sports coat, sending skyward a silent petition that I would find Dr. Kooyman and that the journey would prove to be neither long nor dark. At that moment there was a muffled whoosh outside as the weather front arrived and with it a hard splattering against the window.

Not the answer to prayer I was looking for.

I grabbed a raincoat on the way out.

three

Lorraine Kooyman shook her head firmly.

"No, Mr. Price, Larry doesn't chase women. That's never been a problem. He's a good husband." The way she said it covered a lot of ground but even then, fearing she may have shortchanged the guy and it would get back to him, she added, "A wonderful husband."

We were in Dr. Kooyman's study, a comfortable, converted den in their handsome colonial on a quiet side street of West Roxbury.

We had started off in a room of an entirely different order. The living room was a sterile tableau of pale walls, plush gray carpet, sofa and chairs padded in a demure floral print, and glowing tables with curvy legs that supported gilded, sculptured lamps. A space peculiar to the American middle and upper-middle classes, it was a living room in which very little living ever takes place. I had distrusted the room immediately, sensing a misanthropy that would soon be directed against us, sapping our will to live, and I had suggested a change.

In fawn slacks and a sky-blue blouse, Mrs. Kooyman was happily less formal, less studied, than her showpiece salon. A few years younger than her husband, she displayed no sharp angles or abrupt curves from genes or exercise, nothing immoderate or out of proportion. She was attractive without having to outwit her face to achieve it. Short brown hair with a wave framed dark brown eyes and strong brows. The lenses of her eyeglasses were large and set in pale pink rims. Her lips were thin and, by my reading of the lines around them, given to smiling. She was the kind of woman many a man ought to have married in the first place and then stayed married to. But now,

10

her tired eyes confirmed sleeplessness and darkness lay across her countenance, a shadow I see regularly in the faces of parents with lost children.

Suspense is an exquisite torment, an insidious statistical exercise. Lorraine Kooyman was draining herself living in two worlds simultaneously: the everyday one that strikes the retina and now another one as well, a parallel prison planet without clear horizons or graspable coordinates wherein her husband was trapped, a world where Larry Kooyman could be seen only in his wife's inner vision in scenario after scenario of peril, movie clips continually rewound, re-edited with new details, and then run forward again, over and over.

She was perched on the edge of a love seat that hadn't made the cut for the living room. I was leaning back against the edge of her husband's bulky oak desk. I had been gently bracing her for what she could expect from Frank's police colleagues, should they become involved. In their experience, most adults who disappear do so according to a plan, even if it's a dopey one. They don't *want* to be found. And so I had tossed her a few balls—gambling debts, a boat in a sunset lagoon, the sultry siren—and had had them firmly swatted back.

"Larry has *never* just gone off like this before," she continued. "He has to fly to research conferences every so often, but they're all planned by the school. It just doesn't make any sense. Something has happened to him. I just know it. No one at the lab has seen him since noon yesterday. *Since noon!* His car was there last night and now it's *gone.*"

Her distress was evident and sincere. She was getting wound up but wasn't sure how to release the coiled energy. Doubtless she had been on a continual walking tour of the house, but with me there she was self-conscious. She clasped her hands together.

"Let me ask this," I said, "just to cover a base. Is Larry's passport still here?"

Her eyes widened. "You know," she replied almost apologetically, "I hadn't thought of it. I'll go look. I'll be right back."

I heard her climb the stairs. Knowing where every single object in her house was located, she was able to return quickly, the blue booklet triumphantly in hand. I flipped through its pages. The most recent trip abroad had been to England two years before. Of course, he could have obtained a replacement. And a determined fellow would have prepared a separate kit packed with new stuff right down to the underwear and toothbrush. I handed it back to her.

"Thanks for looking; it helps knowing it's here. There's still the injury angle," I continued. "I know that you've called all the hospitals, and Frank has followed up on that. They'll notify him if Dr. Kooyman or anyone like him comes in.

"He also may have been kidnapped, but that doesn't seem too likely either, does it? You don't have what I'd call conspicuous wealth and you haven't received a ransom demand." It could be a really off-the-wall plot, but then why? And wouldn't they have snatched Lorraine?

I took a new course. "Has he been working on anything really bizarre, any secret projects—you know, X-files stuff?"

"No," she replied, "Larry's been doing the same thing for years. Cancer research. His lab is trying to discover why genes go bad and how they all interact to produce cancerous cells."

I nodded. I had read Marjorie's print from the web page. Bread and butter cancer research. *White mice,* for heaven's sake. Had animal-rights sorts worked their way down to rodentia?

"I don't suppose his Zodiac sign is . . .?"

She soon got it and smiled. "No, he's a Virgo."

"Okay, let's go over this chronologically, Lorraine. What time does Larry usually come home on Wednesdays, or on any other day for that matter?"

"Oh, anywhere from five-thirty to six-thirty. It depends on when there's a convenient stopping point in what they're doing. He does some of the computer work at home, but he tries to do most of it at the lab. Larry says his work isn't governed by the Mickey Mouse clock."

I nodded. "Does he actually have a Mickey clock at work?"

"In his office. It was a running joke at the beginning that has gotten a little out of hand, if you ask me. Mouse gifts by the dozens. You wouldn't believe all the things there are."

"I'm not sure I want to imagine it," I replied and meant it. Thank heaven there weren't any famous cartoon detectives. "Next question: what does Larry do about lunch?"

"Well, actually he brown-bags it. It's a habit we got into years ago. It saved money back then, but I think he just got used to it; he can stay in his office and munch away. He likes the food better, anyway. We were both raised on the four food groups, so he gets a decent sandwich, salad, fruit, and cookies or cake. Of course he does go out to lunch sometimes, when there's a birthday or some get-together or he's over at Cambridge. He took his lunch yesterday, though, and didn't say anything about going out." Lest there be doubt, she ticked off the menu: "A chicken salad sandwich, mixed green salad—actually young spring greens, the kind that come in a bag—Italian dressing, three tangerines, and four butterscotch cookies."

Six cookies would have been better. And was the lunch still there at the lab, I wondered?

"Does Larry usually phone you in the afternoon? Touch base?"

"No. Oh, once in a while if something comes up, you know, or we need to coordinate our evening schedules. But not just to chat."

She stopped, and then was surprised she had stopped, as though her brain didn't know what kind of follow-through was now called for. Another wave of unreality, of suspense, washed over her, and it frightened her. Thirty years of taken-for-granted reality and now *this*? How had it all become so insubstantial, so soft at the edges?

Just to chat. A moment of his voice. What she wouldn't give for just that small, warm connection, an everyday thing, a normal thing.

Where was her husband? Couldn't she just wake up from this nightmare? Surely Larry would walk through the door in the next few moments, or the next few after that. She could hear his voice—here he was! But, no.

The boat was drifting in open seas with Lorraine, the reluctant and inexperienced captain, unable to distinguish floating debris from reefs.

I stood and took a step towards her. "Lorraine, we'll get through this. I wish I could tell you not to worry, but we both know you will. The only way to get you to stop would be to slip you a Mickey—and I'm not talking about the little squeaky guy."

She smiled briefly again, and I continued. "I would like you to worry *less.* You've got people on your side. Your second cousin once-removed is a police detective and I'm a friend of his. Unless Larry was abducted by aliens (*with cancer?*) he's findable. I once found a teenage runaway living under a freeway overpass in Oregon; I can find your husband.

"I've got to tell you, though, that I'm worried about you being alone here in the house, especially tonight." I knew Marjorie would be able and willing, but it proved unnecessary.

"Oh," she replied, "my step-daughter—Larry's daughter—is driving up from New York this evening. And I do thank you for helping. And Frank, too. I just. . . I've never been through anything like this before. Larry's never even had to go to the hospital. He's as healthy as a horse. I just don't know what to do and I don't like it."

"I understand. So here's what we'll do—we'll finish up and I'll get to work. The reason I asked about any afternoon calls was to see whether Larry should have called but didn't. So yesterday between, say, noon and six o'clock there was nothing unusual about the day, correct?"

"That's right. I spent most of the afternoon going through boxes and throwing things out or getting them ready for Good Will."

It was hard to believe anything could slip through Kooyman Customs and hide in the house long enough to later *be* thrown out. With its bookshelves of (seemingly) randomly filed scientific volumes with sheaves of papers wedged between them, the study was likely the home's sole holdout of anarchy. There couldn't be a bed in the house that a quarter wouldn't bounce off of. As for the charity, I imagined Lorraine washing and folding her donations for dignified submission, which brought an image to my mind.

"Are you from the Midwest," I asked.

"No, New Jersey. Why?"

"You remind me of those strong, good-natured Minnesota Lutheran sorts on *Prairie Home Companion*."

"Oh, well, I don't know about that," she said, a little embarrassed.

Silence for a short while.

"Lorraine," I finally said, "tell me about last night."

four

It was difficult to say when concern had compelled action, but around a quarter past seven, Lorraine had found herself moving between the various rooms of the house without purpose. Impatience? Foreboding? She had called the lab then, and talked with Wayne, one of the post-doctorates on Larry's team and the only member still there. He hadn't seen Dr. Kooyman since noon and assumed the doc had a commitment elsewhere. Larry's lunch box? (*Good girl!*) No, Wayne didn't see that either. Sure, he would have Larry call immediately if he returned to the lab.

Lorraine had tried her husband's cell phone next and left a message when he failed to answer. Nothing *too* uncommon about that, though. She turned on the TV for company, Larry by proxy. By a quarter to eight, there had been two more failed attempts on the cell phone. Worry surfaced and swam freely.

Who might know what Larry's plans had been? There was Estelle, the omnicompetent department administrator. Lorraine had her home phone number. Estelle was surprised. No, Larry had nothing going on she knew about, lunch or otherwise. She had last seen him sometime around ten-thirty that morning, but like Wayne hadn't missed Larry the rest of the day; people come and go. Estelle was willing, though, to call around and see if someone else at the lab might know something. She'd phone back soon.

Another dead end, at least for a while. Who else? As a couple, the Kooymans had friends, of course, but most were married as well. Could Larry have some unknown social assignation? It seemed unlikely and it would be embarrassing to call.

What of Larry's friends? There was Jared Timmerman, a pal from his grad school days with whom he occasionally lunched and talked shop. Jared was over in the Bio Lab at the main Harvard campus in Cambridge, which no doubt was as quiet now as its Longwood counterpart. Lorraine had his work and home phone numbers. The same for Steve Schuyler, a former pupil and success story with a team of his own at the Bio Lab. Larry and Steve met regularly to play the dying sport of handball at a campus court. But a six-hour handball marathon? Maybe Larry had finally strayed too deep into heart-attack country—but then someone surely would have phoned. Still, Jared and Steve were at least solid figures she could discern through the mist.

As she feared, neither was at work. On the first call, she got a grad school Cratchit who told her Dr. Timmerman had gone home two hours earlier. No, the student didn't think he knew who Dr. Kooyman was, but he was pretty sure he hadn't seen anyone resembling Larry's description. Lorraine had not gotten the student's name. The second call, to Schuyler's lab, rang through to an answering machine and she had hung up.

With each call she felt more foolish. What a cliché! The wife tracking down her man—what would people think? In any event, calls to both Jared and Steve at home reached only answering machines and each time there was a beep and Lorraine was expected to say something; she was certain the messages she left had lacked both concision and dignity.

Eight o'clock, then a quarter past. More failed attempts to raise her husband's cell phone; she stopped leaving messages on it. Then she had calmed down a bit. Surely there was some reasonable explanation, some oversight. It had only been a couple of hours, really, when you thought about it. Larry would turn up soon and all would be made clear. Estelle called back about then. She'd reached a half-dozen lab members. None had any information; indeed, most had not even been in the lab that day. They hoped everything was all right. The heads of the other labs? Larry had congenial ties with them all, but joined them only infrequently outside of work. There were a dozen of them, but Estelle would see what she could discover.

Lorraine's respite of calm gave way once more to anxiety. Then, suddenly, both a question and an image sprung into her mind—immediate, fully-formed, without conscious antecedent—*what about Larry's car?* The Honda—was it still there at work? She could call Wayne again, if he was still at the lab, and ask him to go check, but then he would have to trudge the quarter-mile to the parking garage.

She drove there herself.

She had disturbed enough people and reasoned that purposeful action would be cathartic, but it had not proved an even trade; instead, nearing the lab had only stoked her nerves. Arriving at the Medical Center shortly before nine o'clock, Lorraine had gone directly to the cramped, multi-level garage grudgingly allowed to squat on prime medical real estate.

And his car was there!—it was there!

The silver Accord was on the fourth level, locked and seemingly undisturbed. Why hadn't she thought to bring the spare keys? Through the window, she could see Larry's gray sweater where it had been tossed on top of some loose papers on the back seat. An empty can of V-8 juice stood in the center of the floor before the front passenger seat. No lunch box. The car had no story to tell her.

She rushed to the New Research Building of the Medical School, where the Genetics labs were housed. The Kooyman Lab on the second floor was locked, presumably by Wayne, both the lab proper and its office, and her knocking echoed hollowly behind the doors. She walked all the floors, inquiring of late-nighters in the few open doors.

Sorry, haven't seen Doc K.

She returned again to the garage and leaned against the Honda and then, wearily, turned up her collar against the cold, naked night and made her way to Brigham and Women's Hospital. And then to Children's Hospital. And then to Beth Israel.

He had not been admitted to any of them.

Lorraine returned to her empty home.

Estelle had called again, hoping Larry had finally returned. A message from Jared Timmerman as well—no, he hadn't seen Larry today, hope everything is okay.

Everything was not okay. Her imagination was in the passenger seat of a speeding car with no driver and no door handles. It was after eleven, and she turned on the TV again. She pulled out the phone book and called the remaining area hospitals.

Lorraine Kooyman spent the rest of the night lingering in the kitchen and moving throughout the house, peering into rooms, sitting on the chairs scattered throughout, some perhaps for the first time. Every light bulb was called on to cast its comfort. Twice she thought she heard Larry's car but couldn't get to a window fast enough, and both times the driveway and street had been empty.

The night deepened and with it the worry, a black hole around which her mind orbited and from whose terrible gravity it fought to break free.

Estelle, the Genetics Department office administrator, had called again early Thursday before leaving for work. She was alarmed that Larry had not turned up. She would conduct a thorough investigation as soon as she got in. Estelle talked Lorraine out of driving again to the lab—let Estelle do the reconnaissance and then they'd see. Had Lorraine called the police yet? No, she hadn't, but she had a relative—a distant cousin really—who was with the Boston Police Department. She was about to call him. Lorraine had the presence of mind to tell Estelle about her husband's car and ask her to confirm that it was still there. No problem, Estelle parked in the same garage and knew Larry's Honda. And the lunch box, check on that. They agreed that Lorraine should wait to call her cousin the cop until Estelle reported back.

And she had called back an hour later with disturbing news.

The car was gone.

Estelle had traversed every level, just to be sure. She was still in the middle of canvassing people in the building, but so far nothing there either. Lorraine had called Frank then, and he had come over. She had phoned her step-daughter Ronnie in New York City as well, who would drive up later that afternoon if her father had not surfaced.

Jared Timmerman called again and was disturbed by Larry's continued absence; other than a medical emergency he could form no theory (as he put it) to account for it. He knew of no professional soiree that might have included Larry, but of course Jared wasn't part of the Medical School. He hadn't heard anything about handball with Steve Schuyler either, but again that didn't mean much. He would check with Steve and get back to her.

For Lorraine, dawn had not brought with it the lift in spirit she'd expected with the retreat of night. If anything, matters were worse. Anticipation had carried her through the deep hours; moment by moment she could believe—did believe—that her husband was just beyond the edge of the porch light, only footsteps from the door with whatever had detained him, whatever problems there were, resolved *out there*, beyond her knowledge and responsibility. The light cast by even the smallest lamp offered an oasis of assurance, an affirmation that darkness could ever be pushed away.

Daybreak, then, should have arrived to sweep the foe before it. But it had not proved so. Perhaps only the direct sunlight is charged with the power of spiritual uplift, but the sun was hidden beyond a dark ceiling that threatened rain.

Worse still, morning had robbed her of the illusion of her home as a safe womb. Daylight was everywhere and Larry could be anywhere out there in it. Now unrestrained, her vision could follow streets block after block, travel instantly along the length of boulevards; why, from a balloon she would be able to see in all directions for miles and miles. Too many possibilities, too many scenarios to evaluate. *Had he turned right at this intersection, or left? And again, after that, right or left—or straight ahead?* Too many parallel worlds to explore and Larry, nowhere in sight in any of them, was unavailable now for the fantasy of quick deliverance at the porch. And so hope, like the daylight, was free to roam, but with so much ground to cover it was spread too thinly to capture her husband and pull him home. Recoiling against an unblinking, comfortless universe staring in through the windows, Lorraine had thrown the curtains tight against it, and turned her face back to the little pools of artificial light.

five

It couldn't have been easy to walk to three hospitals in the middle of the night."

"I don't know," she replied tiredly, "it seems like a dream now." She finally sat back in the love seat and closed her eyes, body and nerves still locked in battle. I hoped that Larry's daughter, should she come, could coax Lorraine back into a routine of rest and refreshment.

"Either Larry will turn up on his own or Frank and I will find him," I assured her. *And bring him home,* I had almost added but demurred at the last moment, not because of any premonition—I had none—but because it might, after all, be a promise I couldn't keep.

To anchor her for a while she needed a concrete agenda, even if it was mine. "I'm going to the lab to follow up on your groundwork. I'll check in with Estelle. It will help to be able to say that I'm working on your behalf; I'm sure I'll get maximum cooperation from Larry's friends and colleagues. I'll call you from time to time with progress reports and probably to ask some more questions. You might recall something else as well. Here's my card—I'll write my cell phone number on it. Call anytime. Oh, one final thing. It hasn't come up yet, but I don't want there to be any awkwardness. My services are free of charge."

She pulled herself upright again and searched for words. I held up my hand.

"I'm running a special this week on scientists. Last week it was lumberjacks. You got lucky."

"Oh no, Mr. Price—Del—I don't know what . . ."

"Nothing to worry about. Frank helps me and I help him. It's a real buddy movie. Do you think you'll be alright until your stepdaughter gets here?"

"Oh yes, of course."

Of course. Certainly. She'd just putter around, whip up a five pound Waldorf salad, maybe paint a bedroom. I had arrived at a somewhat different assessment and laid the groundwork for what I had planned. "If necessary, I may have my office manager stop by. Her name is Marjorie."

She nodded, but then blurted out, *"Where's his car, Mr. Price? Did he come back last night and get it?"*

"I don't know, but it may turn out to be helpful. Frank has already put out the license plate. It may work to our benefit."

In truth, the car disturbed me. Foul play or scheming husband? Neither was desirable. So no, I really didn't like it at all. My assurance was of the kind that, while technically acceptable—the missing car might be a terrific thing, who could say?—was equivocal. It's a topic I've put much thought into, the precise nature of lying. What should one say to the cancer patient, the distraught parent, the mason of a lousy meatloaf? And how about lying to discover the truth? Saint Augustine, not frequently consulted in my church, had some rather pointed things to say about the issue, none of them generous. When trying to balance truth and compassion it can be a tough call. But there's this to be said: the lying mouth at the end of the phone is one thing, face-to-face another.

Before I left, I got the phone numbers of those she had contacted. I called my office from the car.

"Marjorie, I need your help after all. Could you get down here soon? Lorraine shouldn't be alone. A step-daughter may be coming up tonight from New York, but I don't know when that will be. See if you can get someone to bring in some food as well; she's been up all night and I doubt she's eaten anything. I'm heading over to Longwood to Kooyman's lab and I may want to go to Cambridge later. I told her you might stop by—you know, for administrative purposes." Marjorie and I had run this ploy before. "Find out what you can about this daughter, too; I want to know what I might be walking into. And one more thing—check the garage for a silver Honda when you get a chance."

I owned a Honda, too, but it was a white '95 Civic, part of a fleet of invisible vehicles that included a blue '96 Ford Taurus, a blue '95 Dodge pick-up, and a gray '97 Buick Century (the ultimate in invisibility—who notices a Buick?) On those occasions when I need to tail someone I can put different ones in play. I had the Taurus that day.

I retraced my route back to Boston, parking on the fringe of Longwood. Driving into the heart of the medical district is foolish. Between the construction and congestion, your car would move at the same speed that you could push it. And then you had a lottery chance of finding parking. Someday, an entrepreneur will implement drive-though medicine. It could go like this: As you enter the district, your car wheel goes into one of those conveyer tracks used in car washes. A doctor and nurse will climb into the car with you. To process the paperwork, a third person might walk along side or ride in a golf cart. As you move down the street, the medical team does what it needs to do (run a physical, remove a bullet) and then jumps out at the other end, ready to catch another patient heading the other way. A CAT scan could span the street like the Arc de Triomphe. A drive-through pharmacy at either end as well for further fleecing. There has to be money in this.

Marjorie had printed a map of the area, so I found the New Research Building without trouble. Helpfully, it looked like its name—new and consecrated to science. Vertical acres of glass and white stone and stainless steel trim. The Department of Genetics office was on the third floor. It was mid-afternoon.

If you want the fullest picture of what's going on in almost any corporate endeavor, aim low. All depend on the same myriad of greasy parts to keep them going: payrolls, budgets, reports, files, inventories, travel, competent coffee-making, apple polishing. Much of this is blank stare country for executives, but farther down the chain of command you can often find an old salt who does much to keep the ship trim and on course.

Estelle Westerbad was the harbor pilot for the HMS Department of Genetics. A formidable, confident forty-fivish, she was wearing a well-cut brown pants suit with the right balance of shape and rustle. Silver jewelry, no eyeglasses. She was handsome rather than pretty, tending toward Joan Crawford but less severe. It was easy to imagine her referring to the male members of her department as "the boys."

She had tucked right into her investigation that morning. She had driven to the fourth floor of the parking garage where Lorraine had found Larry's car hours before and for all Estelle knew she was parked in the exact space where Larry's car had been, this being made possible by his car no longer being there. Nor was it anywhere else in the garage; Estelle had checked. She had taken the elevator to the top level, climbed the final flight of stairs to the rooftop deck and then corkscrewed down the parking decks (she spun her finger in a spiral) to the street. Hastening on to the office, she had hesitated to call Lorraine but did so because the missing car should probably be reported to the police. Estelle then did a speedy roll call of those she'd missed the previous night.

And here it was: No one knew anything.

Of which, not much could be made. Although comrades-in-arms in the larger genetic corps, the individual labs were platoons that worked independently, pursuing research that might or might not overlap the projects of another. The climate was a harmonious one and Larry Kooyman, the oldest member of the department, was as agreeable as they came.

"A real terrific guy," decreed Estelle and added, just to drive the nail home, "a real straight-shooter." Good aim was important to her.

I had inferred a general picture of the Department, but I wanted to bring it into clearer focus. "There are twelve labs here, then?"

"Thirteen," she corrected. "But that's just the Department of Genetics. The building houses several research departments of the Medical School."

Remembering the organizational octopus Marjorie had described, I said: "Let's just stick with Genetics for now. How many folks are we talking about?'

"Well, it depends on who you want to count." She looked past me and concentrated on a personnel board hovering in space. "There are some peripheral and honorary sorts, but one hundred forty-two will do. The Kooyman Lab has eight."

I liked eight, a manageable number, but Kooyman would have ties with many others in and out of the building. The sky was the limit. But I couldn't cover the sky and wanted to avoid, or at least postpone, a painstaking crawl through the Research building. Either in person or by phone, Estelle had already contacted each member of the Kooyman lab: two post-doctorate fellows, four graduate students, one undergraduate and a part-time office manager. Due to competing responsibilities it was rare for all of them to be in the lab at once. And so on Wednesday, only the post-docs, one of the graduate students and the sole undergrad had been in the lab at any time during the day, ranging from 9 am (Sharon Florenski, one of the post-docs) to about eight that evening (Wayne Carlisle, the post-doc Lorraine had reached).

Dr. Kooyman was already busy when Sharon Florenski arrived. She thought she remembered him going into his office—part of a suite of two small rooms connected to the lab by one door and opening onto the main hallway through another—around noon, presumably to eat lunch. Wayne, who had clocked in at about ten, concurred but placed the time closer to 11:30. Sometime in the early afternoon Sharon had wanted to ask Larry about some lab equipment but didn't find him. She left the lab somewhere around 3:30 PM. Wayne had had plenty to do as well, but nothing that required the boss's immediate oversight. Dr. K had gone somewhere to attend to something—so what? Ryan Rush, the graduate student, had punched in around 1 PM and so missed out on missing his boss. The undergraduate, Brett DeBaker, had come in even later than Ryan and left after a couple of hours.

Professor Kooyman had conveyed to none of them any Wednesday afternoon plans, nor did they know otherwise of any commitment, professional or personal, that he may have had. Sharon had known where Larry kept the just-in-case password to his office computer (was it, like so many passwords of this sort, an open secret?) and she and Estelle had already fired it up, checking his emails, calendar and even the recycle bin for any appointments. They had found nothing even suggestive.

I thought it unlikely that the good professor had dematerialized right there in his office (memo to self: Check floor below for physicists) or, despite precedents, had been assumed bodily into heaven. No, Larry had repaired to his office sometime between 11:30 and noon and shortly thereafter departed, almost certainly through the door onto the main hall. He then exited the building for a destination already anticipated or suddenly conceived. Or he had left the New Research Building later, after first reporting to another lab or office in the building. Or was still *in* the building (grim thought). And all this depending, of course, on whether everyone so far was telling the truth. The police or I could probably find someone who would recall seeing him leave; as the news spread, that someone would likely come forward. But even then, unless Dr. Kooyman had blurted out his agenda at this chance encounter—information he might have imparted just as easily to Sharon or Wayne—we would be none the wiser.

Had he been abducted on an impulse trip to the drugstore as a random target of opportunity? Or had someone hovered around, day after day, waiting to pounce? Both seemed far-fetched. How would you pull it off anyway? There were three hospitals here, for crying out loud. It would be like snatching someone off the floor of the New York Stock Exchange.

And why had Larry taken his lunch with him? It was gone by 8 PM—were we to believe that our hypothetical kidnapper had come *back* for it? How good could Lorraine's cookies be? The car I could understand; anyone with the keys (including, of course, Kooyman) could have nabbed that—but, then again, why wait until midnight to do it? It was all nuts.

"I appreciate your efforts," I told Estelle. "If you ever want to give up this unfulfilling line of work, I'll hire you on."

She laughed. "Thanks but no thanks. I don't think I'd like it; too much running around, following people…" She trailed off, realizing her appraisal was pretty lean. Along with many others, her image of what I do was vague but included generous helpings of tedium, intrusion and sleaze.

"Well," I responded, "you'd have to tone down the bling."

"*This?*" she retorted, holding up her tinkling right forearm and swiveling it. This *was* toned down.

"I'd like you to do me a favor," I said. "Consider yourself the chief sentry at this outpost. Go ahead and spread it around that Dr. Kooyman is missing and that anyone who saw him yesterday should report to you. Don't sugar coat it, but don't make it seem diabolical either; the straight-forward truth will do. While you're at it, see if you can find out if anyone else went missing yesterday afternoon long enough to register. And leave my name out of it for now—the fewer variables for people to react to, the better." I wrote my cell phone number on my card and handed it to her.

"I'll do anything I can to help," she replied. Her face had changed. Larry Kooyman had been missing for over 24 hours. The unsettling novelty of the situation was setting in. "Anything for Larry."

"If he doesn't turn up here pretty soon," I continued, "the police are going to work their way through this more thoroughly than I am right now and with less charm. I'm trying to work fast to play catch-up and I'm going to cut corners. The good news is that we all are on the same side of this investigation."

Or should be: "Let me ask this—do you think everyone in the lab is telling the truth?"

She was startled by the question and became pensive. "Well, yes. Why wouldn't they?" I had tripped an automatic defense mechanism. Mother and cubs.

I shook my head. "I don't mean to suggest that someone must be lying; I was appealing more to your instincts, to any gut reaction."

"No…no," she replied. "I'm sure everyone is as perplexed and concerned as I am. Those guys love Larry. "

"Good. Do what you can to buck up Lorraine, too; she needs it. I understand Larry's daughter is coming up tonight."

"Oh, Ronnie? That's good. Yeah, I bet Lorraine needs help, poor kid. She must be worried sick. I'll stop by after work—if Larry isn't back by then," she quickly amended. "Where do you think he is, Mr. Price?"

How far could someone get in 24 hours now days—half way around the world? I shook my head.

"I've got to find the trail head." I stopped there on the shore of a sea of possibilities, and so we wouldn't begin wading in, I moved on: "I know that the police are going to be predisposed to the wine, women and song angle, an angle without much to prop it up, as far as I can tell."

"And it won't get any support from me," asserted Estelle. "Larry Kooyman is a real straight shooter."

"We'll just have to find him then." I nodded towards the door. "I'm going down to the lab. Maybe bring in a cat to lean on the mice; you know, good cop/bad cop."

She laughed. "No," she confessed, "I didn't grill the mice."

"It's the kind of mistake the amateur will make," I said.

six

The Kooyman Lab was large, bright and reassuringly lab-like. Electronic equipment and glassware in varied shapes were spread liberally across the expansive countertops skirting each wall and atop a large island. White cabinets above and below. Cluttered, yet clean. All in all, a businesslike proposition. Or almost. As a fan of Fifties science fiction films, I felt the lack of what should be a key instrument in any laboratory.

"Doesn't this place have an oscilloscope?"

The five lab members loosely clustered around the island looked at me as though I had asked whether they had a pineapple.

I formed a circle with my index fingers and thumbs. "Picture tube—wavy lines? No? Fine, let's forget it. My name is Del Price. I just left Estelle at the office. Before that I was with Lorraine Kooyman. I'm a private detective. I'm looking for your boss."

My credentials and aura of competence failed to impress.

"Uh, are the police coming?" a stocky, pleasant-looking brunette finally asked. It was awkward beginnings for us all.

"Not for a while, Wendi," I replied. "I'm it." Wendi Sharkley was the office assistant.

Her eyes widened. "Wow." The others shifted nervously.

One person, dissatisfied with this dissembling, let fly with a shot over the bow: "Who are you working for?"

"Well, Sharon," I replied, "that would be Mrs. Kooyman. She knows people in low places." This was Sharon Florenski, one of the post-doctorates and, as far as anyone knew, one of the last to have seen Dr. Kooyman. She

27

was a size four blonde with bobbed hair and diamond stud earrings. There seemed to be plenty of jewelry bolstering science.

The demands of drama dictated that I leave it there, but as Sharon was a key witness and already skeptical, I decided to meet her half-way, pull her over to Team Price.

"Lorraine has a relative on the police force, the BPD—I know how you guys love acronyms—and he called me. It will take a while to get the police ball rolling over here to HMS but roll here it will unless Dr. K turns up pretty soon."

"You already know who we are?" asked Wendi.

"I don't think you're fully grasping the PI bit," I chided.

Sometimes, when the planets line up and a case comes to a quick and crisp end, I allow the parties to bask in awe at my seeric powers, which are remarkable only insofar as they remain unexplained. I was getting some mileage out of this effect now, but confessed before the answer occurred to them.

"There's a photo of the lab on your website. I got Estelle to point out who was who. So in addition to you, Wendi and Sharon, I recognize Ryan Rush, Wayne Carlisle and Brett DeBaker."

They began to relax. Sharon seemed to be mollified.

"Is Dr. Kooyman really missing?" she asked. "It's hard to believe. We've talked with Estelle, but..." Sharon and her colleagues were unsettled, trying with difficulty to fit this unprecedented event into the daily grind.

"Yes, I'm afraid so. His wife is very worried. It seems out of character for him to just take off, so something else must have happened. We don't know what."

"Has someone checked the hospitals and everything?" Wendi asked.

"Yep. Lorraine's cousin, the cop, has tried them all. He's checked crime reports, too."

"What can we do to help?" The question was asked by a guy who was built like a linebacker. He wore glasses with black, plastic frames and had straight, dark hair that swept across his forehead. He could have been Clark Kent, but instead was Wayne Carlisle, the post-doc Lorraine had spoken with Wednesday night.

"I appreciate you asking, and we'll get to that in a minute. Let me ask a few questions first. Right now, Wayne, you and Sharon were the last to see Dr. Kooyman. That was yesterday around noon, correct?"

"That's right," he replied. Sharon nodded her agreement.

"Give me a brief rundown of your schedules."

Each, in turn, corroborated what Estelle had told me, except that Sharon said she had finished at 2:00 PM rather than at 3:30 as Estelle reported. I kept this card in my hand for now. Otherwise, both stories were straightforward and uncomplicated, the easiest to truthfully relate—or fabricate. Ryan Rush and Brett DeBaker confirmed that they had arrived at the lab only later in the afternoon and knew nothing of any plans Dr. Kooyman might have had. Wendi had not been in at all on Wednesday.

It was standard practice, then, for members of the Kooyman Lab to come and go as their individual, overlapping schedules allowed. Each tech had responsibilities, but ones that could be successfully discharged within a flexible work schedule—a wholly admirable arrangement, I thought. As a missionary for my church in Germany, I had been struck by the marked diminution in drivenness. Shopkeepers would shut down for a couple of hours in the afternoon and go home (*In the middle of the day! Lost profit!*) Families would vacation together in the summer in the countryside or on the Mediterranean. (*A month with your family! Away from work! Is that legal?*) An entire siesta culture flourishes around the globe, expressing a very different notion of the bottom line. It was this more humane tempo of life among the delightful *dorfen* of the undulating Rhineland Pfalz that I had brought back with me, the pattern for my own work ethic and target of ribbing (by Frank) or the curious blend of envy and disapproval by others, including members of my Church, who are perhaps too unreflectively American in their bullet train drive down a narrow track, stressed out 24/7.

Back to Wayne and Sharon: "Do either of you remember seeing Dr. Kooyman's lunch box yesterday?"

Wayne spoke up. "I've been thinking about it since Mrs. Kooyman asked about it last night. Dr. K usually just eats at his desk and checks his e-mail. He brings it every day, so I suppose he had it yesterday as well. I didn't notice it one way or the other, I guess."

"Lorraine said he brought it," I confirmed. "Chicken salad. How about you, Sharon?"

She shrugged. "It would have been on his desk, but I couldn't say for sure, either." Fearing this testimony unsatisfactory, she thought to fine tune it. "I mean, I don't *think* it was there later in the afternoon because if it *had* been there I think I *would* have noticed that it was there but Dr. Kooyman wasn't. It would have stuck out, like."

Stuff like this is why attorneys rehearse a client's testimony. Short of hypnosis, Sharon was trying to work it out in her mind and be helpful. Certainly she was no longer able to pronounce confidently on the matter.

"Any phone calls around that time?"

They looked at each other and shook their heads. "Not that I remember," Wayne said.

"One other thing. Did either of you—or any of you," I said, surveying the group—"see anyone who, on reflection, seemed out of place?"

Corporate head shaking.

"Let's look at the doc's office," I suggested. Sharon led the way for me and the rest followed, now participants in the drama. Cancer could wait. We shuffled our way out of the lab and across the narrow, administrative office that lay between the lab proper and Kooyman's personal office.

It was, as his home study, unpretentious. An old (but still solid) wooden desk and a couple of matching chairs, a computer, bookcases, a few struggling plants, a framed generic landscape (Bay of Naples?) and, to be certain, no lunch box. Nothing seemed clue-like. From the wall a black plastic mouse smiled down on us as he pointed out the hour, but nothing else. I nodded toward the monitor on the desktop.

"What about the computer, Sharon?" I had Estelle's report.

"Estelle and I checked this morning," she confirmed. There was nothing on the calendar on in any e-mails that said anything about an appointment."

The e-mail angle was problematic anyway. If Kooyman had responded to an innocent summons he hadn't kept, someone should have followed up by now. If he had kept it then one of Estelle's probes might trigger a response. In either case, where was the original e-mail? If however, something sinister was afoot, why send an incriminating message in the first place? Unless you knew you could delete it later. Or that someone else would. But there was still the surrender of control, no guarantee of what Kooyman would do or say. Wheels within wheels.

"One more thing. I don't know if this has any bearing on events, but I'd like to know what sort of research you do here. Anyone want to tackle this? It'll need to be a plain English version—when I became a P.I., I gave up a promising career in biochemistry."

Sharon stepped up. She struggled occasionally in cutting it down a few grade levels, but did well at conveying an image I could grasp.

Genes are little pieces of genetic information inside cells that direct limited parts of cellular activity. They're supposed to do their thing and then shut up. Oncogenes, the ones that contribute to cancer, speak up at the wrong time or say something wrong or won't shut up. They collaborate with other fifth column genes in some complicated way to produce cells that no longer listen to signals telling them to stop growing and dividing. The goal of the research was to decipher this clandestine intercellular chatter and then interrupt it.

That's where the mice came in. Taken as a group, they served as a model for human cancer. As was the common practice of genetic research, the Kooyman Lab had constructed (Sharon's word) their own designer line of mice with certain genes deactivated, or "knocked out," to test variations from normal behavior, like checking the bulbs in a string of Christmas tree lights. I wondered how many bulbs there are in the human body and what might come from messing with them.

My mind drifted. Where do all the dead mice go? Is each accounted for in the heavenly ledger, receiving back a (cancer-free) material body just as we will? From ant to whale to child of the Most High, we each enjoy our day under the sun before meeting the same end in the dust. What eternal life might mean to a mouse, I do not know, but certainly there's lots of room in the universe for us all. The current census finds more stars in the cosmos than there are grains of sand in all the beaches and deserts on earth. For a presumed immaterial Being, this seems a hefty investment in physicality.

Sharon stopped, and I thanked her for her summary.

"You're a good teacher. Keep at it; it's a gift. Lot's of kids these days are computer experts but good luck getting a coherent, patient explanation out of them."

"Well," I continued, "I don't suppose Dr. Kooyman is out recruiting more mice. Is the research at some crucial stage?"

"Not really," Wayne replied. We have a progress report coming up but we're on schedule."

"I was hoping you guys were on the verge of a miracle drug that would give me a trail to follow as well as a sharp investment opportunity."

"We aren't involved in pharmaceutical development at all," Wayne said.

There wasn't much left to do at the Kooyman Lab. The long and short of it was this: Larry Kooyman had left his office around noon the day before and hadn't been seen since.

"Thanks, everyone. Here's what you can do. It's almost certain that your boss left his office through the door onto the main hallway. Somebody may have seen him leave yesterday, so talk to your cohorts in the building. Talk to everyone. We may be able to track his route each segment of the way.

"I'll be traveling around today. Unless you hear that Dr. Kooyman has returned, I'd like to ask you to contact your absent colleagues and be here tomorrow at 9 AM I'll give you an update. I appreciate your help and I know Mrs. Kooyman does."

On the way out, I checked back in with Estelle. Busy at the keyboard and with the phone pinched between ear and shoulder, she looked up as I entered. "I've been calling around the building," she said, "but nothing so far. I'm sending out e-mails as well."

"Do you think I should talk to the department chairman?" I asked.

"No. You can't anyway. Dr. Lassiter is in San Francisco. A wedding. I called him; he's in the dark like everyone else. He flies back on Sunday."

"Well, I'm off to Harvard to see whether I can track down Jared Timmerman and Steve Schuyler. Do you know them?"

"Slightly. They're over at the Bio Lab. Dr. Schuyler's been around a few times, but mostly Larry goes over there. They play handball. I think Larry and Dr. Timmerman go back to grad school, but I don't see him much."

"Okay. Keep in touch."

On the way back to my car, I called Jared Timmerman's lab at the number Lorraine had given me. He was there and would be waiting. There was no answer at the Schuyler Lab. I phoned Lorraine. Marjorie was not there but had called and was expected. The daughter, Ronnie, had decided to fly up on the shuttle. I emphasized the wealth of good will and helpfulness of Larry's colleagues rather than the meager harvest. I conveyed my immediate plans and said I would return to her home afterwards.

Could this Dr. Lassiter be involved? A fine cross-country alibi, certainly. Motive? Well, motives can be like those legendary treasures which are briefly glimpsed only to slip back into the depths. Nice train of thought, this, one within shouting distance of Lorraine Kooyman's current state of mind. Closer than that, actually, for I follow behind as she wanders twilight, fade-away streets in search of her beloved, confused as one reel is pulled off the projector and a slightly different film is slapped on and she is off again on strange roads. She doesn't see me, but I'm there, an unbilled supporting actor.

It's an occupational hazard. Much of my mental life is taken up counterbalancing the squalid screenplays of mortality. What do you suppose kids do when they run away from home? What they *don't* do as a rule is make a beeline to the nearest Bible study class. They aren't out there playing croquet.

It won't do to speculate very long or very intently on how this world can chew up a teenager.

As a counterbalance, I screen an entirely different kind of movie behind my eyes along with the other, one that is reassuring against chaos, invigorating rather than dispiriting. It has a rather strong leading man and used to be in wider distribution than it is now. A double-feature, the pair of films used to be called in my grandparents' day.

Before you got shortchanged with just the one.

seven

I was near Boston University and crossed the bridge there to Memorial Drive, which runs along the Cambridge side of the Charles River. The dusky, lusterless water slid by on the last leg of its journey to refresh (if that's the word) Boston Harbor. I zipped along at a heady forty miles per hour until I turned in toward the Harvard campus and was reduced to crawling along like Kafka's imperial messenger. I again settled for a spot blocks away from my target.

The Department of Molecular and Cellular Biology is housed in the Bio Lab Building. An impressive, four-story structure enclosing a courtyard, it had been built along the lines of the progressive British factory of an earlier age. The three-door main entrance was guarded on either side by a pair of bronze rhinoceroses the size of cement trucks, textured in a green patina and set atop brick pedestals. They are an arresting and wholly enchanting embellishment to what could have been lazily left as pedestrian institutional architecture. I passed humbly beneath their stern eye.

Jared Timmerman was an anglophile and as with most such that meant Victoriana, in this case the scientific paraphernalia of that age mingled with small *objets d'art* and knickknacks. Shelves had been put up against two of the walls of his office to display the plethora of turned bronze apparatus, microscopes, and calipers for every occasion. On another wall in a gilt frame hung a small painting of bucolic sterility of the type that was attractive only in direct ratio to the fame of the artist.

We shook hands and sat in a pair of comfortably padded wooden chairs. The man himself was tall and dark, serious but not unpleasant. Middle of

34

the road in looks but he dressed to advantage, somewhere in the Tony Blair range. With his dark brown hair, smooth skin and bleached teeth, he seemed to be in his forties but must have been older; he had known Larry Kooyman from grad school. I puffed up my bona fides by name-dropping Lorraine and Estelle. As I had and would with others, I tried to impress upon him the advantages of confiding all to me, that mine was as the voice crying in the wilderness before the arrival of greater authority. He nodded with slow, metronomic regularity during my selective summary of the investigation.

I find the news from the BBC to be more trustworthy than its State-side counterparts because it's delivered in a formal British accent. Minus the accent and falling short of the gold standard of conversation set by *Pride and Prejudice*, Timmerman had nonetheless ratcheted up his conversational pitch to PBS levels. That he had also managed this without a concomitant rise in pomposity put more points up on the board. If later I had to shoot him, I decided, I'd fire to wound. How does one implement this linguistic uplift? Exclusive schools in Maryland? An upbringing by eccentric aunts? Certainly we shared the conviction that contemporary language has degenerated into a tired mush of imprecision, flabbiness, and profanity, a communication mud-slide. But he had done something about it and I found myself now trying to work words like *desultory* and *stygian* into my discourse.

Yes, Lorraine had telephoned the previous evening, and he had returned her call promptly upon his return from the symphony (Mahler, *Symphony No. 4 in G-major*), but had reached only her answering machine. He had phoned again, this morning, assuming the matter had resolved itself. It hadn't and, regrettably, he could offer consolation but no illumination.

"I told her that I hadn't seen Larry at all, neither the day before nor at any time during the two weeks previous." (He lost a turn with *fortnight*, I thought.) "Neither had I any theory to account adequately for his absence. I still don't." I wondered whether this guy got many dates and with whom.

"There could be," he continued, "and probably are, any number of pro-fessional conferences or symposia Larry might attend, but I know of none currently in session. But to attend one, or to travel anywhere for that matter, without telling his wife—no, that would not be."

"Estelle called him a straight-shooter," I prompted.

Timmerman nodded and smiled, sort of. "Of course," he acknowledged, "it would place me in an awkward position had I personal knowledge of a shadow Larry. Fortunately, I'm spared the dilemma; Larry's is an uncomplicated, forthright life. If we are to believe that he is living a lie, then I'm a monkey's uncle."

I couldn't recall when I had last heard that phrase; it had likely been on the wane since the Scopes trial. I considered cultivating Jared as a friend, selfishly using him as a personal trainer to kick my sagging syntax around the track.

"Well," I said, "it's still early days, not yet twenty-four hours since the alarm was raised." I was starting to sound like an idiot.

"Frankly," he replied, I assume that Larry will shortly reappear and all will be revealed. You said he made no apparent prior preparation, took nothing with him?"

"According to Lorraine, a day like any other." I decided to tie up one loose end, in case Dr. Timmerman was of that annoying sort, typically found among adolescents, who hides between the cracks of legal hair-splitting and malicious compliance. "You said you had not seen Larry for two weeks. Have you spoken with him during that same period?"

He sat back against the chair and furrowed his brow. Had he allowed ambiguity?

"No, I have not spoken with Larry, either. It's not unusual for us to go weeks without contact."

Having myself few male friends this needed no elaboration. And as agreeable as it was to sit at the feet of the Higher Elocution, Jared Timmerman, PhD was of no help whatever, other than removing at least for now a fruitless line of inquiry.

"I believe you mentioned a desire to speak with Steve Schuyler," He continued. He's a floor down and the span of the building away. I'll show you to young Schuyler's lair."

We talked as we walked. "I understand you and Larry go way back."

"Yes, that's right. We met during graduate school. I stood up for him at his wedding. To Lorraine, that is—he and Karen had already divorced."

"Did you know his first wife?"

"Not well. She and Veronica returned to her home in New York. Albany, I believe."

"I understand the daughter is coming up tonight to be with Lorraine."

"Is she? Good for her. And good for Lorraine as well. It's been some time since I've seen Veronica."

I launched out on a new tack. "Does your research here and Dr. Kooyman's intersect at any point?" I was shameless.

"Intersect? Not really. Well, part of the same universe of meaning, certainly, but Larry's realm is oncologically focused while our lab is researching pattern formation. We are elucidating the several sequential signaling steps triggered by the decapentaplegic gene. A variety of other genes encode products which interact with the dpp protein and this leads, rather mysteriously, to pattern formation within cells."

Wrong tack. Wrong universe of meaning, too. What universe was I in, I wondered, and was I in it alone?

We arrived at the Schuyler Lab. But no Schuyler, nor anyone else—the door was locked and only the fading scraps of day diffused through its milky window. A brighter light, however, spilled from a doorway further down the hall. This turned out to be part of the Hunter Lab.

And Hunter was on to something. A stunning, pre-Raphaelite red-head sat behind a desk, the architect of an array of neatly stacked papers. She was the complete package: Glossy, wavy, auburn hair that reached to the middle of her back, green eyes, full lips and irenic composure. A Guinevere misplaced in time.

She was doling out pages to the appropriate piles and looked up as we gained the doorway.

"Oh, hello, Dr. Timmerman."

"Good evening, Janelle. We were just looking for Dr. Schuyler, but have been disappointed. You seem to be the only one about. Here is Mr. Price, a detective."

I smiled broadly and tried to radiate desirable male traits.

"Looking for Dr. Schuyler?" she asked.

"Indirectly," I replied, moving into the office and offering my hand. If this goddess wound up in Hollywood one day, I was going to get my brush with greatness up front. "Del Price. I'm actually looking for Dr. Larry Kooyman from the Medical School. As he and Dr. Schuyler are friends, I thought I'd check here."

Janelle shook her head briefly; her cascading hair remained in motion a while longer. "Steve apparently called in sick. Dr. Hunter was looking for him earlier, too." She paused. "That's how I found out," she clarified, maybe because I was a detective and would want to know these details.

"Do you know Dr. Kooyman?" I asked.

"Maybe—I don't know."

"We have a photo," I said, producing it.

"Oh. I think I've seen him around."

"How about yesterday afternoon?"

Another shake of the head and satin folds in motion. "No," she replied, "but I was only here in the morning." I wanted to keep asking questions she could answer no to. I thought of some obvious ones and drooped within.

"Was Dr. Schuyler at his lab yesterday?"

"No—well, I guess I couldn't say for sure. For some reason I don't think he was, though."

I turned to Timmerman. "Did you see him yesterday?"

"Also no, but I didn't venture down this way. I have his phone number; we can ring him."

"I have his number, too, from Lorraine," I replied. He was next on my list in any event.

Improbably, Janelle had a competitor for my attention.

"You know, that's a really big candy bar." I nodded towards the distinctive triangular prism of a Toblerone box. This one was the size of a railroad tie and being held up by a filing cabinet. It must have weighed fifteen pounds.

She smiled. "It's a monster, all right. It's from Steve, actually. Someone gave it to him, I think, from Switzerland—I don't remember exactly. He dropped it off last week."

"What did he drop it off with, a fork lift?"

Janelle smiled. "It's a monster."

The box looked intact, undisturbed. In these dimensions it was more a fetish than a confection and not to be violated by base, digestive desire.

A *Vogue* model and a chocolate I-beam had sapped my detective energy. Oh brave new world with such wonders in it! But except for getting Janelle to marry me by way of a swinging pocket watch, there wasn't anything left to do here. I gave her my card. You never knew.

Jared Timmerman and I walked back to his office.

"If this country wants to invest in the future of science," I observed, "it will send Janelle on a rah-rah tour to every high school."

"Quite possibly. Her father is a renowned biochemist at Berkeley who offered her an alternative to Barbie and later, it seems, to body-piercing."

Back in his office, Timmerman phoned Steve Schuyler at his home. No answer. He left a message mentioning my interest in contacting him.

"Does Dr. Schuyler live nearby?" I asked. "It doesn't sound like it will do much good, but I might as well swing by if I can. Lorraine said she left a message with him last night as well as with you. I think she felt self-conscious doing so."

"Not at all," he returned. "She was right to do so. And right to observe how uncharacteristic of Larry this has been. I was and am concerned. I'll call her and put her mind to ease. I will help in any way I can, Mr. Price. Surely the most likely outcome is that Larry will surface shortly."

"With his health and an explanation," I suggested.

"With both, certainly."

He didn't know Schuyler's home address, but called someone who did. I thanked him and gave him my card, hoping I wouldn't have to start mailing out the things addressed to Occupant.

Outside the building, I hesitated between the two bronze sentinels. They would almost certainly have names. As a race we seem instinctively to imitate the works of Him in whose image we are said to be created, bestowing life of a sort everywhere we can by naming (and addressing) objects like boats, cars, stuffed animals and snowmen. Who wouldn't befriend a big bronze rhino? Both were female, I decided, upon the theory that for a mammal of their stature, maleness should be evident. Having previously passed muster with them, I felt confident in approaching one and stroking its rough, pebbled flank. "There's a chunk of chocolate in there with your name on it," I informed her. Would she share with her sister?

I thought about heading over to the nearby Divinity School to see whether divinity was in residence but demurred, uncertain how much strain an appeal to a material, male, personal Father in Heaven would put on Harvard's theological largesse.

Steven Schuyler resided in Somerville, Cambridge's poor relation to the immediate east, in a recent urban geologic form I call a condo intrusion. From among a well-packed row of tall, tired houses, one is scraped off the planet. In its place springs up a brick and cement column wedged in place like a new tooth. Several residential units replace the single-family home, with tight parking in a bunker beneath. No parking for me, though. Assuming that, as in Boston, the denizens of the neighborhood had unspoken proprietary claims to the "public" street parking, I chose carefully a spot a couple of blocks away. It was ripe evening now and a wet, chill wind punished pedestrians. No sign of the sunset or even of a distinguishable stratum of illumination; as with the day the solar movement went undetected and the sun might have descended at any compass point. A patchwork of lights shone behind shaded windows along the streets, offering weak cheer against the sooty sky.

The condo vestibule held eight mailboxes with a button under each. There was a place for speakers that had not been installed. I pushed the one under the Schuyler box and waited. No buzz released the inner door catch. Schuyler was supposed to be ill, but then illness comes in varying degrees. I tapped at the button again. No go. I tried the number Lorraine had given me and left a message. I took out one of my cards and wrote on the back, "Acting on behalf of Lorraine Kooyman" and wedged it in the miniscule crevice between the mailbox door and the box itself. It would probably fall out, I decided, so I pulled it out, wrote Schuyler's name on the front, and jammed it back in again. Outside, I called Marjorie on her cell phone.

"What's up?," I asked.

"I'm here with Lorraine. Where are you—in your car?" It was a coded response; I knew Lorraine was in earshot.

"I'm standing in the vestibule at Steve Schuyler's condo. Larry's handball buddy. He's either not here or not answering. He wasn't at work today. Ask Lorraine if she ever heard from him."

A brief pause. "No. But Jared Timmerman called a little while ago. Estelle from the lab stopped by, too. What have you found out?"

"Not much. I've been to Larry's lab, then to Harvard. Timmerman says he hasn't talked to Larry in weeks. I might have you look into a couple of things there. Schuyler lives in Somerville, so I bopped over here. Anyone else there yet?"

"Not yet. The daughter, Ronnie, is due anytime; she decided to fly up rather than drive. Frank called; he's swinging by at some point.

"Lorraine a wreck?"

"Yes," Marjorie said evenly, "that's right."

"Is the Honda in the garage?"

"No."

"Okay. I'm going to grab a sandwich and head on back."

And so another forty-five minutes of salmoning my way to the Kooyman headwaters. In the driveway next to Marjorie's Mustang, a white Dodge was parked. I noted the license plate. It was spotless inside and out, obviously a rental.

Larry's daughter, Veronica, had arrived. Would she do credit to the hottie in the Archie comics?

eight

She wasn't far off the mark. Having been recently sensitized to things genetic, I strained to see some of Larry Kooyman in the woman who answered the door. Perhaps her mother—Karen?—was a Russian aristocrat. Ronnie was five-six, mid-thirties, maybe one-ten, a brunette whose short hair, stylishly cut, showed life of its own but not enough to be a nuisance. Her eyes were brown—hazel actually, but the DMV doesn't recognize hazel—and set a little too closely together, and with her high cheekbones, small, slightly crooked mouth and pointed chin they rendered her pixyish. A kind of tough pixie, though, for the shadow of New York Squint lay over a face that said, *"I can be cordial but don't push it."* She wore emerald ear studs and despite her being a smoker I was taken with her. Janelle and Ronnie, both in one day.

So there she was at the door when I arrived, ready to greet and grill. But first, brief amenities.

"Hello," she said coolly, "I'm Ronnie Kooyman." As a greeting it lacked the Hallmark touch. She did, though, extend her hand, setting several bracelets jingling. We shook in the brief, perfunctory manner befitting prosecutor and prey. She allowed me a small beachhead inside the front door.

"Hello yourself. I'm Del Price. I'm the investigator looking for your father. I've been scattering my cards across the greater metropolitan area this afternoon. Want one?"

She ignored this. Amenity time had come and gone. It seemed that probing for a sense of humor might require professional writers.

"Your assistant is in the kitchen," she said. "Lorraine just went up to bed.

41

I'm not sure all this is necessary. It's barely twenty-four hours since my father has supposedly disappeared."

"*Supposedly?* Where do you think he is—in one of the closets? Boy, am I a lousy detective. And her name is Marjorie."

"No, no," she replied quickly, shaking her head, "I didn't mean it like that. I meant…oh, it just seems all this is too sudden, too…"

"Predatory?"

"Your word. By the way, what's all this costing them?"

Given her suspicion, wouldn't this have been one of the first questions put to her stepmother? And wouldn't Lorraine have told her? Was she looking for confirmation? Let her work for it.

"Like I told your stepmother—Lorraine was it?—I was willing to make her a deal. Eighty-five dollars an hour."

"Eighty-five dollars an hour," she repeated flatly.

I shrugged. "She had a coupon."

Ronnie paused for a moment. "She said you weren't charging her any-thing."

"It was a really big coupon."

More of the stink eye. I should probably get used to it. "Is being a smart-ass part of the whole thing? You learn your trade from TV?"

"I looked down and scuffed at the carpet with a shoe tip. "It's more of a calling, really. And yes to the first question."

Stopped her again. Whether regrouping or feeling self-conscious, I couldn't say. Assuming the former, I forged ahead. "Actually, the snappy dialog is part of the written test we take. It's like an SAT but without the math. I scored high. Or highly."

Still nothing.

Fine.

"No, Ms. Kooyman, I am not charging Lorraine a dime. She has a cousin on the force and I'm a friend of his. That's it. And everyone so far agrees that your father's disappearance is both mysterious and wholly out of character."

Having made no headway on the fee, she retreated to her initial theme. "This all seems precipitous."

"*Precipitous?* You sound like Jared Timmerman."

She thawed to 34 degrees. "You spoke with Jared? What did he say?"

"That he hasn't heard from your father in two weeks. He said he hadn't seen you in quite a while."

Bad step, and the rejoinder was swift.

"How am *I* a part of this? What are you up to? You've been on the job for what—*an afternoon?*"

"It was a *long* afternoon, believe me."

We needed a new script or a referee. What I had thought of as amusing banter had apparently been interpreted by Ronnie as baiting. Time to back down.

"Go easy on me. Dr. Timmerman and I were walking down the hall in the Bio Lab trying to scare up Steve Schuyler, and I brought up his long friendship with your father. He put it into a chronological sequence wherein you made a brief appearance as a young girl. You curtsied politely and left the stage. I might add that as far as your father's disappearance goes, *you* seem to have beaten a fast path up here."

"That was because of the whole cop and detective talk. I didn't know what Lorraine was getting herself into. Everything was happening so fast, there was no wait-and-see."

She had a point, but you'd think Ronnie would be happy to learn that her stepmother could shake a cop out of the family tree at need.

She lowered her voice. "What did Steve say?" She had reacted at his name.

"Don't know. Never talked to him. He wasn't in his lab either yesterday or today. Out sick, at least today. I found out where he lives in Somerville, but no answer there, either. Do you know him?"

She paused. "Yes. But it's been a while."

"Well, maybe he'll return *your* call. I hope I don't have to run him to the ground, too."

Marjorie arrived in the living room.

"You missed out on some off-Broadway," I said.

"Shucks."

"Ms. Kooyman feels we're being precipitous."

I was certain Ronnie could pull her weight in any social situation and wouldn't stand there and be talked about. But she was also outnumbered. "Oh, please," she said, "I'm sorry if I offended you. I'm tired and I still don't *get* any of this."

"Nor does anyone else. Your dad's lab is out beating the bushes for witnesses, Dr. Timmerman is concerned and," I lowered my voice, "Lorraine is on tilt. People obviously care for your father."

"Let's go to the kitchen," Marjorie suggested.

The kitchen was surgically antiseptic. Lorraine had probably scoured the place a dozen times in the last twenty-four hours. We sat at a round oak table whose top had been buffed to the point of being frictionless. I was afraid to put my hands on it. The overhead light seemed harsh, but then lights were on everywhere in the house.

"How is Lorraine?" I asked Marjorie.

"She finally dropped off a little while ago."

"She's probably been up for thirty-six hours," I observed.

"So what's going on?" Ronnie asked, more concerned now than angry.

"When your father wasn't home last night by seven o'clock and hadn't called, Lorraine called the lab. She was told that Larry had left around noon and hadn't returned. She was worried. She started calling around. Nix. So she drove there herself in the dead of night."

"Good Lord," Ronnie said.

"Exactly. This morning she called a cousin, Frank Kilcannon, who's a lieutenant with the Department. Not much he could do officially, so he called me. So far, no leads."

"Where's his car?" Ronnie asked. Perceptive gal.

"Good question. Lorraine found it there last night, but this morning it was gone. That's when she called Frank."

Ronnie leaned over the table, alarmed. "Well . . . what does that mean?"

I shrugged. "Your dad came back for it or someone else did or it was stolen that night by coincidence." I added, "I'm not big on the coincidence angle."

Ever helpful, Marjorie chimed in. "Do you think you'd recognize a clue if you came across it?"

"I think so. I have that field guide you gave me at Christmas." I patted my sports coat in various places. "Maybe it's in the car."

Marjorie nodded. Ronnie's mouth moved slightly smile-ward.

"Your father hasn't been heard from in over twenty-four hours. Would you agree that's unusual?"

"Well, yes."

"Universal consensus," I said. "I'm sure your father has more friends and we can try them. Estelle over at the lab is contacting the Longwood and HMS community and constitutes a second front. She has a proprietary interest in her doctors, so we'll see what comes of that. Frank can flash his badge around and see who salutes. He actually should be here soon. He has a thing for Marjorie," I added.

"He can get in line," Marjorie replied.

Ronnie's eyes darted to Marjorie's hand, which displayed a carat and a half's worth of marital status.

"So I just missed Lorraine?" I asked.

"Not by much," Marjorie confirmed.

Lorraine had bounced between hope and despair the entire afternoon with Marjorie diverting her attention as she was able, but it was like moving a compass needle off magnetic north; you could only jiggle it momentarily.

"I built you up as the Sherlock Holmes of our time," Marjorie said.

"No wonder she fell asleep," I said.

"She hung on until Ronnie arrived and then just wound down like a music box. I told her I'd wake her when you arrived," she said, looking at me, "but I had my fingers crossed behind my back."

"Let her sleep," Ronnie said.

"Absolutely," I agreed. "I'll wait around until Frank gets here, and we'll figure out what to do tomorrow. I'll check in with Estelle and your father's lab to see what they've turned up. I suppose I better give Schuyler another shot as well.

"Do you know anything about Steve?" Ronnie asked.

"Well, no, not yet. But I'm sure I can find him on the Harvard website."

"Wait here," Marjorie said. She got up and left the kitchen. I looked at Ronnie some more. Her complexion was that fortunate kind where you couldn't be sure how much makeup, if any, she was wearing. Ronnie looked mostly at the table, finding it more interesting than me. Marjorie came back with prints from the website.

"You're the best," I said. Ronnie seemed impressed as well.

Steven Schuyler, PhD was an outdoorsy, kayak sort with sandy hair and a short beard. Mid to late thirties. I thought he ought to wear round, wire-rimmed glasses even if he had to use plain glass.

Ronnie was frowning slightly.

"You said you knew him," I prompted.

She paused. "Yes. We dated for a while."

"The plot thickens," I observed.

"Nothing came of it," she replied, pushing the page away from her.

"Why don't you come with me when I go back to the lab tomorrow," I asked her. Where was *this* coming from? Even Marjorie pulled back a little.

"Mmm, I don't know."

"C'mon. How often do you get to hang out with the Sherlock Holmes of our time?"

She didn't respond.

"I'll let you shoot somebody," I offered as an added enticement to a New Yorker. "Really, people may be more likely to open up to you than to me. Schuyler, for instance, although it seems unlikely he knows anything; if he did you'd think he would have called."

"I don't know. I'm tired. I haven't really talked with Lorraine yet."

The doorbell rang. "Frank," I said, standing. "Do you want to get it?" I asked Ronnie. She shook her head.

I went to the front door and opened it.

"This is embarrassing, you selling encyclopedia door-to-door at night."

Frank stepped in. "I have a volume right here that'll fit in your mouth."

His gray raincoat was damp. His hair too, but it was thick and stood up to it pretty well. He looked tired.

"Let's go back to the kitchen. Lorraine is asleep; she finally ran out of steam. Larry's daughter Ronnie is here. She seems skeptical of me."

"Say it ain't so."

"As an added bonus, Marjorie is still here."

He brightened. "That gives me at least one intelligent person to talk to."

We entered the kitchen. Marjorie was already up. "Coffee, Frank?" she asked. Where she had acquired her coffee-making skills, I had no idea.

"Sure, why not." He probably would have taken a jar of paint thinner from her.

"This is Ronnie Kooyman," I said. Frank took her hand and introduced himself.

"Sorry you have to go through all this," he said.

"So what's the police take on my father's disappearance?" she asked.

"The take is that we don't have a take on it. Paper hasn't been laid yet." He nodded toward me. "I asked Del here to tide us over."

He looked at me. "So is the tide in or out?"

"Still out," I conceded. I recounted the afternoon's events.

"Just up and left," Frank mused. "It does seem odd. Well," he continued, "your father isn't in any hospital around here. I had someone call our airline contacts at Logan, but so far nothing. Of course, he could travel under an alias. His car hasn't turned up yet. I can get some uniforms over to Long-wood tomorrow to go over the area." Our eyes met. *Going over* meant alleys and dumpsters and a body bag. And leaving this out of any report to Lorraine. Having been down this alley—literally—with Naomi, I was certain Marjorie understood this as well. Ronnie, maybe, maybe not.

I changed the subject and looked at Ronnie. "I tend to reject the idea that your father is in the clutches of some siren. What do you think?"

She shook her head. "No, I don't think so."

We were conscious of being four people at a table in the home of a distraught woman collapsed in her bedroom, the wife of a man who might himself be in serious trouble. At the point when the silence became awkward, Frank said to Ronnie, "Well, your pop's out there somewhere and if he doesn't find you first, we'll find him." The party line.

"I think Marjorie and I will go," I said to Ronnie. "I don't know how long your stepmother will manage to sleep, but the more the better, and when she wakes up you can give her the report. I'll be back tomorrow morning with the Friday agenda."

I didn't mention the invitation to join me; the idea now seemed impulsive, ill-advised. Not very professional, certainly, and the chances seemed good that it would turn into one of those bickering buddy movies but without the laughs.

Marjorie and I preceded Frank out into the night. I thanked Marjorie and told her that I might call on her in the morning, which was ridiculous since she would return no matter what. I sat in my car, staring at the back of Ronnie's rental. A few moments later, Frank slid into the passenger's seat.

"I don't think she's a Mormon," he said.

"Huh? Who—Ronnie?"

"Who else?"

"Does seem unlikely."

After a few moments: "Is it that obvious?"

"Let's just say you seemed attentive."

I smirked. "Great."

"You want her to tag along tomorrow?"

So she had beefed to Frank. "Somebody's gotta do my work for me."

"That's for sure. For what it's worth, I put in a good word for you."

"Thanks," I said flatly. I was embarrassed.

"I don't like this, Frank. I don't like the car thing. Of course, we have only Lorraine's and Estelle's word on it, but I'm not getting any bad vibes from anybody so far."

That Larry Kooyman might be dead lay unspoken between us.

We sat there silently for a few more moments. "Go home and get your beauty sleep," Frank finally said.

"You too."

nine

Sleep.

Sure.

A cup of soup, a soothing half-hour of professional wrestling, and then sweet, sweet slumber.

My mind spluttered along like a lawn mower engine. Foul play vs. accident vs. desertion. I still couldn't catch sight of criminal intent. Mug a guy at high noon in an amphitheater of witnesses? Lure him away, then—but with what? Better dessert? And what stops him from saying something to someone or leaving a note?

Accident or medical emergency? Either should have been reported by now. No, things were tending toward flight, to a rendezvous on sparkling waters or over them in a conspiring lounge. Perhaps within the brooding heart of Larry Kooyman, sin had conceived and finally breached. His life's work tossed aside (interminable? inconsequential?) along with his comfortable, old-shoe of a wife. Freedom!

There was also a combination plate on the menu: A heart-attack, say, at the apartment of his mistress/boyfriend, who was then left with a clean-up job of the sort not provided for in the yellow pages. Could explain the car, too, if the Jezebel waited until she/he could more safely sneak it out. But such outcomes also meant that Lorraine gets blasted out of a cannon aimed at a brick wall and with her husband at the fuse. No fun there. All of which brought forth yet another question: Which Larry is preferable—alive and fallen or dead and righteous? Not the no-brainer you'd think, but again in this, as in so many matters, the world and I have parted company.

I had continued south from the Kooyman's until I hit 128 and then turned north until I left the freeway at Lincoln. Lincoln is a suburb where rich people live. I feel guilty about it but not enough to move. Custom built homes abound, representing every period and style—Tudor, Regency, Colonial, French Provincial, Italianate, even one touted as seventeenth century Japanese Imperial (who could challenge it?)—all might be seen in this residential EPCOT center. I have a condominium in a complex tucked back into the woods on a pond, at the edge of a planned neighborhood of beige houses with high ceilings and a five-to-one room to occupant ratio. It's not Millennial, but away from the concrete perdition of central Boston, it gives you a glimmer.

I wiggled the key in one of the dead bolts to alert the attack animals and hit the light switch as I entered. A lamp across the room responded with a welcoming glow. As usual, the sentinels had deserted their post. I could have been Jack the Ripper for all they cared. Well, I had their number. As I walked to the kitchen, I exclaimed, *"Special taste treat!"* Response was Pavlovian, and they bound into view from the hallway—Ficus and Biscuit, those two fine specimens of rabbitry.

Ficus is a mottled white, brown, and gray mini-lop, four pounds of congealed, neutered sweetness. His female partner, Biscuit Bunny, is a larger, solid New Zealand White with attitude. If I sit on the edge of the sofa, lean back and extend my legs, Biscuit will run up the inclined plane, squat on my chest, and let me spoon feed her. And she'll eat anything—chocolate pudding, Spanish rice, cheddar cheese—you name it. I haven't tried raw meat for fear of what I'd learn. Ficus, a gentlebuck, sticks to traditional bunny cuisine, alfalfa and food pellets, but joins his mate in prizing banana, cucumber, and lettuce. Both turn up their snoots at carrots.

I upbraided the slackers for abandoning their post. "Suppose someone broke in?" I demanded of them. "Well?" They reflected on their poor discipline and vowed improvement. I fed them and then reassembled some leftovers into a meal for myself, reminded of Mexican fast-food places where the menu is forty combinations of six ingredients. As a missionary in Europe, we had called one of these combinations Barfo.

I had spent only a few hours on the Kooyman case, but it seemed longer and I was tired. I tried the TV, for social diagnostic purposes if nothing else. I have an uneasy, ambivalent relationship with television; sometimes I'm watching pleasant people I feel to root for, at other times I understand why Rome fell. This night the range of programming seemed even more limited than that of fast food and less nutritious, all variations of *It's All About Me, America's Funniest Tax Returns, Rx for Sex,* and *The Ten Commandments—Nine Too Many.* Nature shows featured carnivorous insects and history channels were devoted to Nazism. There were also several channels of commercials, interrupted by a few minutes of movie. I have seventy channels and clicked straight through them all.

No reality show, though, on the life of Larry Kooyman. The only cameras trained on him operate within the minds of his beleaguered wife and a perplexed detective, and their product is underdeveloped and out of focus.

I would have Marjorie check out Jared Timmerman's Mahler alibi, but I expected it to hold up. What was it—the Fourth in G-major? Suppose it was C-minor—would that mean anything? Come to think of it, I have plenty of classical music but no Mahler. Philistinism? Maybe I was missing out on a pretty good thing and should flex some cultural muscle.

Ronnie, tugging at me in a forbidden fruit sort of way (along with that Janelle, but Janelle was the Ferrari you'd never own versus the Corvette you just might) now stepped from behind the curtain, stage left. Should I really sign her on as a sidekick? The pendulum was swinging back in favor of the notion. Why not? I could always dump her after a couple of hours, probably to our mutual relief. And she might stir the sympathy of someone who knew something. Alternatively, solid results might obtain from the Death Stare.

Del Price, resourceful PI. Part of me just wanted Ronnie to think better of me, to upgrade me from ambulance chaser. Frank had helped; the man radiated a credibility that reflected off me, yet I was sure more was needed. But we'd see; perhaps she just wasn't interested in either the exciting life of the detective or in me.

I gave up on the TV and took my dishes into the kitchen. Ficus and Biscuit had retired to one of their squeezy places. For me, reading, pondering, and praying before sleep.

Where was Larry Kooyman at this moment, I wondered? What was he looking at and thinking about? Lorraine? Almost certainly, whether out of longing, worry, guilt, or all three. I had to find the guy. But was he already on the other side? I wasn't prepared to follow him that far, although there is a flaky psychic across the street from my office who, to hear her talk, has banked plenty of frequent flyer mileage from journeys Beyond. He didn't *feel* dead to me. Let Frank initiate a quiet quest for a body; I would continue to search for something more animated.

And so I prayed that evening, at the edge of my bed, for the safe-keeping

of Larry Kooyman until, by whatever providences had been set in place by
God, he might be delivered safely to his companion of thirty years. And
I asked for His comfort to blanket Lorraine in her personal Gethsemane.
I remembered Frank and Marjorie and several others. And I remembered
myself, asking for those things I had need of: The grace to see what I should
see, to discern which doors to open and which to pass by and, as always, an
escape from the jeopardy of our mortality.

Acts done and acts left undone, opportunities squandered, people pushed
out of our car of life as we barrel down the street. Or trying to do the right
thing but being unaccountably hedged up in the way. Viewing ourselves as
though watching a movie of a stranger, as we do ridiculous and unspeakable
things.

The Children of Israel shrinking against the Red Sea. Guilt and remorse.
Paul in the dungeons of Philippi. Addiction. Debt. Depression. Abraham,
Isaac, and the knife.

Life is about escape.

Help us, Lord, escape.

ten

A detective? The next day? It had to be Kooyman's wife—the Medical School couldn't have moved that quickly and would, if the time came, rely on the police. Why so soon—was Kooyman on that short of leash? You'd think she'd give the poor guy a couple of days, allow him the chance to slink home with a sheepish grin and a fistful of flowers. And by what criteria had she chosen a gumshoe—the phone book? Women.

Karol had called him in a panic, relaying, no doubt accurately, the state of mind of their colleague who had been contacted by the gumshoe. Not one day had passed and already the sound of hooves on the trail behind them!

Calm down, he ordered. If the wife was behind this, then of course she would begin with her husband's colleagues and friends. The detective's path had been perfectly natural, predictable even. Start at the center and move outwards. Wouldn't the police follow the same route? The gumshoe had learned nothing today and would learn nothing more as he spiraled out into the wilderness. Who was next—the wider Longwood research community and neighborhood merchants? Fine. All contacted will shrug their shoulders. He and Karol had no links to Kooyman in any event—they were invisible.

And the motel? Even if it came into play—and how could it?—hadn't it been scrubbed clean? Hadn't he insisted that they always wear gloves? Not a fingerprint would be found. The Project and its participants had been relocated. There was nowhere for the gumshoe to go. With no clues and no leads the investigation was sure to stall.

So: Relax. All had been foreseen.

He hung up the phone and closed his eyes. He knew Karol wouldn't relax and *would have to be propped up again. Again. But when had it been otherwise?*

He could not allow it to all come tumbling down now. And it wouldn't, not if everyone kept his wits. Still, something nagged at him, that needle in his head. Now it was the tempo. Too quick. Wasn't the woman embarrassed, sending out a rent-by-the-hour peeper the next day? Talk about henpecked!

He wasn't worried, really, but it would be wise to inquire after this Del Price. Threatening the detective seemed a cliché that never worked in the movies, but if it came to it, perhaps Kooyman's wife could be persuaded to call off the hounds, allowing the players to take a breather. Once the money dried up, the detective would slink away.

His phone rang. The department chair-troll, needing him for something of galactic unimportance. This was what was wrong with academia, the latest specimen of the pestering fleabites ever bedeviling his career. His assistant was not in the outer office. Fine. He left the office doors open. He wouldn't be gone long.

eleven

Friday morning found me again on the Kooyman's doorstep. Lorraine let me in. She was rested in some narrow physiological sense, but it wasn't enough or of the right kind. She was wearing fresh slacks (blue) and blouse (green) but was ill-at-ease in them, nervous, working against an invisible mantle that chafed and fought adjustment. She began by apologizing for having fallen asleep the night before.

"Just as well," I replied. "I was exposed as a charlatan by Ronnie."

"Oh, I'm sure Ronnie doesn't think that."

"Doesn't think *what*?" Ronnie demanded as she entered the living room. She was wearing blue jeans of the kind only women can buy—they fit exactly—and a black silk blouse. She had accessorized with a thick, twisted rope necklace of silver with accompanying bracelets. She stared silently.

She was going with me.

"I'm not sure how useful you're going to be at undercover work," I said.

"Let me handle the interrogation aspect," she replied. A vision of Ronnie slapping her palm with a rubber hose flickered before me, and I pushed it into a deep well to join the one of Biscuit Bunny ripping into cutlets.

Lorraine looked back and forth between us, her worry momentarily deflected. "I'll make you some breakfast," she offered.

"I ate at home," I said, "but thanks. Just fix something for Ronnie and yourself."

We walked into the kitchen. I sat again at the oak table and Ronnie joined me after retrieving a yogurt from the refrigerator. Nothing more elaborate was forthcoming; Ronnie wasn't a bacon-and-eggs gal and Lorraine hadn't the appetite. She put down coffee mugs for herself and Ronnie, ignoring me. Marjorie, I figured.

I summarized my Thursday odyssey for Lorraine. I explained that an important aspect of the investigation was to eliminate fruitless lines of inquiry. Many trails there could be, wandering into the wild, but it was too time-consuming to hike down them all collecting stones and leaves and bugs, only to have to retrace your steps. Better to strike the right path at the outset. But how to discern it? How would it recommend itself? In the back of my mind, I felt a Sunday School lesson taking shape. Many fingers pointing this way and that to the Promised Land. How much of our lives is wasted on the kinds of roads marked on maps as "unimproved?"

Tired, depressed, and confused, Lorraine was mostly silent. *Where is he?* hung in the air like burnt popcorn. What other question was there? Could I offer something other than professional competence?

I could.

"Lorraine, let me say something. I suspect that you have gathered from Marjorie that we are religious sorts."

"Yes. Latter-day Saints. I had a girlfriend in high school who was a Mormon."

"Everyone did. We're like Catholics—we're everywhere. At the risk of sounding like Religion Lite, I'll just say it's a Mormon thing to be optimistic. Our faith is such that we expect to get Help as we go along, even when things don't work out as anticipated. That's 'Help' with a capital H."

I looked at Ronnie. "It's kind of embarrassing to be a detective who isn't an alcoholic. I have to overcompensate."

"Don't you have to spend a lot of time in dive bars?" she asked.

"Actually, no. I lose credibility when I order a Shirley Temple. I'm usually looking for kids who aren't old enough to get in a bar and don't have the money anyway. I can slur my words, though, if it will help."

A flash of the Annoyed Smile.

I returned to Lorraine. "Ronnie isn't fully buying into the PI thing. I'm going to take her out and try to impress her. Marjorie will be here soon," I added. "I should have more to report today. We're going back to the lab to see what Estelle has turned up there at Hogwarts. After that, we'll see. Did you get any sleep last night?"

"Oh, some."

"Lorraine, hang in there. We'll find Larry." I was about to ask how she had met her husband but realized just in time that the daughter from the failed first marriage was sitting across from me. I let them sip their coffee.

Marjorie arrived. She had brought a laptop with her, anticipating the need to use the Kooyman's as a temporary field HQ. Lorraine was glad to see her. I wondered whether Marjorie had also brought a syringe of morphine, just in case. She's one of those women, more than a few, who are prepared to do Whatever It Takes. Is it something they're born with, one of those portable propensities brought forward from a pre-mortal realm, or something the stress of mortality equips you with, like disease immunity? For Marjorie, the resolve to stare death in the face had been stoked by her drug addicted daughter Naomi. Deal or deny. Marjorie is a dealer, but whether this is something to be admired for, healed of, or both, I'm not sure. Ronnie seemed flinty enough herself, but there's a difference between tough and brittle and sometimes only a hammer will tell.

"So what do you do in New York?" I asked Ronnie. We were in the Taurus, heading for Longwood. "Ever get back to Albany?"

This got me another look. Mistrust. In the look-shooting department she had lots of ammo and was liberal in its dispersion. I let it go for a few seconds. Let her think of me as a Mormon Fu Manchu, then. I was beginning not to care—even, perversely, to like it.

"Jared Timmerman again," I finally sighed. "He thought you and your mother had moved to Albany after the divorce. You know, it wouldn't kill you to think of me as being on your side, at least until you get the bill."

She opened her mouth and then closed it. What meager portion of her bio did I deserve? Not much.

"I'm in real estate," she finally offered. "Manhattan."

"Oh? Hang out with Donald Trump?"

"No."

"You know, I'm thinking of expanding to New York; I'll need an office. What do you have?"

"Nothing you could afford."

"How do you know what I can afford? I shake down a lot of clients."

"Fine. I'll see what I have."

This was about as far down that path I cared to wander, and I hustled back up to the main road. "Have you met Estelle, the major domo at your father's department?"

"Yes. She's been there for a long time."

"I signed her up on the team yesterday to ask around, see if she could find someone who had seen your father leave the building on Wednesday.

Also to identify anyone else who was AWOL around the same time."

"Do you think he left with someone?"

"Don't know. Having nothing to go on, I have to cast a pretty wide net and see what gets pulled in. I can't afford to throw in one skinny little line with a worm on it and hope for the big one."

I paused. "I think he left under his own steam on Wednesday around noon. He could have just walked down the hall and out the door—who would notice it?"

"Why wouldn't he tell someone where he was going?"

"Oh, because it was just routine, something he'd be back from in fifteen minutes. Or maybe he was coerced somehow or was asked not to tell. It's a good question, though. Hence, the net. But I can't see anyone trying to pull something in a busy building at noon—how could you control all the variables? And if the answer lies somewhere in the lab, I've yet to catch on."

"Which is where you come in. We'll talk to Estelle and then wander down the hall to chat up the lab. If you want to strap one of them down in a chair, I say go for it. You want a gun?"

"Suppose I say yes?"

"We could stop and buy one."

"That's what I thought."

"Ronnie, I *am* worried about your dad and I know you are, too. There's just no clear indication of which way this is going. I've started with a fairly limited number of names; after that I'm going to have to start looking further afield. Lorraine can file a missing persons report but even then the police aren't going to throw the whole force at this. Frank is a big help, but there's a limit. The police will assume, not without statistical justification, that your father has left his fading pasture for greener grass."

"It wouldn't be the first time," Ronnie replied.

Did she mean the police, her father, or men in general? Had Larry Kooyman impulsively abandoned his wife and child all those years ago? I didn't want to believe it of him, but it's tough to know what a pillar of the community might have done long ago with a young man's myopia.

And could Ronnie know for sure? Divorce is like one of those complicated mixed drinks where you have to guess at the ingredients, a libation robust enough for the tempered palate but wholly unsuited to the simple, routinized tastes of a child. What her father had done or hadn't; what her mother hadn't done or had; what each of them *thought* had or hadn't been done; what each of them had told Ronnie or had left unsaid; what Ronnie remembered, surmised, or construed. Tough enough for an adult to process, let alone to ask it of a child.

But I had already tuned in briefly to the Ronnie Channel and gotten static. Maybe later.

"Anyway," I continued, "see what you think as we go along. At this job you keep beating the bush until something runs. It's a real close partnership between your brain and your gut. Tough to describe or to teach."

"How does one get to be a detective?" she asked. "Is there a *school* or something?"

McDonald's Hamburger University hung in the air between us.

"Cops sometimes become detectives, but it's not as common as you'd think. Generally you get there through apprenticeship. You hook up with some agency, put in a couple of years, and qualify for a license."

"So you learn to follow people around without getting caught?"

I was finally getting a picture of where she had been going with this all along—private investigation as an extension of male adolescence. An idea, I realized, not to be dismissed out of hand.

"Searching records, actually. Tedious stuff, but less so now with the Internet. Who owns what. Who *owes* what. County clerk files. IRS stuff, if you can get it. But yes, you have to follow people around from time to time."

"Cheating husbands." A statement, not a question. I was hearing a *leitmotif* in the Ronnie opera.

"Yep."

As a greenie, I hadn't much say in choice of assignment, but I had my reasons for not resisting then, either. Things to work through. I had recurring themes as well.

"When I got out on my own, though," I continued, "I stopped shadowing a, shall we say, certain class of husband."

"Why?"

"Oh, mainly because of the Church. So there wouldn't be a barrier between the members and me. I could anticipate their discomfort with the image of me peeking into the windows of adultery and knowing sensitive things about other members. They know I spend most of my time tracking down runaways, generally substance abusers. Sometimes deadbeat dads. Things everyone can get behind."

"No pulling the lid off the sins in your church, huh?"

I suppose we have New York City to thank for this state of mind, that and Hollywood. You have to go back to Bing Crosby to get much sympathy for religion, let alone a church. Since then, what we're generally offered as entertainment along these lines is the well-meaning but out-of-touch country parson sort, the inflexible, paranoid bigot or, for the more sophisticated, the sensitive story of a religious icon torn between his deep love of God on the one hand and his mistress and money on the other.

"It's not much of a melodrama," I responded, "and I don't feel the need to cast the first stone."

"Do you ever find a kid and just leave them alone, don't drag them home?"

"Once or twice. Some kids make better adults than their parents."

I must have scored some points here. Perhaps she was one of the many arrested believers who associates religion with smiting, and I hadn't smitten, had made allowance for some gray between the black and the white. I stopped there rather than risk sliding back into the ooze. There was mutual silence for a while, but now it was more companionable, less arctic.

We crawled along into Back Bay and parked a few blocks from Longwood.

"How much of this has changed since you last saw it?" I asked.

"More buildings. It looks like they keep expanding the hospitals." It was true; I pitied the mutant bird with this many wings.

I pointed to the northwest. "My office is about a half-mile that way, on Beacon." We tried to locate it with X-ray vision though the intervening buildings. "Ronnie, the important thing is to go with your gut at the lab. We'll compare notes later."

She nodded. I thought she probably had a lot of guts to go with.

Estelle was at her desk, busy at the computer. Today she was in a beige pantsuit. Amble bling, too; several relatives of yesterday's bracelets had come to visit.

"Long time no see, Ronnie!"

"Estelle!" she cried.

They did the woman-hug thing. I would have taken a hug like that from either of them. Maybe I could wade in. A short round of bonhomie followed. I was transfixed by Ronnie, who had gone from tundra to tropics at a snap. I was left out, feeling like I ought to be wearing one of those little black chauffer's caps.

"I can't believe my father is putting you through this. You need to keep a better eye on him," she scolded.

"Well, I guess so," Estelle agreed.

"I understand Mr. Price has recruited you."

"I'm glad to help, Ronnie."

"Thank you."

"And thanks from me as well," I said, seizing an opening. "What do you have to report, Agent X?"

"Well, a few things. The lab team was *quite* unsettled by your visit yesterday. They couldn't wait to beat it down here to me. They weren't expecting a private detective to show up, and one who knew their names. It was their first experience with . . ."

"My sort."

"Well, I guess. They didn't know what to think of Larry's absence, either, and I don't think it had sunk in that it was so serious. They've been busy beavers, though, hitting every lab in the building. I think today's plan is to post flyers around the medical school and out on the streets."

I was impressed; the effort spoke well of them and of Larry. And it was my good fortune, too—his team was doing my work for me.

"We're going down to the lab. I told them yesterday to have the whole gang there. They don't know that Ronnie is here. Why don't you walk down with us and introduce her? They might think my sort is foisting an actress on them, although she's not exactly from central casting."

Ronnie swiveled her head toward me like the ball turret on a bomber. I smiled at her. "You need to work with me," I said. "Show up for rehearsals."

I returned to Estelle. "I don't get hugs."

"That's too bad."

"Did you canvas the scientific neighborhood?"

"Yep. I don't know that I've got that much, though. Here's a list of malingerers."

She handed me a printed sheet of several names and their respective affiliations. "Most of these weren't expected to be in on Wednesday for various reasons. We have some sickies, and a few with scheduled leave. The only ones I'm not sure of are the three I marked in red. I just happened to run into Bonnie on my way out the door last night. She's over at the Bio Lab. I haven't seen her for ages. She was on her way to a baby shower. Katie Olreck, it must be. *Anyway*—sorry—I mentioned Larry to her and she said that Dr. Ermiston left his lab Wednesday morning and said he'd be back in the afternoon, but didn't return. He called in Thursday from out of town with some sort of family emergency."

"Does Larry know Dr. Ermiston?"

She shrugged. "Not that I know of. I'm not acquainted with him, except by name. There's no research connection or I'd know. But I put him on the list there.

"Now, Dr. Stendahl called in Wednesday morning and said he'd be out, but then showed up about 2:00 PM. I don't know what that's all about. Katherine Urpee got called out of town for some reason; I'm not sure whether she was here on Wednesday and then left, or didn't come in at all. Sorry."

"Are you kidding?" I assured her, "Do you know how long it would take me or the police to build this list? You did great."

Estelle shook her head. "I didn't get anything from anybody about Larry. It's weird. I don't like it." She turned to Ronnie. "Sorry."

"That's all right," Ronnie replied, "there's an explanation somewhere."

Estelle escorted us to Lab Kooyman. I was gratified to see the entire corps at hand. With Estelle there to wave blessings over my endeavor, I planned to casually assert some authority and talk separately with each—technician? Scientist? (When do you cross over from student—after a PhD? Is there a solemn bestowal of a white lab jacket in a ceremony similar to that of the Master's golf tournament?)

No doubt the members absent Wednesday had been brought up to speed and, presumably, had no germane information or it would have been quickly forwarded to Estelle. Ronnie was the latest in a series of new things for them. Estelle was talking but their eyes, furtively or less so, were on the boss's dishy daughter.

"Hi. I'm Ronnie Kooyman, Larry's daughter. I'm sorry we have to meet under these circumstances. I'm no more sure than you what to make of this; it's all a bit much, isn't it? We've retained Mr. Price, and Estelle tells me you've been busy as well. Lorraine and I certainly appreciate it. Unlike Mr. Price, I'm going to have to learn your names the old fashion way—by asking you."

It came to me at that moment what Ronnie was about. And what she was about was control. From instinct and experience, she knew what it would take to establish herself as the pacesetter, the alpha. No hat-in-hand woman, she. Her thermostat was responsive and had a broad range. Estelle got socked straight away with a blast of Palm Springs; for the lab, collectively of weaker and unfocused will, a warm breeze sufficed.

And so far, I hadn't rated anything.

twelve

Ronnie and I retraced my journey to Harvard from the day before. Another ashen day, too tired to challenge its predecessor or encourage a successor, inspired the same feeling you'd have facing a thirty-hour bus trip.

Engaging as the Kooyman Lab had been, for clues it remained a dry well. Present this time had been the three grad students I'd missed on Thursday and, while Ronnie huddled with the others, I had taken each into Wendi's office to interview, leaving the door to the lab open. Neils Dorsey, Lynn Dovallen, and Jeanette Kelley had not been in the lab on Wednesday and had no knowledge of their chief's plans. Lynn was what once would have been called voluptuous, but now—what? I realized I didn't know what the going term might be; Mormon women, however attractive, are never voluptuous. Jeanette had short-cut hair and was a no-makeup kind of gal, though her diamond stud earrings suggested an evolving tomboy. She was the most careful of the team, inspecting every answer before its release, an attractive quality I would like to see more of. In neither woman did I detect any reticence or dissembling, none of the little signals of guilty knowledge.

Most intriguing had been Neils Dorsey. He was an Ichabod Crane, long-faced and homely but, bucking long odds, had survived his youth with a healthy self-esteem and a native cheer that rewarded contact with him. Attentive parenting, I wondered? What had brought him to medical research? I spared a few moments to draw him out.

Neil's father, a West Virginian with a long coal mining pedigree had slumped home from work one evening and found little Neils in the front

63

yard rubbing a lump of coal over his naked body. Umpteen generations of coal mining ended right there. Neils Senior and his wife sold everything (not much) and resettled in Lexington, Kentucky. Hard work and steady promotion at the United Parcel Service had put his three kids through college. Neils Junior, watching his father go from health to leukemia, took up the test tube. Mining had died in that family line, but speaking the truth, avoiding debt, and going home with the girl you brought to the dance had not. Neils, whose homeliness may have been his saving grace, was dressed for success by parents who were, first and foremost, in the business of raising children.

"Neils," I told him, "I want to urge you, as a total stranger and with all the horsepower I can muster, to remain true to those values."

For maximum impact, I ended it there, but I could have added that he had received a legacy from his father I could not get from my own. I was grateful that my path had crossed Neils'. Another gift from the Weaver at the Loom, who spins the threads that interlock us, one with another, a history written in the tangled knots on our side of the tapestry, the design revealed on the other.

A microscopic fungus attacks potatoes in Ireland in the 1840s and a child is born in Boston instead of Killarney. The Confederacy counts on the power of King Cotton but, alas!—there had been a bumper crop the year *before* the Civil War. Martin Luther finds a use for the innovations of a recently deceased countryman, Johannes Gutenberg. Neils Dorsey Senior defies tradition and Neils Junior escapes the coal pit; what might he give the world one day?

And all of this, per atheism, the product of dumb atomic particles and, possibly, *multiple universes* as well to overcome the gigantic improbability of achieving both a universe with the critical physical conditions necessary for "our kind" of matter and, after that, the chance emergence of an incredibly complex, replicating molecule for evolution to begin working on. I don't even know religious people with that kind of faith.

Finally, with virtually infinite amounts of time, energy, and matter, what gets coughed up is one species whose members can appreciate but briefly the tiniest smidgen of the cosmos before death and its annihilation of all consciousness.

And that's the best a *universe* can do?

Atheists ought to be sending petitions aloft night and day for some god—any god—to take charge of such a wretched effort. What's the point of anything existing if no one can see it?

The lab members had indeed fanned out after my visit the day before, diligent in the pursuit of every tenant at the New Research Building. They couldn't get Larry to the front door with any of them; a few "may have" seen him in the hall around noon—or was it the day before? The Friday agenda was for the full corps to blanket Longwood with flyers and drop in on area businesses. Ronnie and I thanked them for their extra mile.

Before we left, we tracked down two of the scientists on Estelle's list. Katherine Urpee's lab was located at the other end of the building from Kooyman's. Short—she cleared five feet by will power—solid and with an engaging smile of perfect teeth, the Pakistani scientist was open and affable, aided by a lilting accent and clear enunciation. She was also of no help; on Wednesday morning her mother had fallen down and likely needed hip replacement. Ronnie was more-or-less at ease with her; the slight reserve, I decided, was simply Ronnie's acknowledgement that whereas she herself rationed goodwill carefully, Katherine Urpee had bountiful stores.

Shayne Stendahl looked to be eliminated as well. He was a large, barrel-chested guy in jeans and a plaid flannel shirt. No scientist stereotype was going to hold up, I concluded—no oscilloscopes, plentiful jewelry, and now a guy who could have been a logger. Only Jared Timmerman was close and he could just as easily fill the role of theater critic. Dr. Stendahl's Wednesday alibi? His hot water heater had blown out overnight and he had found his children holding a regatta in the basement. His research? Extracellular signals that pass through the cell membrane enroute to the nucleus. I assured him I was all for it. He had his own designer line of mice as well.

Could I have special-order rabbits, I wondered? Maybe ones that glowed in the dark for easy tracking. What was possible in this genetic enlightenment?

We left the Longwood investigation, for now, floating in Dr. Stendahl's basement.

"Do you know Harvard?" I asked Ronnie. I had parked on the fringe of the Harvard campus near Divinity Row, a short walk to the Bio Lab Building.

"Not really. I didn't spend that much time here growing up. I went to college at Middlebury."

"Vermont?" I recognized it as a small liberal arts college with a good reputation. "And they trained you in real estate?"

"No, that came later."

Of course. The Liberal Arts curriculum, which not so long ago prepared a citizenry (or a certain part of it) to converse and reason intelligently across a wide range of the human condition, from poetry to politics, now prepares its graduates for jobs in customer service.

We could have entered the Bio Lab Building through a side door but, attentive to what drama there is in life, I steered us into the courtyard. "I want you to meet a couple of friends of mine."

She too was impressed with the rhino sentinels. "I have them on the look-out here," I bragged. "I won them over."

"They're inanimate," she noted.

"All the greater challenge."

"And they're female".

"You begin, now, to appreciate the odds I faced." This brought a small smile and a look in my direction. "They probably have names," I continued. "Let's ask. I'd like to find out *something* today."

We paused in the foyer. "Who do we see first?" Ronnie asked. "Steve? Or do you want to find this Dr. Ermiston and tie up that loose end?"

"Mmm, no." I shared my reasoning. "I don't know fact one about him and I hate being in that position, even for something like this where he's almost off the radar. Let's try your old pal Schuyler. If he's not here, maybe we can ask Jared Timmerman whether anything ties Ermiston to your father. It's always good to know more than the other guy thinks you know," I concluded, realizing that Ronnie had probably been onto this by second grade.

"As a matter of fact . . ." I pulled out my cell phone. "Hi, it's me," I said to Marjorie. "See if Lorraine knows a Hector Ermiston; he's over here at Harvard . . . uh huh. Thanks." I looked at Ronnie. "No dice. Let's try Steve-o."

We walked down the hall to the old pal's lab. Unlike the evening before, the rooms along the way were now bright with science, people talking and moving around, life studying Life. Life ebbed when we got to Steve Schuyler's lab. It was quiet, but the door was open and someone was there, someone who wasn't the guy in Marjorie's photo. I looked at Ronnie.

"Oh, hi!" she said brightly, blowing on the embers. "I was hoping to find Steve. He knew I was coming today. Where is that rascal?"

In matters of fibbing, Ronnie wasn't as hobbled as I was. Did I thereby escape culpability? *Stop, conscience, stop!*

The assistant, an Hispanic with a Marine haircut and rimless glasses, smiled at Ronnie. "He's home sick."

"What happened?" Ronnie asked, concerned or seemingly so—who could tell?

"Some sort of pneumonia or bad flu." He shrugged. "He said he hoped it wasn't tuberculosis."

"*Tuberculosis?*"

"Well, that's what he said. I took it he was joking. He was going to the doctor."

"I hope so. When was this?"

"Yesterday."

"Wow," I cut in, "that's too bad. I hope he gets well soon . . . you talked to him yesterday?"

"Yeah . . . well, he left a message on the answering machine."

"I'm Del, by the way, and this is Ronnie."

"Carlos," he reciprocated.

I looked at Ronnie. "I don't know whether we should stop by his place or not, now that he's toxic."

Space filling chuckles. I turned back to Carlos.

"Were you here Wednesday as well?"

"Only in the afternoon. Steve had already gone home."

"So he was ill on Wednesday as well?"

"I guess so."

"I hope whoever was here Wednesday morning didn't get what he's got."

"Marie? I don't think so; she was here yesterday."

"Well, get some chicken soup in her, just in case."

Ronnie's turn: "I think I met a Dr. Scholl here the last time I was here—is that Marie?"

"No, Marie's a graduate student. I don't know a Dr. Scholl."

He would the next time he visited a drug store. I jumped in: "Have you spoken with Steve since yesterday?

"No, he said he'd be out through the weekend."

"Sounds like it," I said. "Oh well, we'll probably get a hold of him but tell him Ronnie and Del stopped by."

"Sure."

I looked around. This lab had a lot more high-tech equipment than I had seen in the others, lots of dials and knobs, a serious electric bill. "What's your research here?"

"We're studying the interaction of protein groupings that lead to cell cohesion and how molecules are transported across resulting membranes."

I was getting used to this kind of talk. Cells. A cell was small and had sub-structures within, like a watch. I could follow it that far.

"And this is what it takes?" I wondered, looking around the lab. I thought it likely they could double their grant money by playing flying saucer sounds from hidden speakers.

We retreated to the hall, but before retracing our steps I led us to the office Jared Timmerman I had visited Thursday evening.

"*Dr. Scholl?*" I demanded of Ronnie.

She shrugged. "It's what I came up with."

"Nice try, though, at getting Marie's last name. I'll get Marjorie to find it. Sounds like the guy's pretty sick."

And sick on Wednesday afternoon at that. What about the TB remark— a joke or a cushion for extended time off with a social quarantine?

"C'mon," I said, "I have something else to show you."

I felt bad about attempting another gander at Janelle with Ronnie in tow, but detectives are supposed to be brazen. Since I'm not allowed to drink, smoke, rough up people, or succumb to *noir*-ish women, I felt I might at least attempt brazen. In this I was frustrated: the door was open but no Janelle or anyone else. The other main attraction was still on display, though.

"You ever see a candy bar the size of a baseball bat?" I asked Ronnie.

"It's a monster."

I started. Life at that moment seemed rich and on track. "Thanks for saying that," I said. She returned a quizzical look.

Up to Jared Timmerman's digs.

"My word, young Veronica!" he exclaimed. "Mr. Price here said you'd be coming down." I was unclear on how Boston was "down" from New York. I imagined myself holding a map—make it one of those classy National Geographic ones—and turning it this way and that, testing new perspectives of the world. Is Antarctica on top of maps you buy in Australia? Looked at that way, the broad land masses of Asia, Africa, and the Americas were there to prop up Cape Town and Tierra del Fuego.

"You remind me of your mother," he was continuing, "How is she?"

"Fine," Ronnie replied in a way to discourage further inquiry.

"What news of your father?"

"No news," I said. "We still haven't got a handle on him. We were just at the Schuyler Lab, where we ran into Carlos but no Steve. The guy's apparently laid up with diphtheria. The police will be getting involved soon, I imagine. In the meantime, young Veronica here is helping out." Another Look.

"I see."

"In the interest of clutching at straws, we're to visit a Dr. Ermiston. What do you know of him?" I was again working up to Timmerman Talk, taking the awful chance of a split infinitive. Brazen.

"Yes," he replied, "Hector Ermiston." He cocked his head. "Hmmm . . . I don't know that Larry is acquainted with him. Perhaps knows *of* him—many do—rather than the reverse." He paused. "Sorry. Dr. Ermiston is our resident cloner." I caught a tone, I thought, to *cloner*. "Cozy with some rather important biotech firms. Attractive ones financially, I should say. How does he factor in?"

Factor in. I could listen to this all day. "We're working from a list of others in the scientific community also absent on Wednesday."

"I see. Lab Ermiston is on the floor immediately above and in the south corner." He didn't offer to escort us. "Veronica, I will help in every possible way to locate your father. An accident still seems to hold the greatest probability."

And the least disturbing.

"You have my card," I said.

"Indeed."

"Thank you . . . Jared," Ronnie said

"Perhaps dinner when we can all be together," he added. Judicially phrased, I thought.

"Of course."

"One last thing," I said. "Do the rhinos out front have names?"

"Most certainly. Victoria and Bessie."

"Which is which?"

He smiled. "Precisely."

The Ermiston spread was substantial, extending along both arms at the corner of the building. The doors were closed, with no lights showing behind the frosted glass. A reception office, however, was open.

A different order of affairs, indeed. This place had a definite *feng shui* that exuded its aura: *Money is here—should you be?* I believe there is a book, a sort of field guide that categorizes the wealthy by their tracks and spoor. In its aggressiveness, this office gave itself away as *nouveau riche*. I could appreciate, though, that with limited space hard choices had to be made.

They'd had to economize on the desk, for example. One as big as a tennis court wasn't going to cut it, but a seven-footer of polished mahogany was angled in a back corner, requiring the petitioner to traverse the room self-consciously in approaching the seat of grace. At least it wasn't on a raised dais. The telephone and computer monitor seemed as lonely on it as polar explorers.

And with a beefy desk you're going to want plush leather chairs and lo!—there they were! Dark chocolate, two of them, with recessed buttons and deep seats. A matching couch kept them company. A couple of squatty, bow-legged oriental tables held twenty-gallon pots of ferns, lush with prehistoric health and ambition. The walls were a rich burgundy with wainscoting. Two paintings, modern abstracts and possibly originals, were situated on either long wall. Lighting was warmly cast from several standing floor lamps. Wall to wall carpeting had possibly been taboo, so a slate floor and oriental carpets had to do. I imagined the decorators going back and forth on a faux fireplace.

And all of this was just a tableau, really, for the most distinctive feature of the office—a five-foot wide, floor to ceiling stained glass representation of the constellation Gemini, with its defining stars and pale outlines of the twins. Modern but with a Renaissance flavor, it was rich blue with golden stars and was backlit. It was truly stunning.

I was still appreciating it when I said to Ronnie, "You're the one in real estate—what's going on here?"

"I don't know," she said, "it seems a bit much."

"It's not saying Bio Lab to me," I agreed, "despite the cloning angle with the Gemini. He must have gotten a zoning variance for this. Probably a showpiece for the biotech angles Timmerman mentioned."

Indeed, there was nothing utilitarian about the place at all; maybe Ermiston had a pre-pre-office we had missed where real work got done by the downstairs staff.

The room was unoccupied. Considering the bare desk there didn't seem much for anyone to do. Why was Janelle down in that cracker box? Were I Ermiston, I'd install her here post haste. In the wall to the right, another doorway opened into what should be Dr. Ermiston's private office. I walked to that.

This room, as expected, was larger than its antechamber and decorated in kind. Floor to ceiling bookshelves wrapped around two walls. The shelves alternated between books and design elements—small sculptures, polished geological specimens, ceramics, photos in frames. Wooden chess pieces from a well-turned Staunton set had been placed here and there across the shelves. Other photographs were hung on a bare wall in a loosely interlocking puzzle-piece array. Leaning near them were what I took to be snow skis in a protective canvas stocking; a red and white airline ID tag dangled from the zipper. A desk, similar to the one in the outer office but smaller was strewn with loose papers. A chair, sleek and ergonomic, was turned with the seat facing the doorway. How long ago had it been vacated? I stepped into the room and placed my hand on the seat. Slightly warm, as was the monitor on the desk.

I turned to the photographs. A silver-framed one in the bookcase showed two men, and since one of them was one of our Senators I took the other to be Hector Ermiston. The latter was showing up regularly in the other photos as well, with other parties who were unknown to me. None was Larry Kooyman. No photos either of a Mrs. Ermiston or of any kids or grandchildren. In fact, no photos at all of anyone in casual clothes. A tall, ruddy man with sculpted, wavy silver hair appeared in several of the photos with Ermiston; they looked to be the same age.

Ermiston himself was a professional everyman. Scientist, CEO, attorney, doctor—he might have played any of these parts. About five-eight, I judged, mid-fifties. Carefully cut dark hair (colored?) over a high forehead, a proportional, straight nose, solid brows over slightly sunken eyes. A firm mouth, but one unstretched by much smiling or laughter. He was always looking straight at you like he knew you were there in front of him. Hazardous to judge from a photos, of course, but I had a dozen to compare and you could almost cut him out of every one, shuffle the cutouts, and replace them randomly without disturbing any compositions. Cool, calm, and collected, as they used to say, but I wasn't completely sold on the calm; I caught something behind the eyes. Or not. Maybe he was a Little League coach and I was being too imaginative. Helpfully, a second opinion was available.

Ronnie had followed me into the office. "I don't see your dad in any of the photos," I said, "but see if anyone else rings a bell. I'm also interested in what you make of Ermiston here."

She studied several photographs. "I wouldn't work for him," she said. "He's full of himself."

We still had the place to ourselves. Were someone to come in, I would simply state my business and confess to being impressed with the layout. Actually, I was hoping someone would show up so I could scratch this off the list.

I unzipped the ski stocking. Rossignol, new and unused. I cocked an eye towards the papers lying carefree on the desk, but nothing popped out. I noted his office phone number. The window onto the campus had what would be called a treatment rather than curtains, and I looked out.

Larry Kooyman, come home.

"I can tell you something else about this guy," Ronnie said, but didn't tell me what the something was.

I tuned back to the door. "Let's see if we can find someone in one of the labs."

We were to be disappointed; at none of the doors I took to be entrances to Ermiston laboratories did knocking produce an appearance.

Well, it was Friday. Maybe it was Gregor Mendel's birthday.

thirteen

On to Somerville for a compassionate visit to the sick.

I was unsettled by Schuyler. Why hadn't he called Lorraine? She, Jared Timmerman and I had left messages; where was he in the hour of need? Were Ronnie and I approaching a plague house?

We rode in silence for a while. We seemed more comfortable with each other; not *comfortable*, just "more." But I was attracted to her and women can sense these things. The timing wasn't right to go fishing for a boyfriend. Did she have many women friends? She was guarded, a tough read but, on balance, didn't seem to be a very happy person. So was I going to heal her?

"Was Steve a student of your father's?"

"Yes. Was that a guess?"

"An educated one. There's the age difference, for one thing. Looks like a good teacher/student fit. Plus, you're in New York. How would you have met him?"

She gave me a sidelong, silent appraisal.

"Dad hoping for a match, that sort of thing?"

She turned to take in the quaint charm of Somerville. "Yes, it was that sort of thing. My father had Steve sized up as son-in-law material."

"I take it he wasn't."

"You may so take it."

Good, I thought—but who was I to feel proprietary?

"I'm sorry. Look, I thought it might be helpful if you talked to Schuyler. I'm not trying to use you to some other end."

"I understand. But he hasn't called Lorraine, has he?"

"Great minds think alike," I said. "But I don't want to expose you to anything, either. The guy might really be wiped out."

"Do you even know what diphtheria is?" she asked.

"No idea whatsoever."

"Me either."

"Well then," I said, "let's hope he doesn't have it."

Ronnie began to laugh, the real thing, and kept at it. I wasn't sure what to make of the fact that it took a communicable disease to do it.

It being a weekday morning, public parking along the residential streets was temporarily available to the public. I found a spot near Schuyler's condo.

"C'mon," I directed Ronnie before we came to the entry, "let's see if we can figure out which car is his." We walked down a narrow driveway into the parking grotto beneath the building. In the dim light we regarded a handful of vehicles.

"Recognize one?" I asked.

"No, but it's been several years."

Cars have windows and the search was soon over. I spotted a green Subaru that looked like a Schuyler kind of car. It was. From the mess within, including wadded clothes, hamburger wrappers and some loose surgical gloves, I made out envelopes addressed to him. Nothing looked suspicious. No lunch box. I jotted down the license plate. We returned to the street.

Again with buzzer and silence. I noticed my card was gone from his mailbox and I didn't see it on the floor.

"I think we're going to have to be a little more aggressive," I said.

Ronnie stepped away from the inner door.

"That's not what I meant." I pushed the other buttons, three short pokes on each, hoping this was someone's code. The machine gun approach can backfire, of course; depending on construction quality residents might hear the progression of muted buzzers filtering throughout the structure. Ronnie was back at the door, looking at the catch as though appraising its strength when a buzz and click rewarded us. She looked at me and pulled the door open, a player now in a real detective drama.

A slow elevator pushed us to the third floor.

"We aren't having much success with Dr. Steve. I'm going to try something that I believe I'm going to call . . . mmm . . . the East German approach."

"You're going to kick the door in?" she asked approvingly. She'd been cheated in the vestibule.

"No. Good point, though. Okay, *polite* East German. I'm going to bang on the door."

"Oh."

"I'm telling you this so you won't be startled. In case I break my hand, I want you to listen for anything in the apartment."

I had ears too, and sturdy bones, but I wanted to give Ronnie an active role in the day's adventure.

The floor was silent. A stumpy, crystal chandelier gave its best against a narrow, carpeted hallway with dark walls. A side table and wall mirror had been thoughtfully provided for whoever might need a side table and mirror in a condo hallway. The residence doors were black lacquer. We were to imagine ourselves in an upscale hotel. I was reminded of the Kooyman's living room and so many others like it. Yes, life is chaos but the ideal is otherwise and we're willing to consecrate a space to achieve it, sometimes a room, sometimes in a cabinet or on a shelf, a little temple precinct within our mundane dwellings. Is this recognition a dim reflection from a former, better ordered sphere?

"This the kind of stuff you sell?" I asked.

"Sometimes."

"Here's his door." I looked at Ronnie, stepped up, and hit it with three sharp, hard-knuckled cracks, enough to feel it in my hand and shake the door.

Response was immediate. Muffled movement—what may have been the swish of papers across a table top—and a thump, not sharp enough to be glass but distinct, maybe a book. Then silence.

Ronnie eyes widened. "*Someone's there*," she whispered.

"Maybe a cat."

"No," she said quickly, apparently speaking ahead of her mind. "*No.* Steve's allergic to cats." She seemed surprised that it had come back to her so easily.

It wasn't a dog, either; dogs bark and run for the door. I pointed at her. "You're on," I mouthed.

"Steve," she cried in good volume, "Steve—it's me, Ronnie."

Had I been alone would he have responded? But Ronnie rapped and called out again and it was enough. "Just a minute," a voice said from deep within the apartment. Ronnie and I looked at each other.

"You're not going to punch him out or anything?" I asked.

She looked annoyed and turned back to the door. "No."

Presently, shuffling within.

The door opened, about a foot. No discernable light came from within. I was disappointed that the door didn't creak.

We beheld the sad and saggy corpus of Steve Schuyler, PhD. Disheveled, as Timmerman would have put it, and a good word it was, one of those words for which you need no dictionary. He looked ill. Tired clothes—you'd think it unlikely that a sweat suit could look exhausted but this one did. Tired face—beard untrimmed, neck unshaved, the sandy hair blowsy, his eyes rheumy red and the skin around them dark, limp, and moist. He had splashed some water around and toweled some of it off and given a quick brush to the teeth, too quick. A little wobbly as well.

Why hadn't he communicated his indisposal from behind the closed door? I could guess: Ronnie.

"Hi, Ron," he said. He tried to sound brighter than his wattage would allow.

Her eyes seemed a little softer. "Steve. We heard you were sick." The "we" stopped her. "This is Del Price. He's, uh, a detective."

This was my standard introduction by third party. I've even thought about printing it on my business card. *Del Price: An, uh, Private Investigator.*

He had been surprised to see two at his door and now he looked at me again. I smiled a polite, non-invasive smile. There are all sorts of smiles.

"We're here about my father," Ronnie continued.

Schuyler was a couple of seconds behind. "Your father."

"Yes, he's been missing since Wednesday."

"We were just asking around," I cut in. "Lorraine is upset and I'm doing the leg work for her. Ronnie came up from New York, and we're checking friends and associates. You're in the friend category," I added in case he was unsure. I didn't mention my message or card left the day before. Would he?

"Oh, Lorraine called," he said. "I thought I called her back."

"You didn't," Ronnie said. "We went by the lab and Carlos said you were ill."

"Carlos," he repeated. You could sense his mind trying to kick into gear. "Well," he continued, "Carlos is right. I'd invite you in, but I don't think it's advisable." I expected a demonstrative cough that didn't come.

"We understand," I said. "The flu?"

"I guess so—something."

"Did you see or speak with Dr. Kooyman at all on Wednesday?"

He dropped his eyes. "Larry? No. Sorry. I haven't seen anyone for two days."

I looked at Ronnie. Tag team.

"When was the last time you talked with Dad?" she asked.

"Oh, I don't know. Maybe a couple of weeks."

"Okay, thanks. You get back to bed."

"That's where I'm headed. How long are you around for?"

"That depends on my father."

He nodded. "Well, I hope he turns up soon."

Ronnie was silent for a moment. Did she think he should have had more to say, to ask? If so, she wasn't alone.

"Take care of yourself," she finally said.

"Sure." He nodded at me once again but with a more appraising eye, albeit a glazed one. "Call me later," he directed at Ronnie.

She didn't reply. The door closed.

"What are your impressions?" I asked. We were back in the car, angled to face each other.

"He looks terrible. I hope he's been to a doctor."

"Oh, he has."

"How do you know?"

"I don't think you're fully appreciating the Sherlock Holmes of our times."

"Not fully," she confessed with annoyed eyes.

"I can even tell you which doctor."

"You found out before we came here."

"No."

She said nothing.

I waited a bit. I liked looking at her. If it made her uncomfortable, she didn't show it.

"Daniels," I finally said. "Dr. Jack Daniels."

It took her a couple of seconds. "You mean he was *drunk?*"

"Well, comfortably numb."

"How could you tell? He looked sick to me."

"Oh, he might be and is self-medicating. I deal with a lot of substance-abusing kids. For one thing, he hasn't been following a strict regimen of oral hygiene. He gave it a quick shot, but it wasn't enough. I was standing closer to him than you were. And there was a wobbliness and weighing of answers. On top of that, for a respiratory contagion the skin around his mouth and nose wasn't chafed. He also didn't seem too concerned with your father."

"No," she agreed, "he didn't. I just thought he was out of it."

"He's had several messages left for him and hasn't responded to a one. But maybe he's been indisposed for two days. You know him—is he a drinker?"

Ronnie shook her head. "No. Not a drunk anyway."

Anyone has things going on in life independent of your investigation and any of them can be made to seem suspicious. That's why there are conspiracy theories, which usually tell you more about their authors than their objects. So the mildly troubling case of Steve Schuyler would probably be left behind to work itself out unobserved in a dark apartment.

"Well, maybe things have changed," I suggested. "In any event, what are the chances that his woes have anything to do with your father? I'm not trying to size up Steve Schuyler for anything, I just think he's acting weird. I suppose we could track down your Dr. Scholl and see what happened on Wednesday."

"I don't know." Ronnie said. I could tell that the visit had troubled her. Did she have *two* people to worry about now?

A change of direction. "There's something else instructive about this experience," I said, "a lesson in detection and, as an added bonus, your religious instruction for the day."

She looked at me. I don't think she had this sort of conversation with many people.

"Actually," I continued, "today's subject is not distinctively Mormon at all, but generally Christian and, for all I know, in accord with World Religion. It's just where my mind has wandered and it does have to do with you."

"So."

"Coincidence. People bump into other people and things happen. Why did they meet at *this* time and in *this* place? Just random atoms banging around? For one thing, I'm pretty certain that without you, your pal Steve would have laid low. But what are the odds that a noise I might reasonably attribute to a cat would need another explanation because *you* happened to be with me at that moment and *you* knew he was allergic to them? The cat thing might mean nothing, of course; some cats bolt and others freeze. There's no telling with a cat. But it's things like that I look for and have come to expect. Synchronicity is probably a better word. It's a marker on the path that says you were expected. The 'by whom' is the religious part. So it made a difference that you were there. Lesson over."

Ronnie took this in for a bit. How many philosophical musings accompany real estate transactions?

"So you think Steve knows something about my father?"

"No, not necessarily. The coincidence itself might be sufficient."

"How could it be? The coincidence doesn't mean anything if *that* time and *that* place aren't important somehow."

"I see your point. I meant that the coincidence might be you rather than Steve, something about you being around. You could be right, of course—but we certainly don't *want* you to be."

Her eyebrows pulled in a little. "Why not?"

"Think about it, Ronnie. If Steve knows something, it's bad juju. Who's he sharing this knowledge with? Not us. Why would Lorraine be out of the loop? If we have to, we can turn you loose on him," I offered, "but for now, he's just a guy who's sick and hung over. We'll let the police know if it comes to that. Here's my cell and here's a list of numbers. Schuyler's lab is on there. See if you can get Marie. Then check with Estelle and call Lorraine—no, wait, make it Marjorie; I don't want Lorraine to jump at the sound of her own phone. We're heading back to the house. We need to powwow with Frank. Maybe your dad's car has turned up."

There was no quick escape from Somerville (many have been trapped for years), but River Street was as good as any.

"So what do you think, so far?" I asked.

The car had been silent for a while. Ronnie was looking out through the windshield but seemed unfocused. Marie had not been at Schuyler's lab, Estelle had had nothing to report, and Marjorie had been apprised of our return.

"You're right," Ronnie said finally, "this is no good at all. Going to my father's lab brought it home to me. Estelle, the lab people, all that ignorance. No one anywhere knows anything."

"No one with whom we've spoken," I corrected.

"No, just everyone who *should* know. I keep turning it over in my mind, thinking of the possibilities. A conspiracy? A kidnapping? Nothing makes any sense. There must have been some random crime that went unwitnessed. The idea that my father just abandoned Lorraine and his work is preposterous."

I hoped so, but I had a case where an entrenched burgher had realized a plan to abandon one life and take up another on the other side of the country, one with another woman and her kids. He had skipped out right after his daughter's high school graduation and arrived in Phoenix in time to attend the replacement daughter's commencement. He had effectively divided himself in half, allowing as little cross-talk as possible. But whereas his final departure had been as abrupt as Larry Kooyman's, the gradual emotional withdrawal from his family and his job of twenty years had been noticed by more than a few. He had made preparations; it had been easy to follow his trail.

"I'm with you," I told Ronnie. "Your father would have to be a lot more convincing than he has been to land the role of a deserter. So did he leave on a sudden notion, did he have an unadvertised appointment, or was he called out unexpectedly? Frank will get the phone records for both office and cell phones. It's unlikely a summons to something sinister would arrive via email; as soon as you send it out you lose control of who sees it and when. In any event, Estelle found nothing telling when she checked Larry's computer Thursday morning."

Unless she had deleted it or didn't find anything because Sharon Florenski or Wayne or someone else had swept clean the email house Wednesday after Larry had gone. Trying to envision the permutations of human interaction is like trying to herd cats; still, in this instance I hadn't smelled a conspiracy there and still didn't.

"I'm afraid that where this is heading probably involves strangers. Something happened after he left the lab, and no one we've talked to has given us any information because none of them *has* any information. The only person near the border of suspicion is Steve Schuyler, and we can hardly accost him because he doesn't have a cat. Let's hope your dad's lab team can turn up a witness.

And what was this thing with felines? I hadn't run across a cat in months and now they seemed to have insinuated themselves in my mind as they would a house, scurrying everywhere. Though I didn't prefer their company, I was no cat hater. With the rabbits, of course, a cat was an impossibility— though I had a dark hunch that in a throw down between Biscuit Bunny and Felix, I would be burying a handful of meow.

It was then, after this image, that I realized what was happening, for it had occurred before during investigations. I had that odd and frustrating sense that my mind was trying to tell me something, was sorting through the information that had gathered like the burrs that grab your clothes on a walk through the fields. It's an anxious and uncomfortable feeling as the brain pulls at the prickles just beneath the surface of consciousness; you feel like running away from it but can't. Concentration doesn't help. And there's no telling where the solution might lie.

But something was hiding, curled up, purring from a small, dark place.

fourteen

Frank had arrived before us. They were seated there, the three of them, at the kitchen table that was becoming our hub, the Round Table to which the questing knights ever returned. An altar, of sorts, upon which we each laid our fears, hopes, and prayers and from which drew on the united spirit to refresh our depleted stores. When Ronnie and I came upon them that Friday afternoon, though, it seemed more like one of those modernist plays of minimal setting just as the curtain rises.

FRANK, a policeman with the aquiline face of a priest and who might once have become one, sits quietly reflecting with his hand curled around a mug of coffee made by MARJORIE, a Mormon who doesn't drink coffee but likely needs it the most as she watches over LORRAINE, wife of the central character, LARRY, who has yet to appear on stage. The dramatic tension arises from whether he will.

Every shade in the house is pulled tight against the outside, and the three at the table share a pool of light cast from a copper fixture above. Other lamps are on throughout the house, but they don't seem to illuminate much, their light clinging timidly to the bulbs. Frank has just arrived, and his eyes reveal a man tired before shift's end. A man who, in addition to his current and pressing duties for the public weal, has quietly arranged some initial, off-the-books probes into a case that officially does not exist yet, on behalf of a distant relative he hardly knows. His silver and black hair is well combed and his clothes—gray slacks, white shirt, black and silver necktie, and charcoal sports coat—hang well on him and, although they haven't been, his hands look manicured. He has greeted and hugged Lorraine, but his good news lies chiefly in the absence of any tangible bad news. He now sits silently at the oak table, waiting to give a more detailed report to THE DETECTIVE, who is just now appearing from offstage with RONNIE, daughter of the missing man. Frank is working his gum, well over the hump from minty freshness to flavorless wad, along the tooth line from one set of molars to the other. There is a rhythm to the chewing, speeding up through the bicuspids and across the dicing incisors, returning to a more ruminative grind at the back. As far as his missing cousin-in-law is concerned, he has opened two fronts—trying to find the man and trying to find his car, the silver Honda. He has located neither. No hospital has taken the man in and, thankfully, the uniforms he had beat the byways and alleys of Longwood have not found him among the refuse. A search of airport parking has failed to locate the car, but here Frank is not betting his retirement against the thoroughness of the effort. He glances at the cousin he hardly knows, yet they share blood and that is enough. He recognizes her torment but discounts the power of words to assuage it. He has never found the right ones. Although it would disappoint Lorraine if she knew, Frank does not think about her husband overmuch; he's seen too much in the last quarter century and has learned not to guess at what might be. He's been wrong too often. Larry is wherever he is and when he's found then they'll know. He doesn't have much else except for a young woman gone missing about the same time as Larry, which information he will offer to the private detective with the same ceremony as a cat dropping a bird at the door. When his mind wanders away from his cousin, perhaps he thinks of his own wife and son and the fragility of the whole human enterprise. It's tough to tell, though, where his thoughts travel because his face doesn't change.

Marjorie, who has discovered the secret of good coffee through intuition and television commercials, also seems to be in a philosophical mood as she stares at a spot on the table where something could be but isn't. Before long her thoughts, as they always do, form themselves into a flowing, silent prayer to, and really, an attempted dialog with, her Heavenly Father on behalf of a daughter who treats her body like a communal kitchen appliance and is bitter that life has been so poorly arranged by either a malevolent deity or a cold, cold universe, that it allows her right to unfettered, radical abandon to fall short of the one freedom she most desires—the freedom from the adverse consequences of her own choices. She invites condemnation and then howls when it arrives. Nothing will either assuage Marjorie's worry or assail her faith. She takes her motto from a famous American theologian and New

York Yankee: *It ain't over 'til it's over.* She's in this for the long haul. What Marjorie can and has done is expand her petition to include a missing man and his beleaguered wife, whom she will accompany on this dark journey like Sam the hobbit, recognizing the burden if unable to personally bear it. Finally, she has a niche remaining for a young detective, whom she thinks of as a son.

Lorraine is also silent and stares out in yet another direction; in her line of vision stands the refrigerator but she stares straight through it, through the door with its narrow shelves of mustard, pearl onions, horseradish, red wine vinegar, and a green can of grated cheese for their spaghetti and then across the glass shelf with the half of ham, yogurt cups, a plate of sandwiches, and larger jars of jam, pickles, and salsa—stares right through the whole of it into a different dimension. She seems as placid as the others, but it's just a temporary equilibrium. Her mind jumps back and forth between a deer frozen in the headlights and a ferret turned loose in a new room. Back and forth, or maybe both at once, like an electron in the cloud of probability said to surround the atomic nucleus, wherein the speeding particle might be anywhere or nowhere or in two places at once. As a wife of some thirty years, she has merged her identity with another and though stronger and more joyful for it, is all the more desolate when cut asunder. More than once, her hands have moved to her chest or hovered briefly in mid-air, searching for something that has gone missing.

All three looked up as we came into the kitchen, three reveries gratefully, perhaps, interrupted. Ronnie, now with more insight into the void swallowing Lorraine, slipped quickly next to her step-mother and put an arm across her shoulders; Lorraine leaned in a little, breaking free from Dimension X to begin a cycle of looking at each of us in turn and then down at the table. I sat between Frank and Marjorie.

"Nothing more at the lab," I began. "It looks like he took wing on a notion or was called out. We need the phone records." This, however, was going to take some time, there being legal hurdles to clear. "Why he took his lunch box, I don't know. *If* he took his lunch," I clarified.

This triggered something in Marjorie, who snapped to, got up, and retrieved from the fridge a plate of sandwiches that had been cut into neat triangular wedges. No one reached for any.

"How did Harvard go?" Frank asked.

"We found out the rhino's names are Bessie and Victoria."

"Wow. You *are* good."

"There seems to be money in biotech stocks, too. Other than that, nothing panned out there, either. It's frustrating," I conceded, "running into nothing but nice people. Steve Schuyler is still laid up, so we took our show to him. We had to finagle our way into his building—"

"You kicked the door in!" Marjorie exclaimed.

"You, too?" I cried. "What's with all the violent women? Ronnie was all for chopping down a tree and battering our way in." Lorraine patted Ronnie's arm and smiled.

"What kind of example are you setting for Frank here?" I demanded. Frank grunted. Marjorie did a slow shrug.

"Anyway, violence of the sort you indicate was unnecessary. I used my wiles."

"I thought you said you got in," Frank retorted, which brought forth a traitorous cackle from Marjorie.

The human punching bag remained composed, added this to a growing list of grievances, and continued. "Anyway, Schuyler seems sick enough; he's certainly been dutifully taking his cough medicine." I looked at Frank. "The kind that *makes* you cough."

Frank nodded. Lorraine didn't react at all.

"He didn't have much of an excuse for not responding to our phone calls, but I don't know what can be made of that. So what's *your* good news, Lt. Kilcannon?"

"More of the same." He reported on the unprofitable hospital and airport sweep. "The airport is pretty big, though." He left it unsaid that the search there was not finished. "I had some men look around the Longwood neighborhood," he continued, "but they didn't turn up anything." He made this search through alleys of urban trash sound nonchalant.

"You look tired," I said. "A million stories in the naked city?"

"And then some. A guy at Star Market barged into a women's restroom with a knife."

"Maybe he wanted to meet a nice girl."

"He did—a body builder. You know that thing in Scotland or somewhere where they throw a log the size of a telephone pole?"

I nodded. "Tossing the caber."

"Yeah. Well, substitute the guy for the pole and you'll get the drift."

All were uplifted by this tale of crime and punishment, but its thin pleasure soon faded. Lorraine's presence was welcomed but cautionary as each of us, in conversation, performed an added calculation of tact and circumlocution.

How did Marjorie while away the hours with her, I wondered? She would hardly smother the distressed woman with patronizing verbal comforters, yet how much silence could they endure together? ·

Frank wasn't through. Leaning back, he said, "There's one more thing, in line with your Who-Took-a-Powder-on-Wednesday angle. I looked through all the missing person reports to see if anything jumped out. Mostly runaways, but a report came in from the roommate of a nurse at Brigham and Women's. The nurse, or rather the ex-nurse—she was fired last week—got a sudden and lucrative job offer and disappeared last Sunday. Odd duck of a job, though. Some guy called up and had the nurse meet him at a pub, hired her for some mysterious short-term gig, and then picked her up a block from her apartment in Dorchester. A couple of hours later and the roommate gets a call from the nurse saying she's at the Garden of Eden. She hasn't been seen or heard from since. At least, that's the roommate's story."

"Why would anyone leave paradise?" I asked. "I don't suppose the roommate trotted along behind the nurse and got the guy's license plate?" It wouldn't have been a bad idea for the nurse to have come up with it, either.

"She did not. Odd but not odd enough for that, I guess. Anyway, it was weird, and so I thought of you."

"And I love it. I just don't know what to do with it."

Back to the matter at hand. "How long before we can get phone records from Larry's office phone and his cell?" I asked Frank. "They're one of the most important things we have left."

He nodded. "I wouldn't count on them for a few days. We're hitting the weekend."

What more to do? I was back contemplating the tedious prospect of joining in the canvassing of the Longwood area's merchants and offices. But I had one final out, it seemed.

"Give me the skinny on the nurse and her roommate. It can't take much time to check out. Tough to see a connection, but I guess you eat what's on your plate. Lorraine, I'm sure it's seemed like an eternity to you, but it's been barely 48 hours. What we have is a mystery, not a tragedy. And Frank, Ronnie, Marjorie, and I are here with you."

"She's been a godsend," Lorraine replied, without specifying whom she meant. It was clear that the drag of gravity was pulling her down and in on herself, physically and spiritually. Her sleep cycle had probably flipped to sporadic day naps and nighttime vigils where her mind worked an emotional swing shift.

"I appreciate everything you're doing," Lorraine said. "I don't know what I'd do without . . ."

Frank smiled at her. "Don't worry, cousin. I have a feeling your man will be back here soon."

It struck me as uncharacteristic of him. Was this prediction or comfort? Either way it struck me odd—wrong, even—but I couldn't say why. Surely we were all solicitous of Lorraine's pain; after five minutes with her you wanted to promise the moon. But whatever comfort they had provided Lorraine, Frank's words had had the opposite effect on me. Back came the anxiety, a realization that in some sub-basement of my brain a few of the scattered jigsaw puzzle pieces had been fit together without notifying my conscious mind. There was still some hidden neural protocol to be obliged, flights of stairs to be climbed. I felt like I would start squirming soon. Most uncomfortable.

"Ronnie," I said to break my mood, "I'll check out the nurse or rather the roommate. You may as well stay here with Lorraine; I can't see this taking very long. Then we can confer on Phase Two." I wondered if I sounded like Eisenhower before a map of Europe.

"Fine," she replied.

Frank and I walked to the front door. Outside, he gave me the names, address, and phone number of this most recent conundrum.

"Something's going to shake down," I told him. "I know something but I don't know what it is I know." I raised my eyebrows and gave him the "who knows" look. I added, "It doesn't feel good, either."

He seemed startled for a moment, as though I had correctly guessed the contents of his pockets.

"Yeah," he said. "I think I just lied to Lorraine."

fifteen

The delightfully named Carmen Rosario lived off Blue Hill Parkway in Dorchester, a primarily black neighborhood in unsegregated Boston. It had been a slog to get there and before the trek I had confirmed that she would be available. I assumed that the interview would hardly repay the commute.

I was wrong. The building in which Carmen and Dorthea Caulley, the missing roommate, resided was as undistinguished as anything in view, a four-story, flat-sided brick box with few flourishes that must have looked old when it was built. The neighborhood, while not oppressive, seemed solemn and a little wary; I saw no interaction among the bundled walkers.

The third-floor apartment was a welcomed oasis behind its triple-locked door, which opened into a narrow hallway leading to the kitchen and living room at the front of the building and the bathroom and bedrooms at the rear. The passage was alive with color—Kahlo, Miro, and Matisse prints hung along both walls, each framed with care and expense. And this was not all; small halogen lights had been installed in the ceiling to illuminate each picture. The walls themselves were clean, smooth, and freshly painted in a pale cocoa. An otherwise forgettable space had been converted into a mini gallery.

The hallway was just the appetizer. The main room was an explosion of greater color still, perhaps even to excess, but was all the more welcomed for being unexpected. One wall had been given over entirely to more art prints; joining the hallway artists were Gauguin, Van Gogh and others, seemingly Latin American, whom I did not recognize. These prints were of mixed sizes but uniformly framed so as to not distract the eye from the artwork. The wall had been transformed into a page from a giant stamp album, evoking exciting life in faraway lands. Elsewhere there were ceramic figurines, art glass, and plants galore, *healthy* plants, many of them flowering and in interesting pots of all sizes. The furniture was a pale wood with neutral fabrics—perhaps so it could be located without falling over it—arranged on a carpet as subtle as the flag of Venezuela. A dark wooden latticework of four-inch squares had been suspended from the plaster ceiling, through which vines weaved and from which were hanging two good-sized mobiles. I wasn't sure what the verdict would be from a home design channel, but I thought the space had achieved maximum impact on a probably limited budget.

Carmen was in her mid-twenties, about five-foot-four with good curves that suggested a fuller-figured future. I was grateful to find a gal with her shape who wasn't wearing skintight jeans. She had a round face, well-spaced and wide-opened brown eyes, and straight dark hair that hung below her shoulders. Carmen was bright and earnest—and a talker. Her accent gave her speech a pleasing melodic quality; does English ever sound attractive to a foreign ear? Clearly she believed that her concerns would become yours too, once you could see them in their fullness and rotundity.

I had anticipated this difficulty before arriving—how to finesse the awkward fact that I was interested in *Larry's* disappearance, not *Dorthea's*—and had tried to lay some groundwork by subtly suggesting this on the phone. Perhaps too subtly—I soon realized I was in a contest of wills I might not win.

"Your apartment is amazing." I told her. "It ought to be in some magazine. Are you responsible, or Dorthea, or both?"

"Oh, I was living here before Dorthea came. She's here only five months. Are you going to find her? She's in some kind of trouble!" She shook her head. "It's not good." She looked straight into my face when she talked, like a child looks at Santa.

"Like I told you, I'm already looking for someone, a professor at the Harvard Medical School. He hasn't been seen since Wednesday. I heard about Dorthea and since she works in the Longwood area, I thought I'd talk to you—"

"You think he is the man who took Dorthea?" she interrupted, energized by an unexpected new angle.

I shook my head. "He's not that kind of man, and he disappeared on Wednesday, four days after Dorthea."

Had I taken a sharp turn into the North American Free Trade Agreement, Carmen could have brought it back to Dorthea. I could appreciate her loyalty, though, so I started us down the road together. "Tell me about Dorthea—how long did she work at the hospital?"

"Oh, for over two years. She likes it there. She works in the emergency room. She works all kinds of shifts, really crazy. She—"

Carmen was down the road in running shoes and would be in Connecticut before the next question. It was Conversation Control time. I remembered a scene in a movie, a Western, where a mountain man brings both arms up before him, palms out, in response to a woman running towards him with a rifle and an attitude. I did the same. *Whoa.*

"Carmen, you're clearly a talker, and the good news is I'm a listener. But let me ask you about five questions first, okay?"

"Okay."

"So Dorthea was working at the hospital before she moved in with you here, and she continued working there after she became your roommate?"

"Yes. She was all the time in the emergency room and she—"

Again with the brakes, but this time I restricted them to one upheld hand. "On what day was she fired?"

"Oh, it was Monday last week. Just before Thanksgiving. Pretty sad, huh?"

"And they said she was being fired because…?"

"They say she stole drugs, but she didn't. There was no way she would do that. I know. She says there was some kind of funny business, you know? She's going to get a lawyer. She isn't going to take a fall. Do you think they took her so she couldn't cause trouble? Maybe you know somebody—"

More palm. I felt like a flashing pedestrian signal. "And when did the man who hired her first call?"

"On Sunday. About eleven o'clock"

"Did you take the call or did Dorthea?"

"Dorthea did. She was standing right by the phone—" Carmen spun and pointed at the confirming instrument, a yellow cordless unit sitting on an end table. "She had just gotten her orange juice and was wearing her sweatshirt that she wears on Sunday after church—"

"Just a couple more questions."

I had used up my five questions, but she wasn't keeping count and so we went back and forth for a few bonus rounds, she embellishing her answers with as much color as she could work in, and I allowing more and more time between the questions. Her responses burst from her as fast as the beam leaves a flashlight, except that flashlight batteries would eventually wear out.

What poor cop had taken her statement? On the other hand, she didn't have the disposition to lie and wouldn't give herself the time to think one up. I thought about taking every fifth word and forming a narrative from those. Soon worn down by her unwavering zeal and irresistible charm, I let her run free like a wild horse, demonstrating my defeat by sinking onto the sofa. As promised I listened, cobbling together a coherent story as she galloped along.

Dorthea Caulley had been fired upon suspicion of stealing drugs, chiefly painkillers. A sampler of such was found in her locker or was said to have been found there—the story wasn't clear to Dorthea, or it wasn't clear to Carmen or maybe wasn't clear to either of them. Dorthea asserted her innocence but to no avail. She was planning legal redress. Then, on the Sunday after Thanksgiving, The Man (to Carmen, he was always *The Man*) phoned, introduced himself as Dr. Rogers, and told Dorthea she had been recommended to him by a well-wisher at the hospital. He needed her for an off-the-books situation, not illegal but private and discreet. It would be only a short-term opportunity but she would be well compensated. A young woman was laid up in a private home outside Boston with peritonitis complicated by hepatitis. Wealth and position were implied by Dr. Rogers or inferred by Dorthea. Was she available? Perhaps, but it sounded fishy. The good doctor allowed that it did—could he meet her somewhere close by, say, at Eddie Winter's place a couple of blocks away from her? He would lay it all out and she could decide.

Dorthea had said nothing then to Carmen but filled her in after returning from Eddie's, which turned out to be one of those bar/restaurant combos. She and Dr. Rogers had sat in a booth. He'd offered to buy her some of Eddie's fare but she declined. He'd ordered some fried mozzarella sticks to keep the waitress from hovering.

Dr. Rogers told Dorthea he was from New York but was in Boston because of his patient, or rather because of his patient's daughter, who, like her father, was not an American citizen. The father wasn't a drug lord or anything like that, but he was a man of affairs and his daughter was illegitimate, an unexpected and unexplained branch on the family tree and a complication to some larger dynastic picture. The girl had been stricken in the States before she could return home and part of a friend's house had been outfitted as a temporary hospital, complete with a doctor and round-the-clock nursing staff. Dr. Rogers said the whole set up reminded him of a four-star hotel. They were in a jam, though, because one of the nurses had to leave due to a death in her family. Dorthea had been recommended. The worst had passed for the patient and it was now just a matter of recuperation. There had been no serious complications, but if there were the young woman would of course be rushed to the hospital (a real one) and Dorthea would be out of a job that paid twelve hundred dollars a day. So really, she was being hired just to be on call, pacifying the father as much as the patient. At twelve hundred dollars a day. From Dr. Roger's perspective, it was lucky Dorthea had been fired, because she was now available at short notice. He was prepared to hire her based on the testimony of a trusted acquaintance at Brigham and Women's who had thought Dorthea was getting a sharp stick in the eye from the administration. Dr. Rogers hoped she got her job back; he was just sorry that this was likely to be a short-term gig for her.

Twelve hundred dollars.

A day.

Church-going Dorthea had seen the hand of Providence bestowing an unexpected Thanksgiving blessing on her to counter recent opposition. It struck her as significant that just as there had been two days between the Monday when she was fired and Thanksgiving Day, there had been two days separating Thanksgiving and Dr. Roger's offer. The symmetry suggested design. And twelve hundred dollars suggested something to her as well. Surely this was a stepping stone to reinstatement at the hospital. The offer was propitious and seemed safe, or safe enough. Dr. Rogers' story seemed plausible, or plausible enough. And if it proved otherwise, she would walk.

So she accepted. Dorthea was to go home and pack a bag for a week's stay; room and board were of course provided. Dr. Rogers would call on her in an hour. He had made it clear that in addition to her professional duties, she was being paid for her discretion. The father had gone to some trouble and expense to protect his daughter. Dorthea should say nothing to her roommate or to anyone else. Such was the father's demand, understandable given the circumstances and easy enough to comply with. In this regard, Dr. Rogers had assured Dorthea that he was in the same boat as she.

Dorthea returned to the apartment and packed. She found her instructions elastic enough, though, to give Carmen the general drift; after all, Carmen would fret if Dorthea mysteriously disappeared and she couldn't give her roommate the names of the parties or where they were located anyway. She would take her cell phone and try to keep in touch each day. Dr. Rogers had called an hour later and asked Dorthea to meet him around the corner, something about stalled traffic. Carmen had watched her roommate towing her wheeled suitcase up the street to a bright prospect.

But maybe not so cheery after all. A couple of hours later, around four o'clock, Dorthea called. Something was wrong. She was agitated and whispering—never a good combination—as though she had had to sneak out the call. It was tough to make out what she was saying, but there was something about a project, a woman, a Garden of Eden, and being blindfolded. Then the call terminated. Carmen returned it but got only voicemail. She had immediately called the police but what could they do? Dorthea had left under her own steam and wasn't expected to return for a while. They told Carmen to give it a few days.

"But Dorthea has no other family, Mr. Price. No parents. They died. I'm all Dorthea has."

By Tuesday, she had badgered the police into taking the report.

It was not what I had expected. This story had more plot than most TV shows. As for being cryptic, Dorthea had hit it out of the park. *The Garden of Eden?* I marveled; Larry Kooyman and now this, within twenty-four hours of each other, just like Janelle and Ronnie. Symmetry. I wished I had a Dr. Rogers I could tie to Kooyman.

"Carmen, that's quite a story. Did you ever see the man at all?"

"No. He didn't come here to get her. I went down to Eddie's too, and asked them if they knew Dr. Rogers. They said no. They don't know Dorthea either, because she doesn't hang out there. "

"I understand. How sure are you that you heard the words *project* and *Garden of Eden?*"

"Oh, pretty sure. She repeated Garden of Eden twice. I don't know what she meant. Maybe something to do with the church, you know, or the Bible."

Perhaps, but that garden had been out of commission for some time and hadn't been near here.

"Okay. Did she describe this Dr. Rogers at all?"

"No, but I think he was an Anglo."

"Why?"

Carmen shrugged. "I don't know, just the way Dorthea talked. She usually called a black man a brother. I think I should have followed her," she said sadly.

"Nonsense," I replied. "How were you supposed to know? You did the right thing and called the police."

I felt an unexpected, sharp vibration in my chest and started. She noticed it. "What's wrong?"

"My cell phone," I said, and removed it from my inside coat pocket with a note to myself to keep it somewhere else. Scare you to death.

It was Marjorie. "Del, you need to get over here pronto. Something's happened. We've had . . . news." She paused, a little too long. At her end, anyone might think she was listening to my reply.

"Lorraine nearby?"

"Yep, that's right. She just heard from Larry."

What? News, indeed. So why did I feel like I'd bitten into a lemon?

"By phone?"

"Yes."

"Is Frank still there?"

"Yes."

"I take it not everyone is waving at this parade?"

"Yes, I'll tell Lorraine you'll be right over."

"Say good-bye."

"Good-bye."

I put the phone in a side pocket. "Sorry about that. That was my assistant, over at the house of the gentleman I'm looking for." I stopped there, and stood up.

"I'll tell you what I'll do, Carmen. Two things. I don't see any connection at all between Dorthea and the professor I'm looking for. Different days, different circumstances, different everything. Nothing in common except oddness, and they're odd in different ways. If it turns out there *is* a connection, then I'll look for Dorthea as well. Second, if Dorthea doesn't turn up, I'll see if I can find out where the police are with their search." I didn't tell her, but if the Kooyman situation resolved itself soon, I might try to pick up Dorthea's trail. It was a bizarre story. But I couldn't have Carmen bugging me every ten minutes.

"Do you happen to have a photo of Dorthea I could borrow, just in case?"

"Sure, maybe. I'll look in her bedroom." Off she ran, and soon returned with a snapshot of a healthily proportioned, smiling black woman in her late twenties, dressed in sky blue nurse's scrubs. She was standing next to a smaller black woman cradling a triangular bundle with a little puckered face exposed.

"That's Dorthea, huh? She looks like a nice person."

"Oh, she is. Somebody's got to do something to find her, you know?"

"I'll check with the police. Let me have her cell phone number, too."

"Do you charge big money to be a detective?"

"Carmen, if it comes to that, what my client is paying me now will more than cover Dorthea as well. Don't worry about it." As we walked to the door I gave her my card and asked, "What do you do by the way?"

"I'm a seamstress, but I want to have my own dress shop. Blouses, things like that. I can make them."

"If this room is any indication, I'd say you'd make great clothes. Do you design them, too?"

"Oh, yes. I try to get them at work to make some of my designs, but they won't do it."

"Too bad for them." The idea of fronting Carmen some seed money presented itself. Might be worth a shot. "I'll be in touch. And I'll bring back the photo."

Had Marjorie not called, I would have jogged over to this Eddie's joint, since it was close, to see if I could find out who was on the wait staff last Sunday. Instead, I said a quick prayer for Dorthea in my car; it would have to suffice.

So Larry had called. Good for him—and better for Lorraine. And you'd think she would recognize her husband's voice, but Marjorie had let me know that not everyone was buying in. What had Larry or not-Larry said? Had anyone else heard it? At least I had warning of what I was returning to—a beaming but exhausted Lorraine encircled by doubters. And what were they supposed to do, dump cold water on the woman—or was that going to be my job? At least I could sound upbeat as I heard her report, then tiptoe out of the mine field if I had to. On the other hand, maybe it *was* Larry and deliverance was nigh.

But my heart misgave me and there remained a stirring in the dark.
Meeow.

sixteen

Ronnie was standing in the front yard, smoking. She held the cigarette, a Benson & Hedges, between the middle and index fingers
of her right hand, her left forearm across her waist. It's useful to
know cigarette brands when tracking runaway teens. She was staring off over
the rooftops. She seemed on edge, perhaps angry. Did she feel cut out of the
phone call?

"I'm out," I said, "can I bum a smoke off you?"

Her expression didn't change, but I could tell she was reeling in her
gaze.

"I left them inside," she said.

"Just as well; I wouldn't know which end to light. It would be one more
embarrassment."

She turned to me. "Do you have any vices?"

I almost replied flippantly that women with vices were my vice but
restrained myself.

"I try hard not to. I take it no one except Lorraine is comfortable with
this phone call."

She shrugged. "Frank rolled his eyes when he found out."

"He gets carried away sometimes. Let me talk to Lorraine and then we'll
huddle together."

She shot me a look.

"I meant the four of us. Ronnie, you're going to be the death of me. Are
you *sure* you want to be a soccer mom?"

Another choice remark better left unsaid. What if she couldn't have
children?

An adrenalized Lorraine ran toward me as I walked through the door, stopping short of a full-fledged hug. Diffident at the final moment, she settled for grabbing my arm.

"Larry called! He's all right!"

"That's great!" I responded, trying to make it sound as good as it should be, but I had already looked beyond her to the two somber masks of the Greek chorus, there to remind everyone but the uncomprehending main character of life's stern demands.

"Tell me what happened, Lorraine. First, when was this?"

"At 3:05."

A time to be seared in her memory and ours as well.

"The phone rang and I thought it was probably you or Estelle or someone but it *wasn't*. At first I didn't hear anyone. I said 'Hello, hello . . .' "

Too bad Marjorie or Ronnie couldn't have beaten her to the phone, but why would they? It was Lorraine's home and she wasn't under house arrest. I could appreciate that, in her telling, she had made that ring of the phone at 3:05 PM seem routine, but surely it was otherwise. Each shrill peal from the instrument must have been a stick against the drum, reviving the warfare within to attend to the thing or throw it out the window. When would the *right* ring come, the one from Larry lifting the siege? BAM! There it was!—but no, no, it was someone else. The next ring then. On and on, hour after hour, the clock also untrustworthy, a co-conspirator. Surely it had been an hour! So why hadn't the hands moved? But then, moments later, they had been spun like a carnival game.

"Lorraine, let's go to the kitchen and sit at the Round Table. I'm beat."

We did so, the four of us taking our assigned places. The front door opened and closed and Ronnie joined us. Marjorie made no attempt to interject food or drink. I disciplined myself to look only at Lorraine. What I wanted was a tape recording; what I was likely to get was an honest attempt at similitude by the person least likely to provide it.

"Go with me moment by moment through the call. So, you picked up the receiver and heard—dead silence?"

"Yes, well, no, not exactly. There was a sort of hissing and static, like the call was from far away. What I meant was that I didn't hear anyone speak, not at first. So I said, 'Hello . . . hello?' And then Larry said, 'Lorraine is that you?' "

I nodded and moved my hand just enough to stop her. "This is important. There was static so maybe he was far away or on his cell phone. Did you immediately recognize the voice, or did he identify himself because the connection was bad?"

She nodded. "That's what he did. After I said 'Hello, hello,' he said, 'Lorraine, Lorraine is that you? It's Larry.' "

"Was his voice as clear as when you normally hear it on the phone?"

"No, it wasn't—but he had the same problem, because he said he was in Canada and because of the static, it didn't sound like me, either."

I stopped interrupting. If I kept at the questions we would soon be doing a "Who's on First" routine. In addition, I didn't want her to see my continual nitpicking for the skepticism it was. There was a tightrope across this call and I would just have to inch along.

Off the witness stand now, Lorraine did better, relaxing to the extent her mind and body would allow.

"He said I had to listen because the call might be lost at any moment. He was in Canada and because of the noise it didn't sound like me at first. He said he was sorry and that there was a huge mix-up he was angry about. He didn't realize I hadn't been contacted. He said he was on a special project for the government that he'd tell me about when he got home. There was no danger, and he didn't want me to call the police or anyone else to find him; he wasn't lost. If anyone was looking for him they should stop; it would only complicate things for him. It would be four or five more days at the most, and then he'd be home and explain everything. And then he said . . . to make some more butterscotch cookies . . . and that he loved me. Then he was gone."

She could no longer staunch the tears. Ronnie put her arm around her stepmother's shoulders. Lorraine's stress was being shed like a body shivers away the cold. It was good to see the tension dissipate—and all the more cruel should the call prove a hoax.

Might as well test the waters. "Forgive me, Lorraine, but with the static and all, it may have been someone impersonating Larry."

"No, I don't think so. What about the cookies?"

I left the obvious unsaid. Conspiracy implied a dark end and right now it would be like pushing her down the cellar stairs.

"Did you mention Ronnie?"

"Yes, but I'm not sure he heard me."

Or he hadn't recognized the name.

"Did he say anything about the lab, or Estelle?"

"No, but I don't think he had the time. Maybe he is going to call them, too. I don't know. I'm not sure I should say anything if the government's involved."

"I think you're right," I quickly agreed. "Don't tell anyone; we'll leave that up to Larry. Has he ever worked for the government before, any special projects?"

"No . . . well, he's with the National Cancer Institute. And most of his funding comes from the federal government."

"That's a good point. Has he ever been away on some sudden project like this before? Has he ever said anything about being on call for something special?"

"No, but he said he'll explain it all when he comes back."

"Okay. We'll talk some more in a minute. First, I need to tell Frank something about the missing nurse report he mentioned. Remember that strange story he told us? Marjorie, you may want to take some notes."

Marjorie, who wasn't going to take any notes, betrayed nothing as she and Frank stood. Ronnie remained seated.

"I've got something in the car," I said and looked at Ronnie. "I'll be back."

"Be right back, cuz," Frank said and smiled at Lorraine.

Outside, the late autumn afternoon was descending from lighter to darker shades of gray. Apollo and his chariot, wherever they had been riding behind the leaden clouds, were in unseen retreat to his nightly home; that this was somewhere to the West had to be taken on faith. Lights were already on in some of the homes along the street. A weak, chill wind swept along the ground, unable to carry the sodden leaves and needles.

We got into my car. Frank opened the front passenger door for Marjorie, then slipped into the back. I felt like we were in East Berlin avoiding microphones. We sat there like stumps for several moments.

Finally, I said: "Is there anyone presently in this vehicle who would like to say something about this fiasco?"

No.

"Marjorie, please tell me about this phone call."

"She took it in her bedroom, upstairs. She came running downstairs crying, 'Larry's all right! Larry's all right!' I tried to get a blow-by-blow from her and got about the same story as you. I gathered he did most of the talking, did it quickly, and hung up—or got cutoff, depending on your persuasion. He seemed pretty clear that search efforts should cease."

"Yes, he seems to have gotten *that* across," I said.

"It seems you hit a nerve, somewhere," Frank contributed.

"So it would seem. Well, let's first consider the possibility that the call was straight up. Larry *could* be part of some special project. He *might* be in Canada; no physical law of the universe prevents it. Calls *can* cut in and out."

Support for this view was not forthcoming.

"Frank," I prodded, "to your knowledge, have relations between Canada and the U.S. of A. deteriorated to the point that our neighbor to the north is jamming phone traffic?"

Frank grunted.

I almost asked him to pull out his cell phone and beam a test call into Ontario but shook off the idea.

"He doesn't have his passport with him, either, although I guess you wouldn't need one for Canada. And what sort of secret government program needs Larry Kooyman on it anyway? Has an alien carcinoma landed in New-foundland?"

Another snort from Frank.

"Maybe the military has some project to introduce cancer to our ene-mies," Marjorie offered. "Project Tumor."

"There you are," I replied. "The Kooyman Lab is a front for Defense research. Why didn't I see it?"

And yet, who knows? In my TV wanderings I've run across a show called *Jackass*, where invincible youth enact all sorts of dumb, dangerous things. I understand lawsuits for burns and broken bodies have resulted from imi-tation. It's the latest evidence, if more were needed, that whatever lunacy the mortal mind can conceive will be attempted by someone. In addition to jumping off roofs and ramming motorcycles into walls, people regularly play financial, emotional, and spiritual Jackass. Why not a scientific kick in the pants as well? The logical, dispassionate Higher Mind is supposed to be run-ning this quest—but men have passions. So is it really a stretch to think that our defense establishment might attempt to reify some cockeyed scheme? Cancer, though? Wouldn't you have to wait years for the results? And would Larry even participate?

The Righteous Call theory left much to be desired.

"This guy's good," I allowed, "a real thinker."

The message of comfort had been concise, neatly hitting every needful topic—I'm fine, I can't be reached, there are reasons, I'll be home soon, take no action, love you, and love the cookies. No time for a dialog that might require improvisation.

I suppose I should welcome a contest of wits with a real contender, but this wasn't a game; a man's life might be on the line while his wife's heart was being wrung out. It was true, though, that I hadn't been tested against any big-league brains. I am generally called upon to outwit teenagers who think they're smarter than anyone else and thus doomed.

"The cookies were a nice touch," Frank added. "She told us they were in Larry's lunch that day. That someone else is capable of looking inside a lunch box apparently hasn't occurred to her."

"She may not let it," I said. "You may be right about hitting a nerve, too. What did he mean by not using 'anyone else' to look for him? No one could have foreseen that Lorraine would have someone beating the bush Thursday afternoon. Sure, she'd be worried and phone around and then maybe call the police, but to have someone out doing face-to-face? I could have drilled into a tooth somewhere—but whose? Someone I talked to or someone who found out from someone I talked to? And why not just let it slide, let us think Larry had been mugged somewhere or took off—am I really that close to something?"

"Close enough," Frank said from the back seat.

"Maybe, but unlike Columbo I can't keep pestering everyone. Of course, he had an advantage because he already knew who was guilty."

"Columbo had an advantage because he had screenwriters," Frank corrected.

"I can see where that would improve your odds."

Having no writers, my mind was left to wander unguided over the cast so far: One (or more) of the eight at Kooyman's lab? Estelle? Jared Timmerman? That Janelle—a *femme fatale*! Comfortably numb Schuyler? Just not enough facts. And having a second run-through with everyone, committing them to a more detailed timeline, complete with alibis, was better accomplished with police authority.

But now there would be no police.

"*Officers, did I mention that my husband called from a secret project on Baffin Island?*" I could just see the cop flop his notebook up and down and look at his partner.

I looked in the rearview mirror. "So, Frank, you want to explain this to your buddies on the force?"

He patted his jacket pocket. "I think I'll just keep the paperwork here for a while. What about the lost nurse?"

"I'll fill you in later. Basically, some doctor or someone posing as one lured her away with the promise of big money and little work caring for a girl at a private clinic. And you're right, the roommate—a real live wire, by the way—says she got an incoherent call from the nurse a while later with a full ration of mystifying references.

"Weird."

"Yeah, a real winner. I don't see any tie-in with Kooyman, though."

We fell silent again, and I had another depressing thought. "I suppose this puts the brakes on getting phone records as well."

"Tough to get records on a man who isn't missing." He patted his pocket again, for effect.

I swiveled in my seat. "Marjorie, what do you think of all this?"

"If I'd known about the phone call I would have picked up the receiver downstairs."

"Good girl."

"It's cruel, that's what it is. It's so hard on her. The phone rings, and it's like a gunshot to her. And she's not going to challenge anything dressed up as good news. She's probably going to want to go to the market now and buy five hundred dollars worth of Larry's favorite foods."

"Cookies," I said. "She's going to bake twelve dozen butterscotch cookies. If that really was Larry she's going to put him into a diabetic coma. Look, I want you to stick close to her for a while. I think I can bargain her into it. I don't know how long Ronnie can stay. I suppose we had better get back in there, see where Lorraine wants to head with this thing. I imagine she'll want to rein me in lest I compromise Larry and national security. I can think of a nifty way around that, or I can just keep poking around on my own. Oh, one other thing. When you're here, see if you can shut off the ringer on the upstairs phone. Let's have some control. I'll bring in a tape recorder tomorrow; I should have done so already."

In the end, I was able to finesse an extended stay for Marjorie. I first tested the strength of Lorraine's resolve, but anticipating the outcome I didn't put much umpf into it.

"Maybe I ought to continue to approach this as though Larry is still missing, see what I can learn."

"Oh, no, I don't think so, Mr. Price. I don't want trouble with the government or anything that might hurt Larry."

"Lorraine, there is hardly anything sinister going on with the government," I said, feeling generous.

"It must be something sensitive, though. I just think we need to . . . stop any investigation at this point." It was part declaration and part plea.

"Okay, look. I'll back off, at least for a while, but only if you let Marjorie stay with you until this is over . . . in a few days. It's what Larry would want," I added, believing it.

Presented as a bargain it looked attractive and Lorraine accepted. She was more animated, brighter of visage. But she could not engage any one of us directly, face-to-face, for very long. Her attention would wander off somewhere, and her body would follow.

How certain was she that the crackling voice had been her husband's? That his had been the mouth enjoying her cookies? I wondered how long Lorraine could remain afloat clutching a paper lifesaving ring that would melt away.

What then?

seventeen

I cornered Ronnie when she came downstairs.

"We need to talk. How about dinner? I know many sub-par restaurants."

"All right," she replied without a fight. "I'll be ready in a minute."

We left Frank and Marjorie behind, though I didn't give Frank much longer there. I drove south, into Dedham. We remained silent en route, perhaps to save the events for the meal, perhaps because I feared becoming agitated to the point of driving off the road. As we approached Route 128, there was a scattering of chain restaurants and independents. I pulled into a small Italian place.

In many things I'm a traditionalist. At Christmas I want Andy Williams and Johnny Mathis; *Metallica's Yule Log* isn't going to cut it. It goes for restaurants, too. Mexican food ought to arrive as a plate of molten goo, not as the Yankee imposter enchilada that lies there like a beached fish, dry and obvious. And small Italian places ought to have checkered tablecloths, candles wedged into Chianti bottles, and music from the sons of Italy.

"How about Luigi's?" I asked. "I'm willing to gamble on any joint named *Luigi's*. I'm seeing a comfortable gentleman with a brush mustache and an apron." I doubted I was going to get him, but that's who I pictured. It was like how, as a kid, you pictured Bible personalities from the stories you heard; you just gave it your best shot.

Ronnie shook her head and smiled.

We settled in on opposite sides of a booth. Happily, a comfortable volume of Italian standards washed the room. I even got the checkered tablecloth (red and white) if not the wine bottle and candle. Compensation was provided by the walls, which were a pale green with murals of Tuscan towns on hillsides and natives hauling grapes. We were waited on by a college coed who was neither round nor had a moustache but was bright and attentive. Ronnie motioned me to go first. I ordered veal scaloppini la cacciatore.

"You realize the risk I'm taking in revealing myself as a veal eater," I told Ronnie. A statement and a challenge.

Ronnie, in whose eyes I had seen the soul of a carnivore, did not disappoint.

"Osso Bucco," she said and closed the menu.

Time now for wine selection. As far as I can tell, oenology has taken its place at the table of secular theologies. Its adherents, as in all substitutes for religion—art, sports, rock music, scientism, multi-level marketing and, above all, politics—run the same spectrum from indifferent, casual partakers to the fully converted priesthood zealously overseeing orthodoxy. Wines are spoken of as though they were living beings who rise in stature through a blessed ancestry and discipline, secular saints with grace to dispense to the worthy.

I was probably not the one to choose a wine to complement a veal shank. *A nice 1997 Welches?* Ronnie, having learned from the coffee at her stepmother's, didn't miss a beat. After a back-and-forth with the server (Do they memorize a list? Get some sort of training? I pictured a long table with a queue of half-filled glasses and little identifying cards) Ronnie selected a Sangiovese.

"Good choice," I acknowledged.

She looked at me blankly. "Thanks."

"My pleasure. Sometimes I'll tip my hat to a worthy raspberry lemonade: *Offers a good nose, tart, sets high goals, and keeps a steady pace, finishing like a whisper of ochre brushed across a sunset.*"

She just looked at me.

I fiddled with a bread stick. I'm sure there's a polished way to eat one. Re-butter the exposed end after each bite? Butter once and go the rest of the way dry? Work it like a squirrel, no butter at all? Yet another gap in public education.

Time to quit stalling.

"I need to apologize to you for the soccer mom remark. It was flip and inappropriate. It was wrong. I'm sorry. So you see, I do have a vice."

She looked at me for a few seconds and then said, "Apology accepted."

"Thanks. I don't know how comfortable the rest of this conversation is going to be."

Ronnie said: "I take it no one except Lorraine believes the phone call was from my father."

"It's a tough sell," I agreed. "There is much to condemn."

I marshaled my arguments. "Assuming for now that the call was bogus, the initial problem, of course, would be voice recognition. How do you get around that? There are limited options. The first is someone with a gift for mimicry. More likely is what Lorraine got—static; just disguise the whole thing.

"It's way too slick," I continued. "It covers all the bases, calls off scrutiny, and is delivered at a breathless pace, no time to respond. Boom. Call over. It was quality con. What a lot of people don't realize about a confidence game is that it works because the con artist initially gives you *his* confidence, exposes *his* soft belly. He distracts Lorraine from focusing on his voice by first focusing on *hers*—it's *Lorraine* who's singing off key—but he can be large and is prepared to trust her anyway with this critical message. Coupled with her predictable emotional state, Lorraine is now prepared to accept the voice of Daffy Duck as that of her husband of thirty years.

"On the other hand, I can't prove it *wasn't* your father, battling cancer out there on the rocky shores of Nova Scotia. If it was, then either he's an international man of mystery after all or he was coerced. But Frank thinks the call is bogus, too," I added to bolster my case.

By now our salads had arrived, a boilerplate offering of shredded greens, a wedge of almost-ripe tomato, red onion, an olive, and pepperocini, served in a faux wood bowl. I was disappointed that no one came by offering a fresh turn of black pepper from a grinder the size of a table leg.

"I don't know what to think about it," Ronnie responded. "What *project* is this supposed to be? He isn't that kind of scientist. Even if he were on call for some program like this, he'd tell Lorraine that such a thing existed, if nothing else. You're right; there's more reason to be suspicious than not to be."

"The worst part is that now the police won't get involved," I said.

"Why not?" She seemed surprised.

"Because no one is missing—*he's in Canada. He called.* Frank is holding onto the paperwork. I really wanted to get the phone records for you dad's office and cell phones."

"Isn't there some other way to get them?"

"Not legally."

She smirked. "So what? Who'd know? And who'd press charges— Dad?"

Here I was again, across from Jerome of Revere from the day before, being pitched a vision of the law as fuzzy and flexible, like a pipe cleaner. The difference was that Jerome was up to no good, and Ronnie was looking for her father. For a Christian, this is where the rubber meets the road. Her argument was perfectly reasonable; in a tug-of-war between people and rules, isn't the answer obvious? Don't you risk a speeding ticket to rush your pregnant wife to the hospital?

In the matter of boundaries, like Mason told Dixon, you've got to draw the line somewhere. If finding Larry required burning down a neighbor's house, would Ronnie light the match? An unrealistic example to be sure, but the daily border skirmishes between principles and indulgence have real consequences.

It's one of the tests of life, identifying sin and steering clear, staying on the road. Those who want the gospel while at the same time clinging to the delights of mortality are in for heavy labor because they are in direct opposition. It's tough serving two masters, hedging bets. The modern West is trying an end run around the conflict by the simple expedient of defining sin out of existence. The believer has no such license. Everyone is born with a map with some of the borders drawn in. More are inked in as we go, separating swamps and minefields from safe ground. After mortality we will hand in our maps, which will clearly show all our forays into enemy territory.

"It's a reasonable point," I allowed. "I'll think about it, but I doubt I'll go down that road. I'm not tapped out yet." Well, not completely—there was still whatever it was that lay curled around the base of my brain, what I knew but didn't know I knew.

We examined the phone call some more, as well as our visits to the lab and Harvard. Our meals were served, and Ronnie opened a few tentative fronts against her joint of meat, eating without appetite. I was willing to invest more in my meal, an appealing and satisfying blend of tender meat, roughly chopped mushrooms, onions, peppers, and tomatoes in a spicy sauce. I tried to impress her by eating in the European manner, keeping the fork in the left hand and the knife in the right, working both together. I don't think she noticed.

Not long into it, she laid her fork aside and looked around without really focusing on anything in particular. Soon, her musings ended and she looked directly into my eyes.

"Del, do you think my father is still alive?"

I had expected the question and could answer truthfully that I didn't know, but I knew that she was looking for something more, something like a betting line.

"Since it's only been 48 hours," I said, "I tend to think the chances are very good. It is a mystery, though. Are you sure he isn't mixed up with any drug companies?" I was probably being unfair, but pharmaceuticals is one of those industries with which I have never felt wholly at ease; along with oil companies, I never feel I can see all the way around them.

"No. My father just publishes his research and other people use it. Drug companies have their own research departments."

"Hmmm. We'll have to get together with Frank and see what more he can do at his end. We may have to wait a few days to see where we're at with Lorraine. We also need to get a recorder on that phone. I should have done it earlier. I'm sorry."

She shook her head to dismiss this.

"I'll also have to figure out how much I can get away with, since it could be argued that I no longer have a client."

Ronnie drew back; this hadn't occurred to her.

C'mon, Veronica.

"I suppose I could hire you."

Hello.

"Do you think you can afford me?" I asked.

"I can if you're going to charge me what you're charging Lorraine."

"I'd have to double it."

"Oh, why is that?"

How soon they forget.

"She had a coupon."

Ronnie picked up her fork again.

eighteen

When the apartments on the third floor had been remodeled into office space, I had the original sash windows replaced with wider, fixed picture windows. I had resisted a potent urge to have my name painted in an arc across them with a single open eye beneath. Since my suite lies in the corner of the building, and my personal office lies in the outside corner of that, I have one of these windows to either side of my desk. They're spaced far enough apart, though, to leave a comfortable angle of corner wall behind me, enough so I won't get shot in the back from across the street.

November was spent and autumn, at least the kind pictured on calendars, was long gone. The final slide from this seasonal purgatory into winter would be imperceptible. It was about mid-morning on Saturday, and I had come in to act like a business owner and sort through mail I could pretend was important. I also wanted to pick up a recorder for Lorraine's phone. Neither task took long. A phone message from Wayne reported no progress by the lab in locating a witness to Larry's odyssey. There were also three messages from Carmen Rosario insisting that somebody should do something. I agreed; someone should.

I walked over to the office window overlooking Beacon. I hoped being three stories up would provide perspective; maybe I could spot a clue from here. Instead, there was Moonique. Moonique is the purveyor of "Psychic Readings," as announced by a small neon sign in the window of her basement lair across the street. She is of indeterminate age and might have been a looker had she upped the maintenance. As it is, Moonique is pretty-eyed but a frump, dressing in tired gypsy. Although mild and benign, in most other aspects—the ones, say, valued by society—Moonique is a perfect dunce. Dialog with her doesn't always achieve full coherence; it's as though she were addressing someone immediately behind you. Moonique would find meaningful and attempt to answer a question like, "What is 64 divided by blue?" I'm not sure how successful her business is, but I could guess: A police unit that hired Moonique to locate a missing person would soon need a second psychic to find its missing cops. A sixties chick born out of time, Moonique is an Aquarian whose moon had left orbit for deep space.

Unsurprisingly, she is an advocate for spirituality over Organized Religion. In prior centuries this frame of mind often manifested itself as adherence to the Bible—and its discipline—while remaining denominationally aloof. In our time most of the Bible has been chucked and all the discipline, as free-wheeling spirituality tends to be vague, permissive, and self-congratulatory. The effectiveness of *un*organized religion has never been clearly demonstrated to me and giving up on distinguishing religious truth from error has simply shifted the penance and donations to ministers in the Church of Perpetual Therapy. Nor has an explanation been forthcoming as to why God, who is capable of organizing cosmos ranging from subatomic particles to galaxies, is incapable of establishing a church with both true doctrines and authorized leaders.

So there was Moonique, her earthly tabernacle at any rate, gliding along the street. I probably shouldn't judge; she couldn't have had any foggier notion than I of Larry Kooyman's whereabouts in this world. I just hoped she couldn't reach him in the next.

I followed her until she floated around the corner. Where to go and what to do? How about Estelle? She would be the most likely to know of any relationship between Larry and the Feds, but then I couldn't have her mention me to Lorraine when she phoned, and swearing her to secrecy might not sit right. Though I now worked for Ronnie by a shadow technicality, Lorraine would certainly view this new alliance as the obvious dodge it was. But I couldn't just stand here waiting for her husband to stroll by and wave up at me. Perhaps I should follow up on Lab Kooyman's tour of Longwood businesses. And yet I was hampered here as well by the personnel changes the weekend could be expected to bring. Maybe I should head to Canada.

It was while pondering this state of affairs that I noticed a few rogue threads escaping my slacks. Probably because they were in the general crotch area, I shrank from pulling them out. What if they continued to unravel? I walked back into the reception area to find some scissors in Marjorie's desk. The first pair I came across were the burly kind with black enameled handles and shiny steel blades eight inches long. What were these for—to cut license plates in half? Too intimidating for this sensitive job, I exercised them open and closed a few times and laid them aside.

It was then that I saw it, half-buried under a lower stratum of office supplies. I didn't even touch it. Leaving the drawer open, I stood and retreated into my office, trying to will myself to stop thinking.

But I knew.

I knew what had been percolating in my mind. The thing of it was, there was no obvious tie-in to Larry Kooyman. And yet . . .

I called Marjorie on her cell. She had again taken her emotional sentry post at the Kooyman's. I told her to tap into the Internet, and I told her what I was looking for.

"I'm leaving the office now," I said. "You'll be glad to know that another issue of *Dirt Bike* has arrived."

"Get it down here," she ordered.

"Why do we have a pair of scissors a foot long?" I queried. "Were they approved in the office budget?"

"They were. I use them to clip little grocery coupons out of the paper."

I drove to West Roxbury in a serene state. I was doing what I often do at the moment of discovery—back off. Perhaps it has something to do with delayed gratification, stringing out the anticipation when the payoff is assured. It isn't worth psychoanalysis, but it is a delicious feeling.

Marjorie met me at the door, holding two pieces of paper. She handed one to me, but I was distracted. Something was different. The curtains had been pulled back; the siege of Fortress Kooyman was lifted and daylight readmitted. I was both glad and anxious.

What I had found in Marjorie's desk had let the cat out of the bag. It was one of the most hand-friendly of devices, with its smooth, rounded body, its deep red casing and identifying silver cross, its myriad folding blades and tools, especially the little scissors.

It was a Swiss army knife.

I had seen too much of something, and that something was Switzerland. An industrial-sized ingot of Swiss chocolate in Janelle's office and a Swiss airline luggage tag on Hector Ermiston's skis.

I read the paper Marjorie had handed me.

On Friday, the day after Thanksgiving, Dr. Ulrich Roessner from

Schliemann-Schmidt, a Swiss biotech firm, and two of his staff had been killed in a traffic accident outside Boston. Roessner, Marie Pestel, and Elsbet Vanderheit had perished when a semi jumped the median. The collision had been head-on and the damage decidedly one-sided. The truck driver was in satisfactory condition at the hospital. The trio had been in town as guests of Prime Meridian Technologies, a biotech in the suburb of Waltham.

It had taken Marjorie a half hour to earn her day's pay. She had begun her search by tying together in various ways Switzerland and the Harvard Medical School. Most of the returns identified those HMS faculty with degrees from Swiss universities, joint research and the like, but with no mention of Larry. Marjorie had jotted these down and expanded the parameters to include Harvard in general and then outward to Boston. The accident had been briefly reported in the following day's newspapers.

This was intriguing but what did it have to do with Kooyman? Was there a connection, after all, between his cancer research and a Swiss biotech firm?

I asked Marjorie about Roessner.

"Nothing so far," Marjorie said. "I'm still looking. I slipped the name by Lorraine but she drew a blank. Larry's never been to Switzerland."

"How about this Prime Meridian?"

She handed me the second sheet.

Prime Meridian Technologies was a recent player in the booming biotech expansion. Its blue steel and blue glass complex in Waltham bespoke a twenty-first century vision and competence. Prime Meridian was devoted to—what else—"innovative solutions," in this case to the development of something called "biotherapeutics." This booster blurb was accompanied by a photograph of the CEO, Karol Vyridiak, a handsome, broad shouldered, wavy-haired captain of industry and Daniel Boone of a new frontier. Nice name, too, with its east European flavor suggesting scientific precision. He was posed outside before the main entrance of his flagship, chin up and facing into the future, which was somewhere off to his left.

I recognized him.

He was the ruddy man in several photos with Hector Ermiston.

Which was also interesting, but there was nothing sinister about any of it. I would call Estelle and run Roessner, Schliemann-Schmidt, and Prime Meridian past her, but if Ronnie was right about her father, a tie-in was unlikely. The Swiss referents that had bedeviled me were at the Biological

Sciences Building, not at the Medical School or Larry's home. Jared Timmerman had already told me that Ermiston was up to his waist in biotech
dough (would cloning money be different than counterfeiting it?). Also left
unanswered was how Steve Schuyler fit in; Janelle had thought that the
chocolate had been given to him by someone from Switzerland—had it been
Roessner?

"Good work," I said. "You get paid this week."

"You said that last week."

"I'll tell you what. I'll give you *half*"—I made a chopping motion with
my hand—"*half* of everything I make on this case."

"That's generous. Would this be the right time to mention that the battery on my laptop is dying?"

"Keep looking," I encouraged. "I may be just exchanging one mystery
for another, but I don't have anywhere else to go. Working Longwood on
Saturday doesn't seem productive; I might as well throw a couple of hours at
this. And try not to let Lorraine paint the house," I added.

"Did you bring a dart gun?"

"No, but I brought a recorder for the phone. Where is Lorraine?"

"Puttering around somewhere. She's been up since 5:00. I got here at
7:00."

"Was she out chopping wood?"

"Not quite, but she was in the garden."

"Marjorie, this is New England. It's December. The ground is granite.
What garden?"

"I'm sure it needs clearing out. And it's good to see her in the daylight for
a change. The drapes are opened, too."

"I noticed." *Goodness,* I thought, *the woman was out trying to clean dirt.*

We managed to lure Lorraine back inside. She was initially doubtful
about the recorder; it smacked of subterfuge and legal complications. I sold it
to her on the basis that if Larry called again, as would be likely when he was
on the way home, she would be able to replay it to hear his voice. "You'll be
the one in control of the tape," I told her, "not the police." True enough, but
it reminded me uncomfortably of my crash course for Ronnie on confidence
men. I was glad she was still upstairs.

Lorraine asked what I was going to do. Her tone suggested that something non-investigative would be appropriate.

"I have some business in Waltham," I replied. I had considered a revisit to
the Ermiston show room; but again, it was Saturday and Bessie and Victoria

were likely presiding over a quiet building.

I left a message for Frank. What could the police report of the accident tell us?

I next called Jared Timmerman at his home from my car. It was 10 AM. People should be up at 10 AM.

"What luck?" he inquired.

"Bum luck," I replied.

"You've learned nothing?"

"No, but let me run some things by you. They may have nothing to do with Larry, they're just odds and ends that have come my way."

"I understand."

"How about a Dr. Ulrich Roessner?"

"Mmm . . . no, I don't believe so."

"He hales from Switzerland," I prodded.

"He's not alone. Still no, I'm afraid."

"Let's try an outfit called Schliemann-Schmidt."

"Your luck is still, as you say, bum."

"Okay. Karol Vyridiak. Karol with a K."

"My sorrow only increases at my ignorance."

I was tempted to start in with Red Sox players, but forbore. "How about Prime Meridian?"

"It runs through Greenwich, England."

"So it does. Prime Meridian Technologies."

"Ah, yes. A biotech concern. Somewhere along 128, I should imagine; biotherapeutics, I am certain."

"Which are . . . ?"

"The construction of healing agents using live biological materials. Unlike mixing chemicals to arrive at a medicine, biotechnologies employ biological elements themselves—DNA, proteins, and molecular structures already created by life—to repair failure at the molecular level."

"Can you think of any connection to Larry?"

"I'm afraid not. Prime Meridian will certainly direct its own cancer research and Larry would not be a part of it. Have you come to believe otherwise?"

"No. What about Steve Schuyler?"

"Young Schuyler? Even less chance of a connection, I would imagine."

"Okay, just checking. Thanks."

"You're certainly welcome. How are the police progressing, if they are?"

"Uh, they're doing their thing." Well, Frank was.

"I see. Give my regards to Lorraine."

"I shall. Thanks, Dr. Timmerman. I'll keep in touch."

Next phone stop, Larry's world. I bypassed Estelle this time in favor of Wayne. The results were only marginally better but not enough to tip the scales. He thought he recognized, by name only, both Schliemann-Schmidt and Prime Meridian Technologies, but drew blanks on Roessner from the former and Vyridiak of the latter.

Fine.

Time to fill in some blanks.

nineteen

unches don't always work out, of course, but they never work out if you don't follow them. And as this one led to only one place (or two, if you wanted to count Switzerland) and as I had no other productive alternatives at the moment, I donned a crisp shirt and tie and headed to Prime Meridian.

Route 128 is the chief beltway separating Boston and its closest relations from the more distant, standoffish suburbs. Technically, for much of its arc it doubles as Interstate 95, but the freeway is a latecomer and it's still 128 to the locals. For part of its length it also claims to be America's Technology Highway. Scattered liberally along either side and in defiance of all tax sense to themselves and housing costs to their employees, are the citadels of Raytheon, Polaroid, Digital, Sun Systems, and now the next generation of scientific ambition.

Waltham isn't far away and soon my genetic Olympus was in view from the freeway, gracing a high point north of Brandeis University. I navigated by sight to the complex of Prime Meridian Technologies.

High tech seems to demand a lot of steel and reflective glass to promote itself effectively. With New Hampshire and Vermont close by you'd think you get granite, but no. The future is leaving terrestrial geology behind in its reach for the heavens.

And a grand statement PM was making. A wide, three-story arc of aquamarine mirrors, almost a half-circle, from which rose a cluster of shimmering prisms of varying heights, suggesting the Emerald city and its corresponding wizardry. I pulled into a guest parking spot, one of a smattering of cars distributed across the lot. Two stainless steel rectangular monoliths, about fifteen feet high, smooth and bright, denoted the entrance. They were anchored in the grass twenty yards away from the building, facing and parallel to each other and twenty feet apart. The walkway between these sentinels spilled into a cement plaza that conformed to the curve of the building. The lower part of Prime Meridian, the smooth arc, presented a sweeping, undifferentiated façade. The entrance was cleverly designed to be one with this face; as I approached hidden doors slid open silently like the panels on alien spaceships.

The foyer was an immense, largely empty space with a vaulted ceiling, a secular cathedral impressing upon the pilgrim the sublimity of the human achievement. I was embarrassed at the pitiful statement my own office must be making and vowed to knock down walls and seize neighboring territory. Confronting me was the second oversized desk I had seen in two days. This one must have taken an entire tree and three carpenters to realize. Repeating the lines of the building, it was a twenty foot curve of dark wood, clean and smooth with a satin finish and no other embellishment. The desktop was a separate slab of what seemed to be petrified wood, also polished to a muted glow and hovering two inches above the base. I wanted to squat down and see how it was attached but demurred, not wishing to play the yokel. The countertop was largely bare; a flat panel computer monitor and a large, bright yellow, cone-shaped glass vase of stunning dahlias were the only squatters allowed.

An even grander wonder awaited, catching the eye at the threshold. To the right and supported several feet off the floor by a steel rod that looked too thin to hold it up was a huge, rotating, glowing crystalline sphere. It took me several seconds of blinking to figure out what I was looking at.

On the clear surface were etched the continents of the earth with some of their major geographical features. The interior of the globe was given to a three-dimensional representation of the structures of the cell. Obvious enough was the nucleus, a clear bubble encasing its own glowing constituents. I summoned what memories remained of core-course college biology. Mitochondria I recalled (I had liked the name) and thought I could spot them glowing in crimson outside the nucleus. Vacuoles, lysosomes—I assumed that these and all other cellular components were accurately represented as well.

As North America swung into view I saw a gold line, perhaps a half-inch wide, which ran from pole to pole. No longer did it run through Jolly Old;

the new longitude from which bearings should be taken now transected the eastern United States, nicking Massachusetts Bay. I was standing where the macrocosm and microcosm had come together at a new prime meridian. Jared Timmerman would need to be notified.

"May I help you?"

The woman at the desk, somewhat lost behind it, was about twenty-five with sharp, genetically blessed good looks that she was currently augmenting with a retro TV anchorwoman hair style—it started on one side, swept across her forehead and then swooped down the other side, like an off ramp. A gold name plate identified her as Leigh.

"I hope so, Leigh. Impressive globe, by the way. Can I buy stock?"

"You certainly may. It's PMT on the stock exchange."

"Great. I know it's Saturday, but I was driving by and thought I might as well stop in now to make an appointment to see Dr. Vyridiak. I don't suppose he's in now?"

"No, he isn't. I actually can't make the appointment," she said apologetically and seemed to mean it, "but I can have Dr. Vyridiak's assistant call you on Monday."

"That would be fine."

I handed her my card for big shots. I have two cards, one for big shots and one for folks. The big shot one has the fancy font of a British publisher. If big shots think I do work for the Queen, so much the better. (I had thought about introducing a third card for teenagers, a black one with a blood-red font, but a run past Marjorie had not proved encouraging.) Leigh took it, arched her eyebrows, and gave me a reappraisal; maybe I was cool and dangerous. I would have to keep the truth from her.

"I'm a private detective looking for a missing person, a leading cancer researcher at Harvard. His wife is pretty upset, as you can imagine." *Go with the flow, Leigh.*

She looked sympathetic. "That's too bad."

"Anyway, he has a wide range of colleagues, which means that I have to go around and *talk* to this wide range of colleagues. I won't take much of your boss's time."

"Yes, like I said, you need to talk to Dr. Vyridiak's assistant, Robin."

"Let me have her number, if you could."

She could.

"Do you work during the week too and get stuck here on Saturday as well? Seems like a raw deal."

"Actually, there are two of us. Carmen and I take turns every other Saturday for a half-day."

Two greeters. Progressive Prime M, cheaping out on the employee benefits.

"That's interesting. I met a Carmen yesterday, but she's a dressmaker. Her roommate got lured away to some pie-in-the-sky job and hasn't been heard from since."

"Yikes!"

I liked a girl who would say "Yikes."

I cocked my index finger at her. "Exactly." Then, "Were you here Wednesday, by any chance?"

I could work with either yes or no; on the drive here I had anticipated and rehearsed several combinations of dialog.

"Yep, Wednesday was one of mine."

"Well, you almost saw me on Wednesday, then, but I think I had heard somewhere, maybe from *my* assistant, that Dr. Vyridiak was out. Do you remember? It would make me feel better about not stopping by."

"You might have caught him Wednesday morning, if you got here early enough. He was here for a little while but then he left; he's been out the rest of the week, too."

"Wow," I said, "is *he* missing *too*? You know, Leigh, there's only so much I can do."

She smiled. "No . . . well, I don't think so. He's got to be at the reception tonight."

I hadn't anticipated this. "Over at the hotel?" I prodded.

"The Magellan."

I nodded. It was a four-star hotel on the Charles River in Cambridge.

"I guess I ought to start writing all this stuff down," I said, making no effort to do so. "A wedding?"

"No, a reception for PM investors."

"Ahh. Well, thanks, Leigh. So I'll call Robin. Is Monday one of yours?"

"No, that's Carmen." She pouted. During the conversation something had shifted, and she was now staring into my eyes every time she spoke, broadcasting availability. I was being invited to do the same, do the eye game thing, and go from there. Or I could play obtuse, which is what I did. The fact is, most non-Mormon women I'm attracted to scare me. So much for cool.

"One more thing. The newspaper had a story about a traffic accident involving a Dr. Roessner from Switzerland. It mentioned he was visiting Prime Meridian; that's why I noticed it. What happened?"

Leigh went blank and then pensive. Clearly, she wanted to come up with something. I was surprised. It had only been a week ago; how could it be hush-hush if it was in the news?

"Wow, I don't know anything about it," she finally responded. "Are you sure it was Prime Meridian? When was the accident?"

"A week ago Friday."

She pursed her lips, trying again to retrieve something helpful, but no go.

"Don't worry about it," I said. "He may have just been visiting one of your staff here. You know, a colleague from school or something."

"Yeah, maybe. I guess," she replied without confidence.

"That's okay. I don't see how it has anything to do with the guy I'm looking for. Thanks, Leigh, maybe I'll see you later."

"Hope so."

Well, it *could* happen.

She'd at least put in a good word for me with Robin. Would she tell Robin to schedule me on a day when she'd be at the front desk? I walked over and stood at the base of the glass globe and watched it silently revolve. It must have cost a bundle. Perhaps God considers His creations as moving within a vast sphere and watches the waltz of the stars and galaxies, the beauty of everything, in one eyeful.

I left that crystal Valhalla for the low tech, low glow world below.

Only hours before I had realized I'd seen too much of something. Now, I'd heard too much of something else. I felt a theory coming on. On my way to the car, I pulled out my phone.

I asked a strictly rhetorical question.

"Ronnie, can you do swank?"

twenty

The sky had brightened to dull silver while I had been inside. I appreciated even this feeble solar effort and sent a compliment skywards: *Keep it up! You'll break through someday!* I faced a dilemma. What I wanted to do was have another go at Steve Schuyler and run Roessner by him. But what if he were to then call Lorraine and report this second, unauthorized visit (or harassment, depending on how he might present it to her?) So far he couldn't be bothered, but I had to think ahead to mitigate possible damage. I thought of a preemptive strategy and called Marjorie.

"Ronnie is all aflutter," she reported, "or at least to as much flutter as she is given. Anyway, she's moving around a little faster. She's going downtown."

"Of course she's aflutter. She has a date with me tonight."

"Or she could be packing up to flee town."

"Thanks, Marjorie. It's a wonder I have any self-esteem left. If she's thinking of an evening dress remind her I'm a Mormon and only human. But that's not why I called. I'm going back to Schuyler again and I want you to mention it to Lorraine in your subtle way. Make it sound like a sympathetic visit to the sick, which of course it is."

"In case he calls her later."

"In case," I agreed.

I put another call through to Estelle at her home. I didn't need her calling Lorraine or stopping by, putting Lorraine in the awkward position of concealing what she considered to be a call from her husband. I told Estelle I was following up on some information, but the hunt looked like it might take police resources after all. We'd know more on Monday and until then Lorraine should take it easy for the weekend. Estelle understood.

Next challenge: the quickest way into Somerville from where I was in Waltham. It was Saturday and I wasn't up against a time restraint, but still, it was Boston traffic and you wanted to win. I finally decided on Route 2, speedy enough to its termination in Cambridge but thereafter I faced a slowdown to Somerville beyond. I chose deliberately, though, so as to pass beneath another temple on a hill, also of recent appearance, where macro- and microcosms meet to a wholly different purpose.

After much legal wrangling our Church had been able to build a temple on a high point in Belmont overlooking Route 2. Although hindered by anti-Mormons (a confederacy, not quite a conspiracy, unknown to most Americans) and cautious neighbors (at one point there was an objection to the shadow cast by the spire,) compromises were reached and the edifice was raised. Local feelings were greatly ameliorated during the public open house that preceded formal consecration. After touring the simple, quiet eloquence of the rooms and noting the absence of any imagined weirdness, misgivings were set aside and the temple took its place in the New England religious landscape, providing yet another ensign for orientation.

And good bearings were exactly what I needed. Where was I headed with this thing? Was I abandoning Larry Kooyman to indulge my curiosity about big shots and Swiss chocolate? Doubtless a couple of hours in the temple would do me good, yet I hesitated, edgy with a low-grade anxiety and a feeling that I was moving but to no set purpose, like a restless bird before migration. So I passed by the temple and my uplift was brief and insufficient.

Freed by the weekend for escape or other errands, cars were fewer and parking was no problem near Schuyler's condo. I trotted down into the parking cave to confirm that his Subaru was there. It was. There was the same awkwardness in the vestibule, though, with another cycle of trying to ring through to Schuyler, failing, then tapping out entreaties to the other units. Someone was expecting a Saturday visitor and I slipped into the building.

This time there was no response to my knocking and no sound from within.

"Steve," I said loud enough to penetrate the door, "we need to talk.

I tried to sound more peeved than angry. I had begun suggesting some of the items to be put on the table for a frank discussion when the elevator door opened behind me and out he stepped, laboring with a clutch of plastic grocery bags.

He was surprised to see me and drew back; for a moment I feared he would retreat into the elevator. He hesitated and then found some meager store of resolve. I helped him out.

"Sorry. I've been here shouting into an empty room. I could have just left a phone message or shoved a note under the door, but your history of returning calls doesn't inspire confidence."

"I've been sick," he said. He seemed somewhere between angry and scared.

As he approached I could see that although he had showered he hadn't washed away the reddened eyes or sagging, pallid skin. I was about to ask how the Johnnie Walker was working for him but bit my tongue, eschewing that cheap pleasure for the more robust one of hitting him in the face with a brick.

"That's not good," I replied. "Something's definitely going around"—he started to nod—"but I guess it's preferable to a ride with Karl Roessner."

The appeal of this approach is that guilty knowledge should produce shock whereas innocence ought to return incomprehension. A slick guy might pull off some quality theater, but my guess was that Schuyler's slick had been washed away by an even slicker whiskey.

And he did react—but I was left with an unanticipated problem of interpretation.

He passed out.

I saw it coming; like the mercury dropping in a thermometer the blood fled his face and neck, his mouth opened, his eyes fluttered, and he crumpled, twisting to the floor. At least he didn't fall backwards like a wooden plank. I was able to grab the collar of his jacket and guide him in for an awkward landing, preventing his head from striking either the wall or floor.

"Steve," I said, "I don't think this medical regimen is working for you."

I found the keys in his jacket pocket and dragged him by the armpits into his condo until I could prop him against his sofa. I went back for the groceries, which were split evenly between junk food and beer. After closing the door I looked around in the dim light. Another curtain puller, like Lorraine. Why did he shrink from the light? I dismissed the thought of throwing open the shades, unwilling to chance a curious neighbor across the way. I switched on a lamp.

Has anyone studied neatness? As either a socio-economic, educational, psychological, gender-related, or even religious phenomenon? Not the compulsive thing where the strings on a rug's fringe must be combed hourly, just ordinary tidiness. There seems no rhyme or reason. A man can be as dapper as Cary Grant and yet keep a home arranged by dynamite. You'd think a scientist whose work demanded the meticulous might bring home some of that discipline, but Steve Schuyler was a slob, the genuine article. He had a frat house worth of contents crammed into his few rooms. A family of refugees could have sneaked in and lived undiscovered for a week.

I wasn't going to toss the place, although I would have liked to have seen him persuade the police that I had. I wasn't adverse, though, to looking for low-hanging fruit like, say, a Mickey Mouse lunch box. A scan revealed sports equipment (a bicycle and enough parts for two more, a kayak stored on one wall and a lacrosse stick on another, balls in enough sizes to make a model of the solar system); camping stuff (a couple of backpacks, a loosely rolled up tent, a sleeping bag, white-gas lantern, compact camp stove, and hiking boots); books (in precarious stalagmites); a computer; a TV and video equipment; and the standard bachelor debris (castoff clothes, bags of chips, candy wrappers, empty beer and soda cans, pizza crusts in cardboard boxes).

I found the kitchen (yes, a sink full of dishes,) filled a coffee cup with water, returned, and tossed it on his face. He jerked and spluttered his way back to awareness, falling slowly over until he rested on the carpet. His eyes blinked as he tried to herd his roaming senses into the corral. I helped him up and onto the sofa, a sad and sagging beige affair. I shoved some paper plates back from the edge of a round dining table and perched there, one foot on the floor.

He put a hand to his head. "Wha . . . what's going on?"

"You passed out," I said.

"I'm sick. What are you doing here?"

"I couldn't just leave you in a pile out in the hall."

"How did you get in?"

"I pulled the door off its hinges."

He tried to make sense of this and gave up.

"Steve," I said, "I can't help feeling that in your case confession would be good for the soul."

"You shouldn't be here," he said. Maybe he hadn't located his soul yet. I was patient.

"So call the police." I looked around. "If you can find the phone. Or call Ronnie and see how that works out for you."

"What do you want?"

"I'm getting edgy. I'm still looking for Larry and so far the ratio of answers to questions is going in the wrong direction. Perhaps I'm not getting the cooperation I should be. Or that Larry deserves."

I waited a few moments. "Which brings me to you."

He gave me the same look he had given me the day before as Ronnie and I were leaving. Wariness.

"You belong to a club, Steve. Do you know that? I'm not sure of the official name, but I like to call it the Order of Wednesday Runaways. The OWR. Maybe it's more of a network. Anyway, people come to work on Wednesday just to leave a couple hours later. Makes you wonder why they bother to come in at all. I'm going to run the names of some of the members by you, see if you know them. Then we'll get back to Roessner."

A few more moments of silence. Nothing was preventing him from demanding that I leave, but he must have been curious. Besides, he faced certain practical considerations in tossing me out.

"Let's start with, oh, let's see . . . Karol Vyridiak."

His eyes tightened and he looked away from me. "Who?"

"Do you know him?"

"I think I've heard of him."

"Ever meet him?"

"I don't know." He put his hand to his head—to remind me of the pain?

"Oh, c'mon, Steve. How many Karol Vyridiaks do you think there are?"

"I don't see where any of this is going or what it has to do with Larry. I don't like the way you're asking these questions, either. You're not the police."

He hadn't made it past the first name. Had I really caught on to something? And even if I had, was it something to do with Larry? I had been weighing a decision and now I made it. If there was a pot to stir, I would introduce an outboard motor.

"Some people actually prefer talking to me rather than to the police. Cops make reports and arrest people and talk to the media. I'm just trying to help Lorraine find her husband and Ronnie her father. A feel-good story. But no, I'm not the police. What I *am* going to do, though, is give the police a report of my labors. A list of the sheep and the goats, you might say; in this case, those who seem concerned about Larry and those that seem . . .

less concerned. That means *you'll* get a chance to talk to them. I'm going to
tell them that Karol Vyridiak and Hector Ermiston are joined at the hip at
Prime Meridian and that I can tie them to Karl Roessner and I can tie Karl
Roessner to you and I can tie you to Larry."

The effect was electric; Schuyler's eyes popped open and his face turned
red. I continued to bore into him.

"You see, Steve, I've been fretting since day one over how Larry disappeared. It's like he turned into smoke and blew away. But suppose he got a
phone call from someone he trusted, a friend or colleague who asked him to
slip away quietly and tell no one. Now, that could hardly be Vyridiak or Ermiston, and Roessner was dead, so you tell me who that leaves? There would
have to be a good reason, of course, and maybe Larry was told then or maybe
he was told all would be revealed later, but whatever the pitch it was enough
to get him down the hall and out the building. Anyway, it's a theory and I'm
going to share it with the police—did I mention that Lorraine has a cousin
who's a Boston police lieutenant?"

Another pause. "He tells us he can get the phone records of Larry's
incoming calls on Wednesday."

Schuyler didn't respond. He now had his head in both hands and his
elbows rested on his knees.

"Steve, if you want to say this is all nuts, go ahead. Right now it's all I've
got but if there's something to it I'm going to find out. I admit there may be
a few gaps here and there, but for two days work I've seen too much Switzerland and too much Wednesday absenteeism. Maybe it's the Harvard work
ethic. Maybe it all means nothing. But that's where I'm at." I slid myself off
the table.

I adopted a softer tone. "Let's clear this up. Did you call Larry Wednesday?"

"I already told you, no." He was still talking to the floor. "What do you
mean about Switzerland?"

"It's not important . . . okay, a number of little things. In your case, it
was that log of chocolate Roessner gave you. It was crushing Janelle's filing
cabinet, the last I saw it."

Another jolt. *I knew Janelle?*

"She said it's mine?"

"You brought it in," I countered. "Tell you what—I'll have the cops dust
it for prints."

"I want you to leave."

"I bet. Okay. I apologize in advance if this turns out to be a nutty conspiracy theory. But understand that right now my reason for living is to find Larry Kooyman. I'm tired of what I see in Lorraine's eyes. I'll look under every rock and if something squirms out, oh well. Nobody *has* to like me. They'll be missing out, of course, but . . ." I shrugged. "Steve, if you know something, now's the time to talk. It's just going to look worse later."

He shook his head as much as he could while cradling it between his hands.

"I don't know where Larry is," he said. "I really don't."

"Then I'm wrong. Here's another one of my cards in case I'm not." I laid it on the table. "I believe I can find my way out."

I turned at the door. "Wish me luck."

He raised his head but his look was inscrutable.

twenty-one

Schuyler was distressed—but by what? I called my chief minion, Rex Yeakel. Rex is a jazz pianist and composer polishing his skills at the Berklee College of Music. Like Marjorie, he has discovered a latent attraction to (or weakness for) detective work. Maybe it informs his music. It probably helps that I pay him more than he makes at most of his gigs. Tall, lanky, and with straight, limp hair, he could reasonably pass as a musician, math grad student, or unemployed slacker. He is also quiet, smart and patient, and had proved adept at tracking down leads or trailing those whom police call *persons of interest*. If I had to canvas the Longwood district on Monday, I'd want his help.

I told Rex what I needed. Within a half hour he slid by me in his own invisible car, an old Ford beater. He took over the surveillance of Steve Schuyler.

I considered a courtesy call on Carmen Rosario but knew it would only wind her up again to dervish pitch. There's only so much you can take of another's righteous zeal. All that energy reminded me of Lorraine. Was she up on the roof yet with a hammer and a mouthful of nails? I called Marjorie.

"No, not quite," she reported, but Lorraine was working up to pillaging the market. Marjorie would accompany her to keep her from buying a side of beef. Ronnie had gone, planning to hit both Bloomingdale's at Chestnut Hill *and* downtown. I winced. I weighed my options and decided to stop by the Kooyman's on the way home. What had Marjorie unearthed about our now international genetic community?

She had been able to delay Lorraine until I arrived. Lorraine was dressed befitting her new, upbeat mood: bright white slacks with a blouse that wasn't shy with primary colors. A blue scarf was tied close to her neck.

"What's up for today?" I asked her.

"Oh, we're going to the grocery store. I need to get some things."

"Great. No phone calls?"

"Not yet, but he said it would be a few days."

"I know. I was thinking more of Estelle or Jared Timmerman." I didn't mention Schuyler.

"Oh. No, not today."

"What's Ronnie up to?"

"She left a while ago to go downtown."

Sure. For stuff you couldn't get in New York. Had she told her step-mother of her evening plans? Probably not—but that led to another consideration. How would Ronnie later explain dressing to the nines? Would I be expected to produce a ladder to reach an upstairs window? Ronnie would have to dress at my place. It was not a disagreeable thought.

"I suppose I should go shopping, too. For something."

"How about spats?" Marjorie suggested.

I'd been getting a lot of sauce of this kind lately from someone whose paychecks I sign. Like Carmen, I thought someone should do something.

"I won't keep you, Lorraine," I said. "I'm just going to check in with Joan Rivers here about some office stuff."

"Okay." Lorraine smiled and left us in the kitchen.

"Spats?"

She shrugged. "If anyone can bring them back, it's you."

A challenge for another day.

"I suppose most of the Schliemann-Schmidt stuff is in German."

"Some, but their home page allows you to choose a language. It also turns out that the international language of finance is English."

So money talks and the loudest voice (for now) was the dollar.

"Good. So what are S and S up to?"

"Well, Hans Schliemann and Joachim Schmidt are two immunologists who left another biotech to start up their own. Switzerland apparently provides fertile ground for this sort of thing. They specialize in engineering—that's the word they use—antibodies to reset T-cells so they won't attack healthy tissue."

"As in organ transplants?"

"I guess. Anything you put into someone that you want to stay there."

"Will it work for common sense?"

"They don't say."

"And Roessner works for them?"

"That's the interesting part. According to them, no. I couldn't find him on their website; they seem to list most of their staff but he wasn't among them. So I called them up in Basel—they're only a few hours ahead of us. It's Saturday, but I thought I'd give it a shot."

"You called Switzerland?"

"It's where most Swiss companies are located," she said tartly.

I chose not to argue. "And?"

"I told them I was following up on the story in the *Boston Globe* about Dr. Ulrich Roessner's death and wanted to confirm his relationship with Schliessmann-Schmidt. I got put through to an Anna who said that Dr. Roessner was not associated with Schliemann-Schmidt. I asked if he ever *had* been associated with them and after a pause she said she didn't have that information, which seems odd, since they've only been around two years and have a staff of fifty."

"Does seem odd."

"I'm trying to find him somewhere else, but there are dozens of these firms. There's a few large pharmaceutical outfits like Roche and then all these biotech start-ups."

"Well, keep looking. I want the police report to see what they found in the car. The *Globe* didn't just throw a dart at a foreign phonebook and hit Schliemann-Schmidt."

Lorraine returned, car keys jingling in her hand. "Ready to go?"

"Yes," Marjorie replied brightly.

"I need to make a few more phone calls," I said. "Let's walk out to the cars."

Off they went to market, Lorraine lacking only a wicker basket swinging from her arm. I realized that I wasn't as comfortable around her as I had been, nor she with me. I was the reminder that, after all, her husband might still be in peril.

"Bye, girls," I called after them, "don't—" but I couldn't think of what it was they shouldn't do.

I tried reaching Frank but had to settle for a message. I wanted him to file the missing person's report for Larry Kooyman. It could be useful as leverage, but really I was just following my gut, that it would prove more beneficial having it there than not. True, as things then stood the phone call from pseudo-Larry tended to invalidate the report, but it would take into the next week to process, anyway, and who knew what would happen by then? I regretted the subterfuge and would have to come clean with Lorraine later.

Next: Rex, hunkered down in Somerville. Any movement by our man? Nope. Maybe he had uncorked another bottle of medicine. I told Rex to give it another couple of hours and then take off.

Third: I called the Magellan Hotel in Cambridge. The Prime Meridian reception began at eight.

Finally: Ronnie.

"You know," I said, "I'm going to wind up paying *you* for this gig."

"You just might," she concurred.

"Where are you?"

"Filene's Basement."

The Basement, a beacon of capitalism, is where a ton of department store stuff is discounted, sometimes to ridiculous levels. Twice a year there is a wedding dress sale where the behavior of the women provides the kind of evidence for evolution that's tough to refute. I count on Filene's for the only Ferragamo neckties I own. My rationalization is that whereas any necktie over fifty bucks is a slap in the face to the third world, the same tie at twenty-five is okay. It's an argument I don't expose to rigorous examination.

"I'm sure you can find a nice dress there," I said lightly.

"Funny. This is for knock-around stuff. I'm heading to Nieman-Marcus."

Nieman-Marcus is another mercantile establishment with a somewhat different slant on economics, although it could occasionally surprise. The Armani suit I was going to wear that evening had been purchased there, another guilty pleasure indulged in on the same thin theological grounds as with the neckties; it had been marked down from eighteen-hundred dollars to eleven hundred.

"You'll look terrific," I said and meant it, "but in the interest of complete disclosure, I should tell you that since we're sort of crashing this shindig, we might not actually be *staying* for an appreciable length of time." Of course, they might sensibly keep her and toss me, but I didn't mention this.

"We'll see. What are you planning to wear?"

"I have a Nehru jacket. And a fez."

"Seriously."

"As a matter of fact, an Armani suit."

"What color is it?"

"Charcoal gray. Wool, pinstriped. Notched lapels. Flat-front pants with cuffs." I still remembered the salesman's spiel. "*Tres chic,*" I added.

"Thank you."

I wasn't sure if I was being thanked for the information or the effort.

"Um, something else. Did you tell Lorraine about your plans for this evening?"

"No. How could I? You're not looking for my father, right?"

"Right. So . . . I can't very well pick you up at her place, can I? Good as I am, I'm not sure I could convince her that we're going bowling."

"Gad, you're right."

"So here's an idea." I took a breath. "Come over to my place, and we can leave from there."

Silence for a few moments. "Okay, that makes sense. I'll have to stop by my father's first."

"I understand. It's pretty simple to get to my place."

"Don't tell me now; I'll call you when I leave my father's. When do we need to be there?"

"It starts at eight, so I figure at least a half-hour after that. It might help us if everyone there is well on the way to locking arms and singing *Kumbaya.*"

"I don't think that's likely with this crowd."

"Maybe not, but I still think it's in our interest to let everyone get a snoot full. I could score points as a designated driver," I suggested.

"Not with me you wouldn't."

"They're on their own then. Lorraine and Marjorie are out buying six months worth of food. I don't know how long they'll be. I'm probably going back to my place now."

"All right. I'll be there by six."

"Sounds good. Happy shopping."

Something had changed in Ronnie, a softening in her attitude and demeanor. I was a beneficiary of this reassessment but, perversely, was accordingly less at ease, the *frisson* of danger when with her all the greater. Her disdain had been easier to deal with.

I was standing in the Kooyman's front yard, as Ronnie had been when I had driven up the day before. I too stared beyond the defeated autumn into some other invisible season of clear, golden skies and bright, dry leaves and perfect stillness. A period of quiet melancholy is not to be underestimated as a spiritual gift, a corrective to both scarecrow hopes and corrosive pessimism. A childhood memory came back to me at that moment, the memory of an odor. I flared my nostrils and tried to catch it once more, the smell of burning leaves.

My father and I would rake them up into piles in the fall and then ration them into a garbage can riddled with holes to allow for burning. (I imagined that it had been shot up by a German machine gun.) At first there would be flames, almost invisible as they caught the leaves, and then smoke, thick and pungent. We would stand there together, leaning on our rakes while the leaves were consumed and the smoke thinned to a shimmering of air over the can, transfixed by the metamorphosis of beauty to ash. I was unable then as now to adequately articulate my feelings at that autumnal rite.

Why hadn't I kept the burning can? So easily discarded as a utilitarian nullity when I sold the house after my mother's death, so precious now. I'd passed through many autumns since, but it was there at the Kooyman's in the fading light, presided over by the sad, enduring trees, that the memory of burning leaves hit me keen and hard, and I missed my father, an old garbage can, and a lazy twist of smoke taken by the wind.

twenty-two

There were several things I needed to do. On the way home I stopped at a high-end grocery and bought high-end eats; if Ronnie was to arrive at my place at six we wouldn't have time to eat out before the reception.

Once home, I called a former client, a Lincoln high tech millionaire who belatedly discovered that his millions hadn't automatically produced happy kids. That time, a good result had been forthcoming; largely free of the self-absorption and self-contempt crippling many wealthy kids, the boy was now doing well at college. The father was one of those men who saw the world as a kind of living organism running on the give-and-take of influence, favors, and money. Upon the return of his son, I had been absorbed into the system, another component declared worthy to receive of the life-giving flow of nutrients. More work got directed my way. Now, I had a favor to ask.

Granted. I drove to his home (thirty rooms, four people) and returned to mine (seven rooms, one person, and two rabbits.)

Next, in anticipation of the Prime Meridian reception, I made a purchase over the internet.

Was the condo presentable? Pretty much—no Steve Schuyler, I. Once organized and tidied, two simple rules (put things back in their place, clean up as you go) and minimal time commitment keep things that way. I touched up with a little vacuuming and dusting. I investigated the refrigerator for refugees and cast a narrow eye around the kitchen. I tightened up to Marine standards the spread on the queen-sized bed in the master bedroom, where Ronnie would be installed for her transformation from casual to formal beauty. I got out heavy, hyper-white Indian cotton towels and distributed them liberally throughout the master bath, saving a couple for the hall bath. New bars of soap were laid out. A chlorine spray in the tiled shower removed any biological trace of me; I even wiped it dry and buffed the blue tiles to a shine. On some previous whim I had filled a pill bottle with M&Ms and attached a label advising the patient to overdose. Would she notice it in the medicine cabinet? I removed from the bedroom the items I would need that evening and placed them in the guest room. I put out a coffee table photo book of Paris, suggesting the sort of place with which a person of class ought to be acquainted. Finally, I counseled Ficus and Biscuit on proper etiquette toward guests. "Go easy on her," I pleaded. "Biscuit, be a lady—no gnawing. You two are lucky I don't give *you* a bath," I added.

With the apartment prepared I turned to some Internet research. Hector Ermiston was retrieved from the Harvard website and I learned that Dr. Go-Getter was currently forging a path into the wilderness of xenotransplantation, the insertion of animal organs and tissues into humans. Since this procedure was neither anticipated nor allowed by nature, misdirection was necessary; the human body had to be tricked into accepting the xeno. A regimen of harsh drugs could be used, but a better way would be to turn off the genes that trigger the human immune system to reject the transplanted tissue. Ermiston was using a knockout pigmy pig; swine, apparently, having more in common with people than just manners.

Other than his research, there was little biographical information offered on Ermiston. The blurb began with his college degrees (Columbia and Harvard) and didn't mention Prime Meridian or any other private business interests. No photo of his office or the Gemini screen either, which you'd think would provide an arresting visual element. There was a list of publications and I wondered, without any particular justification, if he was the sort to have his minions do most of the work and then drop in his name at the top as the keystone.

The Prime Meridian website was more forthcoming on Karol Vyridiak. Here was the photo Marjorie had given me of the confident shipmaster facing into the wind. His parents had escaped Hungary ahead of the war and found their way to Ohio. Karol, born there in 1938, went on to biology at Columbia in the 1950s followed by an MBA. Since Prime Meridian had been founded in 1992, that left a fifteen year gap sketchily accounted for ("active in area business.") He'd hit pay dirt, though, as one of the founders and CEO of Prime Meridian.

The website extolled the glories of PM. Operating revenues were within shouting distance of a billion dollars. Although to my mind not a very encouraging term, "diluted earnings" were at forty-seven cents per share. The flagship in Waltham and a manufacturing facility in Greensboro employed over 1,000. Trade marked products included mostly oncological and immune system agents, all of them biotherapeutics produced by manipulating genes and proteins within cells. The current goal was to bring fifteen new molecules into clinical development. Hector Ermiston was not listed as a company officer and I couldn't find him anywhere else on the website.

I tried my luck with Ulrich Roessner but was disappointed. My rusty German was about as good as the joints of the Tin Woodsman and made all the tougher by a vocabulary of biochemistry and genetics that had not played an overlarge role in missionary work; I had trouble enough with their English equivalents. Eventually I tired of this and switched over to a crash course in genetics, cancer research and xenotransplantation; it's hard to resist a word beginning with an x.

It was mid-afternoon. I dealt myself a hand of What Goes With What? It is a card game of my own device. It is interesting in that it has no rules and each game is played with a different deck of cards. This day's hand was dealt from a stack of unlined, white index cards that I had chopped in half to produce small, nearly square blanks. I took them, one by one, and wrote a name or object on each: Larry Kooyman, Lorraine, Schuyler, Jared Timmerman, Vyridiak—so grew the deck. The Kooyman Lab got one corporate card; subdividing the lab into its individual lab members still seemed unnecessary although, at the last moment and out of respect for her many talents, Estelle Esterbad was awarded her own ticket. Ulrich Roessner and his entourage, Prime Meridian, Schliemann-Schmidt, Larry's Honda, even his lunch box increased the number of cards in play. Ficus and Biscuit were represented as well, just because. The deck didn't need to be shuffled, since in any order the cards expressed my confusion.

One challenge to a game with no rules is that there's no set beginning. I swirled out my cards across the dining room tabletop. I looked at them for a while. There was Larry, of course, but since I had no idea where he was in the physical universe it was difficult to anchor him anywhere. On the table edge? That didn't seem very optimistic. My eye fell on Hector Ermiston and I scooted him over next to Vyridiak. The Prime Meridian card joined them. Roessner got grouped with the two women, Schliemann-Schmidt, a chocolate bar, and Ermiston's skis. The Swiss cluster in turn gravitated toward the

Prime Meridian trio of cards. I wasn't sure what to do with Steve Schuyler, but soon placed him between the PM boys and Larry. This perspective suggested a new possibility—perhaps the boozehound *was* one because he was caught between these two poles in some unhealthy, inextricable way.

And so with the other cards, moving them around like lost planets looking for an orbit. What went with what? The Bogus Phone Call circled like a low satellite. Or maybe it wasn't bogus and should hook up with Larry's card. Many of the cards seemed to congregate in a roof above the tableau, like cloud cover. I couldn't find a way to work Jared Timmerman, for example, or many of the other cards down into the arena. I couldn't even be sure that Larry's Mickey Mouse lunch box, let alone his car, was still with him.

I had a few motive cards floating around up there, too. The Big Five—money, power, acclaim, revenge, and love—were each represented but no one of them could fully recommend itself. Money? Prime Meridian was certainly a big bucks concern, but how did Larry fit into any of that? Had his research turned up something even *he* hadn't recognized? If that were so, had one (or more) of his lab team found it? Revenge? Power? Love? Equally difficult. In the game of What Goes With What, avuncular Larry Kooyman didn't seem to go with much. That left acclaim, the hunger to be recognized, the adulation more important than the work itself. But how could Larry be dressed up for that? Product endorsements?

So the motive cards remained hovering above the human drama, dark and fat with rain that hadn't fallen.

Yet.

twenty-three

onnie called around five-thirty from Lorraine's. The shopping road had run straight before her and all had gone well. I gave her directions to my place and went into the kitchen to prepare a rather undisciplined, if well intentioned, appetizer buffet. There was more food than both of us could eat on a wager; perhaps I was trying to impress Ronnie with my caveman competence as a hunter-gatherer.

I took a Polaroid shot of the current status of What Goes With What? and scooped up the cards from the table. I spread a lace tablecloth I had purchased in Bruges for my mother after my mission and put out trays of tidbits. I uncorked a bottle of a fine sparkling cider that had been laid up in the fridge for all of three hours. I screwed it down into a bowl of ice.

Then I waited, nervous, pacing.

Ronnie arrived in her second skin of blue denim, black blouse, heels, and street pixie allure surrounded by enough packages for a family of seven at Christmas. An image of Steve Schuyler dragging along his pathetic plastic life flashed unbidden behind my eyes. I blinked it away; he'd blown it with her somehow and she was mine now.

Mine? All I needed was a club and a bear skin.

"You might as well keep moving to the bedroom and drop this cargo there," I instructed. I helped her pile the load on the bed.

"Some of this is for you," she said as she sifted through the packages.

"What?"

"Here." She handed me a shirt on a clothes hanger covered by opaque plastic, a narrow box, likely a necktie, and a small turquoise Tiffany bag—cuff links?

"Thank you," I said, "I don't know what to say. Do you always throw this kind of dough at detectives?"

"All the time."

"I can't be bought," I said unconvincingly.

"Of course," she agreed.

"We have time; let's go back to the dining room. I prepared a snack."

We surveyed the spread of goodies. It fell short of Martha Stewart but was well above cocktail weenies. Melon and prosciutto, fresh mozzarella, basil, and tomato finger sandwiches, fruit, tapenade, and salads of random organic elements. I had tried for a broad spectrum of variety and color while excluding sushi, which I mistrust.

"Oh!" she exclaimed. It was more than she had expected.

Nibbling and experimentation commenced. She looked the place over while she ate, a glance here and there, sizing it up and therefore me as well. How was I stacking up, I wondered? Would a Picasso have helped? A fencing saber?

"Successful shopping, I take it?" I finally said.

"Mmm . . . yes," she said.

"I hope this event doesn't turn out to be a waste of time, but I should tell you it's a stretch. We're going through this to see what reaction we get. That's about it."

"Are we hoping for a reaction?"

"That's a good question. Arguments can be made both ways. I lean toward a reaction just so we'll have something to work with."

I laid out my reasoning, acknowledging the many gaps. She followed me on the trail to Prime Meridian via chocolate and Alpine skiing.

"Initially," I began, "we proceeded on two fronts. Could your father's trail be followed, whether by plane, train, or automobile? Frank and the police are initially best for that. I did what I could with Lorraine and the lab and Jared Timmerman. So far, nothing. Not counting the phone call from Canada, which . . . well, I'm *not* counting. So, no trail so far.

"The other angle was to look for anything out of place elsewhere on that Wednesday. Any others missing in action? You and I followed those leads to no avail. So where are we? Your dad either sneaked out on his own, in which case we're still looking for his path, or he left on an errand and got waylaid, or someone called and he was lured out. As far as the errand goes, his lab team is hitting up the neighborhood. As for being lured, what if he got a call asking him to leave but not tell anyone? It would have to be someone he trusted. But was it to do him harm or did something go wrong and now the caller is afraid to come forward? Between the two I'd choose the latter. I tried it out this very afternoon on Schuyler—"

She put down her cracker. "You saw Steve again?"

"I did. I went there again after the visit to Prime Meridian. He's not looking any better, by the way. He still says he doesn't know where your dad is, but he's nervous about something. I know a bunch of people leaving work on a Wednesday doesn't demand a common denominator, nor does a visit to several people from a Swiss scientist make a conspiracy—but both involve the same people and so it doesn't seem so trivial to me. I have no proof of anything, but . . . " I shrugged.

She was in mid-chew and couldn't reply. Suddenly, her eyes popped and her hand flew to her pursed lips. She wanted to cry out but couldn't because of the food and had caught herself at the last moment. She did point, though, at the floor. I leaned over the table but could guess.

"Meet Ficus," I said. "Ficus, this is Veronica." The little guy had hopped in and was facing Ronnie head on. "He's one of the attack bunnies that guard the place. No sudden moves," I warned, "he can smell fear."

She held a hand to her mouth and finished swallowing. "You have a *rabbit?*"

"Certainly. There's another one around somewhere. Biscuit. She may be put out that I didn't allow her to draw blood."

Ficus scooted himself around so as to be perpendicular to Ronnie, regarding her warily with the side eye.

"Don't they make a mess?"

"Nope. You can train them, like cats."

"Oh. Don't they . . . ?"

"Nope. Been fixed."

She continued to stare at Ficus. Maybe in New York anything other than a dog, cat, rat, or pigeon was exotic wildlife.

"I'll have them guard your door while you're getting ready."

"Thank you. I suppose I better start now."

"Okay. Take a plate of food with you."

She prepared a plate and we walked back to the master bedroom and confirmed that Biscuit was not lying in wait therein. "The place is yours," I said. "I'll be out in the living room." I shut the door behind me.

I wasn't worried about running out of hot water, but I showered quickly in the other bathroom anyway—why compete? I tried to drag out my prep and dressing time. The only adjustment I had to make was due to Ronnie. She had indeed bought me a dress shirt, light silver with a slight metallic sheen and an Italian tie, narrow strips of silk in shades of black, silver and gray braided in a tight, thick weave. Together they were probably four hundred dollars. As a bonus she had thrown in a pair of bean shaped Tiffany cuff links in silver and black enamel.

We have a hymn wherein we bid a hearty farewell to Babylon; I seemed now to have defected to the other side, waving to the departing faithful. *Enjoy the desert! Good luck living off the rack!* I had, in fact, never worn the Armani (*to church?*) or the black Zegna shoes that went with it. I also had a square-faced watch that looked expensive from twenty yards away. Only the belt and socks were under a hundred bucks and no doubt stood out to the practiced eye. I checked the results in the mirror. Work clothes, I told myself. All things to all men. The jacket was cut in at the waist and broad in the shoulders. I looked pretty sharp. I practiced looking unflappable, as though receptions for investors were ho-hum.

The bunnies had abandoned their post at the master bedroom. No bonus for them this year. I put the food back in the refrigerator and looked at my imposter watch. How much better time does a $5,000 watch keep? Do the wealthy need to measure atomic decay? The Prime Meridian reception would soon begin. Who would be there? On the basis of his office photos I had assumed that Hector Ermiston was a player at Prime Meridian, but the website knew him not. I had hoped to find both him and Vyridiak at this thing but might have to settle for the latter. Well, something else to do on Monday.

I picked up the book on the living room table and flipped through the photos of Paris. Looked like a fine place. I put the book back. I could read for a while but that would require concentration. What would she look like? I hardly knew her and suspected we had little in common. I couldn't even say whether she had a boyfriend. *What was I thinking?* Baptism and happy ever after? It had never occurred to me to get serious with a non-Mormon and now I was falling for one I didn't really know. Hadn't I skipped over several steps along the way?

I shook my head. What I needed to do was gaze outward at the world rather than peer within, measuring every subtle psychic discharge. And yet I was almost as disconcerted by the objective world as the one wherein Ronnie awaited me in a castle tower. What, really, might I learn at a tony affair to which I had not been invited, for which Ronnie had almost certainly invested over a thousand dollars and from which we would either be expelled or learn everything we needed to in fifteen minutes? I was hit in the gut at this late hour with the self-indulgence of the whole charade. Was I just striking a pose? I was at the center of an amphitheater being watched by a lifetime of church attendance.

There was soft rustling and I looked up.

And then stood, instinctively.

I was off by a thousand bucks.

"You're going to need a bodyguard," I said.

"I thought I had one."

I shook my head. "I'm going to be the problem."

Ronnie was posed for inspection, on an occasion that legitimately called for posing. She was in a full length sleeveless evening gown, black, with a V neckline and halter straps fastened behind the neck. The top was pleated, as was the full skirt below. Across the broad waistband were sewn a thousand shiny rice-shaped black beads aligned side by side in four rows. Around her neck was a thin diamond choker, with matching ear studs. I dragged my eyes down to the bottom of the gown and raised my eyebrows. She lifted the skirt enough to reveal a black, three inch heeled open-toed satin pump with lace and patent leather trim. There was a bow on the vamp with a rhinestone buckle. I pointed at it.

"Dolce and Gabbana," she said.

I pointed at the gown.

"Carmen Marc Valvo."

"He's a genius."

I couldn't take my eyes off her. She had arranged her short, dark hair to be freer, with as much sweep as she could get. It had a sheen. Her hazel eyes, a little too close together, her asymmetric mouth, now a deep red, and her bare arms, white and softly rounded, had transmuted the pixy-rocker appeal into something different, into an exotic Slavic beauty.

"You look stunning, Ronnie," I said, looking in her eyes. "I mean, really beautiful. I feel like the country mouse."

"No, you're very handsome. The Armani was made for you."

"It's the shirt and tie."

She smiled.

"You know," I said, "on mature reflection I have a different idea now of what we could do. Why don't we elope?" I might have meant it.

She might have thought I was serious as well because she hesitated. It meant a lot to me that she did, and that she responded with the perfect reply.

"Maybe later."

Ronnie went back to the dining room to retrieve the black shoulder wrap and clutch purse she had tossed onto the table on her way out to the reveal.

I was glad to have a surprise for her, something worthy of her efforts. We walked across the lot to the car.

"Welcome to the upside of detective work."

She looked down at it, wide-eyed. She had to look down because it was a red Ferrari Modena, and it hugged the ground, a helpful trait in a horizontal rocket.

"You own a Ferrari?" she exclaimed.

If there were ever a time to lie, this was it.

"I do tonight," I replied as I helped her into a sinuous, metallic expression of herself. I hustled to the other side. Climbing into the seat was as satisfying as settling into a warm bath. Ronnie was looking at me, eyes sparkling.

"You deserve the best," I explained.

I ignited the engine and looked around for the kind of controls that would take us out of Earth's orbit. We slid out of the parking lot at a low growl.

"I helped out a rich guy once, and he let me borrow it," I confessed.

"It's wonderful. You wouldn't dare drive this in the city, in New York," she observed. "A gang would pick the whole thing up with you in it, engine running, and carry it off."

"They won't catch us tonight," I promised. "You can drive it home if you want."

"Really?"

"Of course."

With no one behind us, I took the on ramp to 128 at about ten miles per hour and then punched it at the last moment. We were at 60 in five seconds.

"I'm showing off," I said.

"Go for it."

We enjoyed the drive in companionable silence. Though the distance was the same for any vehicle, the Ferrari seemed to annihilate it more quickly and smoothly, even at the speed limit, which I would exceed, tempting fate, and then back down.

Our destination, however, was not so very distant, and we exited the Mass Pike after a few miles at the Allston/Brighton exit. I had to toss the change *up* into the toll basket. Should our quest at the reception prove short-lived, I resolved to take Ronnie on an extended night flight on the Pike into the wilds of Western Massachusetts. As we approached the hotel, a fifteen story ziggurat of boxes and balconies on the bank of the Charles across from Boston University, I reviewed strategy with Ronnie.

"We want to divide and conquer," I explained. "Of course, if Ermiston isn't there that leaves only Vyridiak. I suggest we schmooze for a while, drink in the ambiance, allow you to humble all other women present and bring grown men to their knees, that sort of thing. The best situation would be for Vyridiak to approach *us* and walk into a face full of Kooyman. But either way, when we introduce ourselves, it will rattle his cage or it won't. That's really all we're here for tonight. Afterwards, I'll take you out to a 7-Eleven for a Slurpee."

"That would be grand."

"If *neither* of them is there we'll stay as long as we want and put on airs."

I was silent for a few moments. "To me it's all worth it to see the way you look tonight."

"It's nice to dress up every so often," she replied. I had hoped for more.

As we drove into the hotel, I concluded our strategy briefing. "If Ermiston is here then we still want to approach Vyridiak first." I remembered the photos of the two of them and the way Ermiston's eyes had looked straight into mine. Mr. Control.

Parking valets live for nights like this. I hoped he got as much as he could out of the fifty yards he drove the Ferrari to its space. We walked through the lobby into the atrium, a huge open space reaching to the top of the building; the hotel was basically a shell of boxes artfully arranged to create this interior space. Balconies lined the sides and telescoped into the heights. There were hanging vines and plants everywhere and little lights hanging at the ends of almost invisible wires scattered randomly throughout the volume, like stars in a three dimensional planetarium. It was a struggle to channel my thoughts, much more so than usual, and I didn't think she was even consciously using "the Power" on me. Did I want her to?

The Prime Meridian reception was in a banquet room on the second floor. The doors were open and the hubbub leaking out was subdued, befitting refined decorum.

"Ready?" I asked. "Sure you don't want a weapon?"

"Who says I don't have one?"

I couldn't think of anyone.

twenty-four

There was no problem in blending. I was sufficiently camouflaged in dress and decorum and Ronnie, whose eloquence was unsurpassed, could have towed a longshoreman behind her with the grace she had to spare. Probably a hundred were there, displaying openly tokens of wealth, position, and desire. The men noticed Ronnie, of course, and wives pulled the double duty of eyeing both Ronnie and their husbands. Their gaze passed across me and lingered, when it did, on my necktie.

Just inside the entrance was placed a table of brochures, slick and glossy, touting the expansive vision of Prime Meridian. A quick thumbing revealed another portrait of the Leif Erickson of biotechnology, this time in front of the crystal globe in the flagship foyer. It seemed that the company was going to open a front against viruses, which were relentless and impervious to antibacterial agents. PM had assembled an expeditionary force and was beginning the push into enemy territory. The reception was a stylish sales pitch to the wealthy champions of social Darwinism. A screen had been set up in one corner of the room; a rousing video would be forthcoming. The brochure had the added benefit of giving me and several others something to do with our hands.

"Look at that." Ronnie gave a slight nod of her head toward another corner. A Lucite sphere, much smaller than its parent, had been set spinning slowly. "What is it?"

"It's a globe of the earth but with the structure of a cell within. Its mother is at their headquarters and is ten times larger. I had to study it a while, too, to figure it out. When it rolls back around, you'll see a gold longitude running through Boston—the new prime meridian. Get it?" I wondered if this idol had a trough around it to throw cash into. Maybe the sphere would glow brighter and spin faster as donations grew.

Most of the guests, who had doubtless rubbed elbows at similar functions, stood in clusters chatting but there was a sluggish current flowing around the edges and we joined it. It led eventually to a table of hors d'oeuvres, social kibble prepared along lines similar to my appetizers but snazzier, better sculptured, little works of art. I took note so as to improve future efforts, while rejecting greener-than-thou nonsense like the soymung bean-plankton loaf. Along the way, a waiter scraped by us with a tray of drinks. Ronnie selected a flute of champagne. I asked for a soft drink but without much expectation; like a comet, the server might not reappear in my lifetime.

"Why didn't you ask for a Shirley Temple?" Ronnie asked, trying not to giggle.

"I have to drive," I reminded her. Actually, if I thought I could have gotten away with ordering one I might have; I like the things.

As he was dressed in a tux and stood a head taller than almost everyone, I had already spotted Karol Vyridiak across the room, working a clutch of investors. I pointed him out to Ronnie. I did not see Ermiston but my line of view was often obstructed. No worry; the current would eventually wash us along every shore.

Ronnie and I began a series of introductions. A networker by reflex, Ronnie had warmed to the appropriate level. She admitted readily enough to being in New York real estate and, when it fit into a conversation, would also mention that her father was a cancer researcher at HMS, opening a protective parasol of genetic research above us. I just stuck to being one of the investors. The first time I introduced myself thus, Ronnie gave me a sidelong look.

"What's with the investor thing?" she asked skeptically at the first opportunity.

"What's with it is I *am* an investor. I bought two shares of stock this afternoon on the Internet." She went blank, unable to find the words.

I wasn't going to lie about my profession but I wasn't going to trumpet it. This was not because I feared social quarantine but quite the opposite—people are generally fascinated by my trade. I could anticipate that someone would want me to follow her spouse (who was of course standing there, har-har) or wonder whether I carried a gun or used to be a policeman. I might be asked to voice a strategy for any number of speculative situations. Some would drop their voices to talk about their kids. Wanting to field none of these inquiries, I laid low.

And so we circulated slowly throughout the reception, chatting with Tom and Miranda, Carl and Kitty, all smiles and pleasantries. But, as it must, the moment of truth arrived. And it came, to my disconcertion, when my back was turned. Ronnie was next to me but facing the opposite way. I heard her say, "Hello, I'm Ronnie Kooyman. I believe you know my father, Larry. Have you seen him here?"

I wheeled around. Ronnie's hand was in that of Karol Vyridiak. He was looking down at her but upon catching my rotation, looked at me. I smiled and lifted my eyebrows.

"Del Price," I said, "Private Detective." Technically, in Massachusetts, you're an investigator rather than a detective, but only cops made much of the distinction and I wanted to suggest a tough guy rather than a claims adjuster.

Vyridiak looked back and forth between Ronnie and me, saying nothing. Ronnie still had a hold of his hand.

"We understand you and Dr. Ermiston might know where he is," I said pleasantly, despite understanding no such thing.

The normally robust color in Vyridiak's face was draining. He began breathing harder and his eyes could not hold either of ours. I feared he might do a Schuyler on me and hit the floor, but he fought to recover and pulled back his hand.

"No, I'm afraid I don't," he stammered. He opened his mouth to continue but either thought better of it or was running on empty and closed it again. "Excuse me."

He turned and moved away at good speed through the archipelago of guests, several of whom turned their heads to follow him as he brushed quickly by. I followed his single-minded retreat to the opposite side of the room.

"Would you call that a reaction?" Ronnie asked pointedly.

My eye was still on Vyridiak as I replied. "Tough to be certain without medical tests but, yes, I believe so. Nice going, by the way; you were perfect."

In truth, I had not expected it. A possibility to be considered—hence our presence—this had always been a long shot. There was nothing, really, but some disconnected, circumstantial facts, nothing that rose to the level of evidence. More to the point for me had been the excuse to preen before Ronnie.

And now her father was there with us, his face once again taking shape in my mind, annihilating the mood, hitting me in the pit of my gut.

I grabbed Ronnie's arm; she was about to take off after him.

"Hold on. Let's see if this flushes anyone else out."

We watched as Vyridiak took a sudden left and exited the reception.

"Could be incontinent," I offered.

"I hope so," she replied. "I may as well choose this moment as well to visit the ladies room."

"I'll be over by the globe. He's got to come back sometime." Money is a jealous god.

Ronnie steered her way through the crowd. I liked watching her move and I wasn't alone. I worked my way back to the Prime Meridian icon. Presently, I sensed someone moving in close to my side.

"I don't believe we have been introduced."

I turned. We shook hands, no hesitation on his part. "Oh, hi, Dr. Ermiston," I said casually, "I wondered where Dr. Vyridiak ran off to. I'm Del Price. I'm here with Larry Kooyman's daughter. We're looking for Larry. Let me ask you something. This globe here, did you get it for half price when you bought the big one?"

He was shorter and older than I had envisioned, about five-eight and certainly in his sixties. Otherwise he was much as he was in his photos, immaculately dressed and groomed, the lips full and well shaped, the forehead high, the brows, plucked and straight and strong over intelligent, cold, eyes. But there was something else, something a camera couldn't catch. I am not much of a believer in auras, the idea that each of us radiates the spiritual equivalent of the Northern Lights. Moonique is, of course, though she could hardly be put forward to validate anything except the failure of public education. But there was something about Hector Ermiston, and that something wasn't good. He seemed to me like a man who had stepped out of a dark room and had brought some of the dark with him. I took a visceral dislike to him, unusual for me. It was possible that it was Vyridiak and not Ermiston who had guilty knowledge, but I was struck that it was the latter to whom the former had fled for refuge.

He wasn't rattled. "No," he replied. "It was quite expensive."

"Are you behind its design? The reason I ask is that I admired the Gemini in your office and wondered if yours was the visual flair behind the globe as well. You ought to make desk-sized ones, maybe six inches in diameter, battery operated. You'd make a bundle."

"Yes, the idea was put forward once. It was felt paperweights would be tacky."

"I see your point." Had he seen mine?

"I'm interested," he said, "how you would come to ask Karol or myself about Dr. Kooyman."

"Oh, both of your names came up early on and I'm simply following up on every lead. You know, then, of Dr. Kooyman's disappearance?" If we were going to cat-and-mouse this, he was going to have to hold up his end. Of course, my end was held up by nothing, but he couldn't be sure of what I knew.

"I'm certain that the unfortunate news has spread throughout the research community."

"How would it get to Dr. Vyridiak, I wonder?"

He gave a slight shrug. "I don't know. There is certainly staff at Prime Meridian who studied at Harvard."

"True, but he hasn't *been* at Prime Meridian since Wednesday morning."

He hesitated. "There are telephones, Mr. Price. You might have used one yourself and spared yourself this trip."

"And someone phoned him up just to mention Larry? How odd. As for tonight, I assumed Dr. Vyridiak would be here and probably you as well. So, two birds with one stone. Make that three birds. I'm also an investor in Prime Meridian."

"You're an investor?" Ermiston asked flatly.

"Yes. I bought two shares this afternoon."

"I see." He didn't seem impressed and he didn't thank me.

"You know, I couldn't find you anywhere on the Prime Meridian website or in here." I held up my brochure, now warped from the attempt to roll it into a tube.

"I'm a consultant for Prime Meridian."

"And an investor?"

He smiled.

"So, here we are. Where's Larry Kooyman?"

"I have no idea, Mr. Price. And now your investigation here seems to be complete."

"With you, maybe. But not with your pal."

"Didn't Karol inform you that he has no idea of the whereabouts of Dr. Kooyman?"

"He tried. But he's lying."

"You need to choose your words carefully, Mr. Price—or don't the laws for slander apply to your trade?"

"You didn't see his face."

"Is that your proof?"

"Heavens, no. But it's the reason I'm going to step up the investigation. That and my client." I looked past Ermiston, and he turned.

"Ronnie, this is Dr. Hector Ermiston. You remember his office. Dr. Ermiston, Veronica Kooyman."

"Hello," he said and extended his hand; Ronnie took it after a too obvious hesitation. "I'm sorry about your father's disappearance, of course. I am acquainted with his work at the Medical School. I assure you and Mr. Price that I will help in any way I can."

"I may hold you to that," I interjected. His jaw tightened.

"Dr. Vyridiak knows something," Ronnie said to Ermiston. "Let's begin with him."

"She saw his face, too," I explained.

"Both of you seem to assume I have influence or authority over Dr. Vyridiak."

"Both of us have seen the photos of the two of you in your office," Ronnie replied.

"And you're the one he ran to," I reminded. "To consult. You should keep a closer eye on him, run through some role-plays."

Ronnie and I were working well together at Gang Up. Now I picked another lane to travel down, an unexpected one I had not previously mapped.

"Can we cut out the nonsense, Doctor?" I asked, upping the volume.

Ronnie's eyes widened and Ermiston flushed. At least it was a reaction. Maybe he was warm-blooded after all. Others around us let their conversations fall to the floor and inclined an ear our way. Dinner theater!

"Vyridiak knows something, and it's dollars for donuts that whatever he knows, *you* know."

"Perhaps we should discuss this at another time, Mr. Price. I must tell you, though, that I don't take threats well."

"I haven't even started in on the threats, and I don't care *how* you take them. The police are going to be firing up their inquiry into Dr. Kooyman soon enough, and I'm going to move you and Thor Heyerdahl to the head of the line."

A circle of silence rippled away from us. As a rule, parties and police don't mix; perhaps for some it brought back memories from college.

"Mr. Price, *please!*" He was angry but kept in control. *No one* told Hector Ermiston what to do.

It was a cheap, unworthy pleasure, tossing this cold fish up onto the rocks to flop around. There was another part of Del Price standing back, observing with some interest this indignant Del, and not for the first time I reflected on how thin is the veneer of civility and how tenuous are the conventions and poses governing the social interaction of beings so opaque to one another. The New Testament offers another kind of relationship, one where each participant is in and through all the others, as Jesus was with his Father. How frightening! That, then, is the real basis for the call to repentance and righteousness—not because God needs or wants puppets but because He desires us to become heirs and heiresses of the kind of life He lives. What kind of person would you need to become in order to embrace, rather than flee, *that* sort of interpenetration, your inner self transparent?

But for now, veneer.

"You want to talk, fine" I was saying, "I'm *glad* you want to talk. I'll be in your office Monday. That is, if I don't have to fly to Switzerland to figure out this Roessner angle. Another headache." I pointed a finger at him, gave him the laser-eye, and lowered my voice: "But I will figure it out."

Hector was still heating up, but he was also off-balance and needed to keep face.

"I don't know what you're talking about. Are you going to leave or do we need to summon security? You simply cannot disrupt this gathering with threats and innuendo! Miss Kooyman, I'm sorry that you have chosen this route to locate your father. He would have been embarrassed!"

"*Would have?*" I asked quietly.

He was flummoxed for a moment. "I mean, if he were here," he stammered.

"If he were here, we wouldn't have to locate him, would we? Let's go Ronnie." I looked at him a last time. "I'd get used to the disruption."

But going was easier said than done. I don't think many told Ronnie what to do, either. Her agenda was not wholly swallowed up in mine; why should it have been?

"*I swear to God . . .*" she began.

Whoa.

I took her arm and started hauling her away. "Save it for later, Ronnie," I pleaded, "save it for later."

She glared at me. *"Let me go! I don't care—"*

"Save it for later."

We had some momentum going and got space from the guests who were parting to let us pass. A murmur followed us out. I felt bad for Ronnie—how would she react outside? The rest of the night seemed shot. I raced through options for damage control. But then, near the doors of the reception room our way was suddenly barred by a familiar face.

"Your drink, sir."

I smiled. Life is like this, sometimes.

"Thanks for remembering. You're a good man. I appreciate it. I suspect I've been demoted from a 'sir,' though." I fished for a loose bill and pulled out a twenty. Oh well. I probably wasn't going to need it for much else that evening and didn't anticipate an increased investment in Prime Meridian. How many millions would it take to buy up most of the stock, I wondered? Wouldn't that be a hoot. I dropped the bill on the tray, took the soda and gulped it down as we continued to walk out. I set the glass, a nice stout one that felt good to the hand, on a table in the atrium. We continued toward the hotel entrance. Ronnie was beside me, but had said nothing further.

"Do you think he bought that?" I asked lightly, grinning.

"You mean that was an *act*?" Ronnie exclaimed, incredulous.

"It was my Oscar bid. Why—you've never seen anyone behave like that before?"

"Not sober."

"I'm sorry I didn't cue you somehow. I didn't know until that moment. It must have been embarrassing for you." I stopped and looked at her. "I apologize for that."

"Are you kidding? I thought it was great. You shouldn't roll over for those guys. If you hadn't stopped me I would have . . . well, never mind. I'm not sure what to do now. We may have burned a few bridges behind us."

"You think? And I was so looking forward to the Hamptons. Ermiston's smart; he would have clammed up anyway. I'm certain he will insist on a similar course for Vyridiak." I smiled. "Neither of them knew we'd be here tonight."

The valet brought up the Ferrari, parting with it reluctantly. I couldn't blame him. He got a twenty, too. "One last thing, though. A favor and a tip. Don't swear to God at a cocktail party. Trust me, it's the wrong venue."

"I'm sorry."

"Don't worry about it. It wasn't a criticism. Let's go for a drive," I suggested. "West. Nebraska. The wide open spaces."

Ronnie smiled, a little crookedly, a smile that went to my heart.

We had lasted at the reception all of forty-five minutes.

twenty-five

What happened back there, Del?"

We had cleared 128 and were cruising along to Worcester. It was a challenge to keep the Ferrari under eighty. Ronnie had put her seat back and gazed with a contended smile out the window at the lights punctuating the darkness. I imagined how the car would look from an overpass, sleek as a porpoise, the freeway lights dancing and glinting off its polished skin as it fled into the night.

"Well, we seemed to have hit a sensitive tooth. By the way, I did a careful study and you were the most beautiful woman there by a mile—except maybe for Kitty."

She laughed. Kitty was in her fifties, fashionably thin but with skin like a saddlebag from too much sun in her youth and ineffective epidermal repentance since.

"I'm sorry we couldn't have stayed longer," I continued.

"Don't be silly. I just hope you don't get in trouble."

"What for—being a bore? They'd have to arrest the Legislature. Look, if it turns out the two of them really *don't* know anything about your father, I'll apologize personally. *My duty to Lorraine and his daughter—I'd do the same if I were looking for one of your kids.* How can they resist? They'll be fine."

Ronnie rose up. "You saw Vyridiak—he practically passed out!"

"I know," I assured her. "That was just 'if.' As for the other side of the coin, I can't see either of them wanting to call more attention to this. Del Price is a crazy man—who *knows* what he'll do? I told them some of the things I know, or appear to know, without telling them how I know them.

155

It's got to be bugging them that the search for Larry unearthed them so soon. I showed up at their *reception*, for heaven's sake. And with Larry's daughter, to boot. Ermiston, at least, will realize that his best course is to simply say nothing and deny everything. And that's where our problem lies—what else can we do, except tell Frank and have him pass along my lurid imaginings to whoever gets the case? We'll sit down with him and Marjorie, probably on Monday, and figure out our next move. We'll find your father. Let's just relax for a while."

On we knifed through the night. Despite Larry and the stress, I felt serene. It was odd. Maybe we would just drive all night, see how far into tranquility we could go.

After some time Ronnie said, "I owe you an apology."

"What on earth for?"

She turned toward me. "I thought you were some kind of hustler."

"How could you know? Besides, I'm hustling *you* pretty hard."

"That's different. When I saw the affection you and Marjorie and Frank have for one another and your concern for Lorraine, I realized I was seeing something else."

"If Lorraine finds out about tonight you probably *will* see something else."

"If that happens, I'll take care of it."

"Thanks."

We sailed past Worcester. It was close to eleven o'clock. From here to Springfield the population thinned. We might have seen the stars had the clouds relented; as it was we were cocooned by the dark and comforted by the low glow of dashboard lights.

"Shouldn't you be married with three kids by now?" she asked out of nowhere.

I paused before answering. Though I detected no guile in the question, I also knew that with women, despite their disclaimers, there is assuredly a correct answer to personal questions and the more personal the less scope there is for error.

What to say? That, yes, per Brigham Young, who regarded as a menace any unmarried man over twenty-five, I should indeed have stepped up to the plate before now? That the last woman I had dated had wanted to spend more time talking about the relationship than actually having it? That the one before her already had three children by a skunk of a man who had abandoned them and that I just wasn't up to it?

That my mother had died of a broken heart because of my father?

Dad had spent twenty years at a prominent insurance company headquartered in Boston, his shoulder to the wheel, rolling it along from promotion to promotion until his ambition had finally carried him to a vice-presidency. He had a sideline as a motivational speaker. He looked good in a suit. And he had met people along the way, many of them women. He had become close to one married woman in particular, too close. He could have turned away at many points but hadn't. The two spiraled in on each other until the gravity proved too powerful to escape. As is often the case, emotional intimacy preceded the physical. And which was worse—the sharing of the body given to the spouse or the sharing of feelings to be spoken only to her? The two-paycheck marriage, desirable or necessary as it may be, has not been an unalloyed boon. The scope for adultery has vastly expanded and its invitation frequently proffered. The bill put to marriages and children by guilt, resentment, divorce, and single-parent fatigue is immense and probably unpayable. Shouldn't these things be added to the cost of doing business?

The affair proper began a year after I had left for Germany on my mission. By temperament and experience, my mother would have been oblivious to any signs. My father, who could ordinarily compartmentalize responsibilities and thus endure hefty amounts of stress, buckled under the psychic and spiritual weight of betrayal. He would have held up longer, and arguably been better off, as a prisoner of war. He confessed all, lost his membership in the Church—while I was out seeking to increase its numbers—and searched hard for the kind of glue that could put a marriage back together.

To his credit, he succeeded after a fashion. Repentance and rebaptism were in time forthcoming. The woman, who might have played it a number of ways, chose self-effacement. Her marriage failed and she moved away. My mother, like Lorraine Kooyman, found her life was like walking through wet cement. Embarrassment, anger, and a questioning of faith were her lot. She had done her best to do everything right—and *this* was the payoff? Even so, she never would have divorced Dad. What did they say to each other? What ratio of small talk to silence did they fall into? She skipped church for a while. His motivational speeches ended.

They were in a tough jam between wanting to spare me while I was focused on things spiritual and fearing lest I found out from someone else.

It was Dad who finally wrote me. Not the sort of letter you record in your journal. As it was near the end of my service, I was able to sleepwalk to the finish line in a clerical post at the mission office. I have no idea whether I went through the "normal" grieving process.

Things improved, though. I was at school and so better able to detect the change in my parents at return visits; like the progress of a plant, growth undetectable in daily increments was visible at longer stretches. And it might have gone on so.

It was winter and Dad had a routine business trip to New York. Usually he took a flight but sometimes he would drive, probably—if I got this trait from him—to be alone with his thoughts. He drove this time. It was raining hard and somewhere in southern Mass he was cut off by another driver, lost control, and sailed out over the shoulder and arced down into the hard trunks of old trees.

This second blow, massive in itself, hit too soon after the first, and my mother never fully recovered from either. She followed her husband two years later, taken by a cancer that she battled half-heartedly. My father had revisited his finances soon after his confession (feeling vulnerable?) and left my mother set for life. In turn, my mother, who would never think of moving to Florida, buying gems, or going on safari, bought a ridiculous amount of life insurance before there was even a shadow of malignancy—at least one detectable by medicine—and it all passed to me, her only child. I hadn't moved to Florida either, but I was still young.

I wondered whether my father foresaw any of that during those last few seconds before Ford met fir. Did he get a glimpse of the different destiny for his family that he had set in motion? Had he faced the recapitulation of his life said to occur at that moment? I like to think he thought of Mom, the bride of his youth. How precious she must have seemed, how much he loved her.

How he must have loved her, then.

✑

"Why aren't you married?" she asked.
"I don't know," I said.

twenty-six

A shakedown, that's what it amounted to, and a ham-handed one at that. If he knew so much, why hadn't this Del Price gone to the police? He smelled money, that's why. Who did this clown think he was fooling in his Armani suit and cheap watch—oh yes, he had seen it. Tall and well-built, the sort who looked athletic even without sports credentials, the sort he had hated in high school. This one was just shy of preppy, his eyes a little too keen, a pickpocket's eyes. A sleazeball all the worse for putting on airs. So this was who Kooyman's wife had hired, a thief who was peeling bills off the Kooyman bank roll as fast as he could, taking advantage. A parasite and its vulnerable host, just as nature had intended.

Obviously, the phone call hadn't worked. It had been a side thought anyway; it might have helped and couldn't hurt and with no ability to control its effects, he hadn't cared much either way. Was Mrs. Kooyman made of sterner stuff? But wait. The Kooyman daughter—Victoria? Valerie?—maybe that's who the detective was working for now. He smiled at his perceptiveness. What additional services was he providing that hot ticket? This guy was working the entire family!

He snorted. A gumshoe, taking him on. A welterweight who had climbed into the wrong ring; what a punch in the gut this guy would get.

Now, how much did Price know and how did he know it? He had been pretty elliptical about it, suggestive rather than concrete. Probing for a reaction, no doubt, like a fortune teller who holds your palm but reads your face. Still, there was no way either he or Karol should have surfaced, even more astonishing that Price had crashed the reception. He had not foreseen it; how could he have? And so Karol, unprepared, had been blindsided. Clever, that.

159

Clearly, they had been inside his office. When had they been there? Had they broken in? Perhaps not; they may have lain in wait until his minion had taken a restroom break. But what could his office have told them? The woman had mentioned the photos, presumably of him and Karol. And Price knew that Karol had been out since Wednesday. Was that it—was the gumshoe working through a list of Wednesday absentees? But how had their names been added, and so quickly? Most troubling had been the dropping of Ulrich's name. Where had that choice tidbit come from? The newspaper?—but what had led the detective there? He shook his head. Too many questions. Was all this investigative competence supposed to give him pause? Scare him?

There was another explanation. Loose lips—and the pool of blabbermouths was fairly limited. Something didn't add up though; it was clear that Price didn't know everything or he wouldn't be fishing. So what had been said? Was the detective being played somehow?

In the meantime, Karol was a wreck. The detective had been right about that—Karol was an oak with shallow roots, crying out to be propped up at every breeze. Had he known he would have prepared Karol.

He had always prepared Karol.

Karol had come to him in the fall in their Cleveland high school, looking for help. The pairing of them was unexpected. Karol was a big, good-looking, popular kid who had gotten good mileage with an exotic European charm and an (implied) desperate flight into exile. Karol had little talent for academics and less motivation, but wits enough to realize that someday credentials would matter and that these seemed (sadly) to involve a record of sustained achievement. Maybe there was a short cut into the Gold Club.

He was night to Karol's day, an outcast from society—a status arrived at by mutual consent. Smart, but on the short side with a big head and a funny name—a rotten hand to be dealt a boy. Born old, he was dismissive and off-putting; even teachers were hesitant around him, especially the women. But his intelligence—dare we suggest genius?—was first rate and could not be gainsaid. No petty Duma of a student government for him, and no proms or drama or sports either. Chess club, though—you could do that with minimal social interaction and schools didn't have poker teams. Maybe this cold oddball could help Karol, a little.

Indeed, the outcast could. And did. He realized early on that tutoring wasn't the solution for Karol—the kid was a twenty-watt bulb. What was wanted was not learning but answers, the kind that appear on answer keys. He was a year ahead of Karol and this had helped. Karol had at least some short-term memory and could retain answers as long as comprehension was not also required. Soon, he was supplementing test answers with essays and papers in Karol's name. By the next report card, Karol was on the honor roll. In the spring, he ran, from the backroom as it were, Karol's successful campaign for student body president. Administration and faculty were impressed, and so a dim bulb was lifted up as an ensign to inspire youth. Let the others play with their dogs and cats, he thought. He had a boy.

He saved everything from his senior year and before going off to Columbia passed it on to Karol, like an inheritance. The mail and telephone calls would fill any gaps. He instructed Karol to enroll in the same senior classes that he had taken (excepting math and physics—here reality prevailed) and with the same teachers. When a different teacher was assigned, Karol got his mother to plead him into the class with the "right" instructor for her sensitive son.

Karol, for whom the Ivy League had once been as remote as Valhalla, began toying with the idea of following his mentor to Columbia, though which of their minds had originated this was unclear. No matter—the Gold Club was unaccountably now within sight.

He had laid the groundwork at his end. He approached the Admissions Office to put in a plug for another hometown lad, a Hungarian boy who had overcome long odds—poverty and a foreign language at home—and had pulled himself up by his bootstraps, mentoring others along the way while working two jobs after school. He trowelled it on pretty thick to be sure something would stick. Should this new Abraham Lincoln happen to apply to Columbia, he felt obliged to recommend Karol, the better man, for admission.

*And so the molding of this fraudulent human being continued. Karol arrived in New York in equal parts exultant (*the world is my oyster!*) and terrified (*but I'm a fraud!*) The biochemistry at which his creator excelled would not serve for Karol and a lower protein diet was found. He advised Karol to think of biology as a sort of stroll through a zoo, giving him a grasp of the matter he could manage. Later, as the idea of Karol conducting scientific research was preposterous, a new heading would be given—business administration.*

All these years.

Surely his original expectation had been that after the amusement of messing around with Karol's life for a season, pulling and distorting him like a spiritual Gumby, he would cast off his creation and let him flounder. But godhood was heady stuff, and he had found that the time to cut Karol loose had never come. Indeed, Karol had surprised him with occasional bursts of business acumen— only tentatively attached to any notion of ethics, certainly, but ingenious and profitable. For them both. Eventually, genetics and business had been wedded into their biggest enterprise together, Prime Meridian. He had made an empty shell into a CEO.

For him, genetics had been an extension of the drive to control life, to get it to do what he wanted it to do— fetch, beg, or roll over. And it had the brightest of futures. He had been there at the beginning, rushing in to claim his piece of the lush, virgin lands discovered by Watson and Crick. But research was time consuming, advances more incremental than he had supposed, and he had had to depend on so many other, weaker links without his vision and drive. He had often sensed hesitancy about his research from colleagues and blamed this for the insufficient acclaim he had been accorded. So he had conceived the Project with Ulrich, his Swiss doppelganger. Why wait twenty years for what everyone knew was coming in one form or another?

Why had Karol come to him, the outcast, those forty years ago? Had the Hungarian hunk assumed the oddball kid would be dazzled, grateful for the beau geste, and so swept starry-eyed into allegiance? What a monumental mis- calculation! What was it like being Karol, he wondered? Never entirely sure why or how your success had come, waiting for the day when the rug would be pulled out from under you and an accurate accounting of your achievements demanded. Karol had been married, once, during a period of relative autonomy, but his orbit had inevitably carried him (people being more like inanimate objects than they realized) back to his mentor, and she had not been able to compete. There had been no children.

So: Monday at his lab office. Clearly, Price meant to barter. An incentive to back off, keep a zippered lip. Was he supposed to have a blank check ready? How big of bite would the barracuda try to take?

Well, they would see.

He had teeth, too.

twenty-seven

I awoke late to a chilly Second Saturday. Second Saturday has been a fairly recent adjustment to the calendar, insinuated there as a solution to the demands of our harried world. It used to be that one Saturday per week was sufficient to haul kids to soccer, put the machete to the yard, shop, golf, wash the car, barbecue, or catch a movie. But with the explosion of two-paycheck families and the steady amplification of secular demands and ballooning wants, Saturday was overburdened and an additional day was found to catch the overflow, a bonus day whereon remaining idolatrous duties could be discharged. The Fourth Commandment was ground away like rock beneath a glacier. Second Saturday used to be called Sunday.

Early Mormon leaders walked the line on the Sabbath, and present ones still do, albeit with less muscular rhetoric. In pioneer Utah, if your livestock broke through the fence, you waved good-bye to it on the way to the chapel. Farmers and ranchers were told they would lose five times as much as they would gain by working on the Sabbath, and many believed it. There was a great deal of frowning on recreations like skating and buggy riding. By divine design (and mercy) early Utah antedated malls and professional sports.

I rolled out of bed after four hours of restless sleep. Normally, I could operate pretty well on that amount, but this time it had been difficult to drop off and then to sleep soundly. Dreams were odd and fragmented. Thoughts of Ronnie and the frustrating enigma of her father's disappearance roiled, complicated by the drama at the Prime Meridian reception.

We had returned to my place at 3:00 AM after a drive that had taken us to the New York State border. Gliding through the night, Ronnie and I had examined (and found wanting) my love life, though not much of hers, except this: She had no current boyfriend.

We tried to weave together the loose threads of our joint venture into some sort of cloth, but couldn't. Roessner had died on the Friday before Larry's disappearance and maybe had handed out skis and sweets—so what? And yet, of all the biotech concerns he might have visited it had been Prime Meridian that claimed him, and it had been its CEO, Karol Vyridiak, who had imploded at Larry's name. Perhaps something was up with the women in Roessner's car. No doubt Marjorie would remember them in her searches. And what connection, if any, did Steve Schuyler have with the others in this mystery? I had put it to him that he was in bed with Vyridiak and Ermiston, but it was a bluff based on a hunch, aimed at provoking flight. It hadn't worked. Of course, he might have phoned someone. And, as I had told Ronnie, even if all three were part of the *dramatis personae* in this melodrama, their silence was an effective roadblock. I would be left a boor who disrupts cocktail parties and persecutes sick drunks, neither of which would do much to enhance a business card.

I still had hopes for phone calls taken or placed by Larry that Wednesday, though their legal value might be nil. "*Sure, I talked to him,*" the caller could say, "*but Larry said he had to run an errand.*" Kaboom. It might even be true.

We had stopped at my condo so Ronnie could change and get her things before she returned to her father's house. Surprisingly, neither of us found ourselves tired at that hour. Perhaps we had absorbed some of the zoom from the Ferrari. We lingered inside my door.

"You show a girl a good time," Ronnie finally said. She seemed a little punchy.

"Sure. I got us thrown out of a party after a half hour. That's real class."

"Don't worry about it." She paused. "It's kind of nice to go on a regular date for a change. One where you don't have to worry about who's going to end up where, and . . . Oh. I'm sorry."

"I understand."

"You're a better person than I am."

"I could go out and rob a liquor store if it would help," I offered.

"It might," she allowed.

"Before you change, I'm going to ask you for something."

"Oh?"

"A kiss."

"You're asking?"

"I thought I might." It's awkward being nice.

She didn't reply, but looked up at me. I took her in my arms, and she slid her bare arms around my neck. It was a good kiss and long enough.

"I've never met anyone like you," she whispered.

"I bet."

"A man with rabbits."

"You may have deduced that I like you."

"I know. You know how I could tell? It was the shower. You buffed every tile in it, including the ones on the floor."

"Maybe I never shower."

"I'll *never* see that again. I could tell before, but I knew then. That and the Ferrari. You're an A minus, by the way."

"I'm being graded?"

"On the kiss. There are two kinds of kisses. A minus or C plus."

What if I had missed and hit her jaw—wouldn't that be an F? But why push for details? I almost told her I hadn't had a lot of practice but thought better of that, too. Maybe I was a natural.

"Nice to know I made the grade. I'd have to give you high marks as well, but then I'm prepared to give you high marks in everything."

She pushed her head into my shoulder. "Oh, Del, not everything."

Neither of us made another move. It seemed we both knew that a second round would only destroy the lingering magic of that first kiss. But I didn't want to let her go, either. We stood clasped together and swayed back and forth for awhile. What would it mean to fall in love with this woman? What future would there be? Could we make it work? How much would each of us have to give up?

"I can drive you home in the Jet-mobile," I finally offered. "We can figure out the car thing tomorrow." Technically, of course, it already *was* tomorrow.

"No, I'll drive home."

We released and she started for the bedroom.

"Do you want to take some food back? I have a ton."

She shook her head, a swaying of black satin. "Give it to the bunnies."

Wherever she was, I was certain that Biscuit perked up.

Ronnie left a short time later. We kissed again briefly at the door. Rotten detective that I was, I failed to notice something important. When I got back to my bedroom, I found her dress, laid out purposefully across my bed. She had left it behind.

✺

So then, after all that had happened, followed by a few hours of surface sleep, it was time for church. I had intended all along to invite Ronnie but forbore after our late night jaunt across the state. What would likely be for her an anthropological field trip to a strange tribe should not be undertaken after a scrimpy slumber.

Church for us is a three-hour block of meetings on Second Saturday, with a good probability of some additional ones thereafter, the LDS equivalent of committee meetings. The general tenor of our Sabbath worship is Low Church Protestant, but well above snake handling. Like the church in New Testament times, meetings are dignified yet simple. We renew the covenant we made at baptism to reject sin, lighten each other's burdens, share sorrows and joys, and set a good example at all times and in all places. To be the same inside and out. In return, we receive the peace promised by the Savior, the peace not of this world, and are settled. We get to be happy.

I enjoy attending church; six days of this world are enough for me. But this day my mind was a revolving door: Ronnie, especially, but her father, too; Lorraine with her desperate hope; a dead Swiss scientist; a shaky CEO and a pair of shadowy Harvard sorts—all were coming and going.

I whitened the sepulcher and gave it my best. Wisely, I did not drive the Ferrari to church; I would never be able to leave without running a rotating carnival ride with the youth (if not their fathers) who, caught between Sunday School and a Ferrari, might view it as some sort of object lesson. I was a little late and slid into a seat towards the back of the crowded chapel. I saw Marjorie and her husband several rows ahead. Although Marjorie would have certainly invited her, Lorraine was not with them. I tried my best during the service to jam the revolving doors and focus on what the speakers were imparting. I generally didn't have this much trouble compartmentalizing my work, but now it wouldn't leave me in peace. Time seemed to crawl.

Between sacrament meeting and Sunday School, Marjorie found me in the crowded hallway and we swam out of the current into a shallows.

"How's Lorraine?" I asked.

"Cheerful, in a brittle sort of way. Before, she was waiting for anything; now, she has something definite to wait for but it's still *waiting*. It's really not much different than before. Did you and Ronnie find out anything?"

"I guess. Karol Vyridiak had a meltdown at Larry's name. He ran to Ermiston, who then drifted over to get the lay of the land."

"Did he get it?"

"I gave him some geography to survey."

"You didn't make a scene?"

"Define *scene.*"

"Del! At a snazzy affair in a hotel!"

"Interest was lagging. Besides, Ermiston didn't know it was a routine. Neither did Ronnie; it freaked her out," I said, smiling.

"You're making quite an impression all over," she observed.

"Yes, aren't I? Somebody needs to crack. Maybe I should go back to Schuyler and stare at him until he cries uncle. Nice Sabbath talk, huh?"

She patted me on the arm. "Go to class. Oh, I did find out something about Karl Roessner. It was last night while you were at your event not making a scene. It got late so I waited until today."

"Just as well. I had my arms full."

Marjorie, whose womanly radar was second to none, looked at me. "Be careful, Del."

"I will be. Now, dish."

"Well, to make it short, it seems that Ulrich Roessner is, or was, a doctor—a medical one. I found that out by trying different spellings of his last name; it isn't consistent across the web. It looks like the women, Marie Pestel and Elsbet Whats-her-heit are, or were, obstetric nurses. If that's what a *Sauglingschwester* is." She got it out by chopping the word into separate syllables.

"More like a baby nurse, I think, but they might be the same."

"They were linked to a U. Roessner, who is a *Frauenarzt.*"

Literally, a doctor of women, a gynecologist. I nodded.

Marjorie continued: "He may be into genetics as well, but so far this is the only definite thing I've found out about him. I have to go. Come to Sunday School."

"In a minute."

She disappeared down the hall.

A doctor and two nurses. Why had that struck something?

Oh-oh.

A wholly unexpected character now pushed her way through the spinning door. This was just too weird. This case was a bunch of puzzle pieces fighting connection. I couldn't even find the edge pieces that would frame the rest. Now this, the wackiest one yet.

Two Swiss nurses had died in a Friday car smash-up. Did I know of another nurse who had received an improbable job offer shortly thereafter? An urgent plea, even, made by a total stranger willing to dump a bag of money over the head of a nurse who had just been fired for suspicion of drug theft?

twenty-eight

An hour later I walked into Eddie Winter's in Dorchester. On the way, I had phoned Carmen Rosario. As expected, it took ten seconds to learn that she had heard nothing further from Dorthea and an additional ten minutes to indulge her entreaties, exhortations, and forays into crazy conspiracies. That girl was a talker. Charming, but charm can be smothering. I didn't tell her where I was heading.

Eddie Winter's was indeed established to cater to the neighborhood at large. One half was demarked as the restaurant section. Booths defined the perimeter and between them rectangular tables were set in two parallel rows. Each table was coated in shiny brown enamel pitted with wear. The restaurant would work through early evening for casual family dining before yielding to the later pizza and beer crowd. The other half of Eddie's, separated from the first by a shoulder high wall, was given over to a bar and lounge with the same brown furniture; TVs were mounted high on the walls and set to a sports channel. This area served the family of the inebriated, a clan with interpersonal ties as complex as on any genealogical tree. There was likely cross traffic between the two sections.

I took a booth on the sober side; I couldn't see Dr. Rogers courting Dorthea on the booze side, and alcohol couldn't be served until the afternoon on Second Saturday, a final handhold of the Blue laws and one certain to be pried away one day. What's a bar but another kind of altar? A cheerful middle-aged black woman named Debra approached with a menu.

"Hi!" I said brightly. "Maybe you can help me before I order. I'll make it quick. I'm looking for someone who was here last Sunday." I laid on the

169

table the photo Carmen had given me. "This is Dorthea Caulley. She's a nurse who lives a couple of blocks away. She was in here last Sunday with a white guy sitting at one of these booths. I think they sat there for a while but didn't order much. He offered her some kind of bogus job. She hooked up with him later in the day and hasn't been seen since. I'm hoping you remember the two of them or know who was working here last week who might remember."

Debra seemed transfixed, looking between me and the photo. This was not her usual customer experience.

I helped her. "I'm a private investigator, like the ones on TV but more boring. My name is Del Price."

She smiled. "I kinda remember them," she said. "I think. But it mighta been Claudelle." She looked around. "*Claudelle!*" she yelled in a voice that would crack a windshield. Maybe this was the ambiance that reminded patrons of home.

Claudelle, another black woman, had her arms full of breakfast for another table. It looked pretty good too, to a man who shared crackers and cheese with rabbits. Claudelle threw Debra a look, but after dispensing the dishes she came over. Younger than Debra, she had ironed her hair flat and colored it in alternating shades of rust and gold.

"You remember those two people from last Sunday?" Debra prodded. "This gentleman says the woman hasn't been seen since."

I took over. Debra had started in midstream and Claudelle was confused and would soon become annoyed. I handed her the photo. "This is Dorthea. She was here with a white guy. I'm a detective and Debra here is helping me," I said, nudging them over to Team Price. "Dorthea told her roommate before she disappeared that she hadn't ordered anything and the man had French fries or something—maybe mozzarella sticks."

Claudelle had begun nodding. "Yeah, I remember them. You're right, she didn't eat nothin' and he finally ordered some mozza' sticks. They just sat there talkin'."

My turn for nodding. "I'm pretty sure he was some kind of con artist," I continued. "He offered her a job out of town somewhere. I've got some more photos here. If you see the guy, please holler." I fanned out a stack of them like they were baseball cards. My starting lineup.

The response was immediate.

"That's him!" Claudelle exclaimed, pointing. She seemed excited that she could make a contribution. Other patrons began turning around to look at us. Only a few minutes had passed, but I knew that restaurant demands would soon reassert themselves.

"Uh-huh," Debra confirmed. "I remember him. He was wearing the same jacket."

"You seem pretty sure, Claudelle," I said.

"I am. He *was* wearing the same jacket. His hair was neater, trimmed up more."

"Thanks," I said. "I don't want to take up more of your time." I handed each of them a twenty. I was developing a disturbing habit of passing out double sawbucks. "When I find Dorthea, I'll tell her to come back here to thank you two."

They looked pleased. They had a story to tell.

I pushed back my thoughts until I left Eddie's. Unlike the protracted struggle with the Swiss connection, ideas now came to me in a rush. They both excited and disturbed. Naughty Dr. Rogers was not a doctor at all, but an impersonator out to deceive Dorthea Caulley. Why the subterfuge? It was too big of coincidence to believe that this act was unrelated to the deaths two days before of Marie Pestel and Elsbet Vanderheit.

And now there was another question to answer, even more troubling, and something I had learned early on came back to me, accompanied by a feeling wholly unexpected: Fear, even dread. It was like a door opening into darkness, with something in there looking for me. I fumbled with the keys at the car and dropped into the seat. I called Ronnie's cell phone. No response. She might still be asleep. I could have left a message but didn't want to wait for the reply. I called Lorraine.

"Oh, hello, Mr. Price. I think Marjorie is at your church."

"I know; I saw her there. I'm in Dorchester now. I take it you haven't heard anything yet?"

"No. It's probably too soon."

"You're probably right. Is Ronnie still asleep?" I felt like a teenager trying to sneak past my girlfriend's mother.

"No, she got up a little while ago and went out. She didn't say where."

That seemed odd, but I was being inundated with odd.

"Uh-huh. Say, by the way, I was just wondering about something. Something about Larry . . ."

I waited a short time until church ended (or should have) and called Marjorie.

"You played hooky," she upbraided.

"Judge not. Unless you can find it quickly, we need to put something out on the PIN. Mark it as urgent."

The PIN is the Price Information Network. I like to picture the PIN as a cadre of sharp operatives embedded at the centers of power, information, and wealth who jump when summoned by special pagers. Others with less vision, like Marjorie, see the PIN as a list of email addresses. Although its members are a Noah's ark of experience and wisdom, almost none can see either power or wealth with a telescope. And if they don't jump, they usually respond.

I was going to put out to the PIN a piece of information none of the major players in this mystery could know that I had.

"Other than the obvious biblical reference," I directed, "I need to know whether something floats anyone's boat."

"What's that?"

"The Garden of Eden."

twenty-nine

I sat in my Ford parked down the street from Eddie's. Compared to the Ferrari, it seemed like the boxy wooden wagon you see in Westerns. Maybe I should just buy a Ferrari and achieve uplift and well-being through spending. A wild indulgence never before considered now looked reasonable and justified. It bolstered my professional image and was a hit with women and kids. On the other hand, this course of action ran counter to proscriptions regularly voiced in scripture. Was it Ronnie? Because I didn't want to give her up? Nope, not much of a Sabbath at all.

I was alone and felt alone. I called Frank but had to leave a message. I asked him to call back without dropping the big news on him. He wasn't on call 24/7 for this thing and in helping Lorraine, he had already squeezed in time he could ill afford. Marjorie would send out the electronic smoke signal; no reason to bother her anymore, either. Big news but what to do with it?

The obvious thing to do would be to confront "Dr. Rogers" and explain to him that the axe was laid at the root of the tree. Confession was the rational course. It was only my third day on this search and it was a shock—and I was surprised at the shock—to realize that it might be over today, Larry Kooyman's whereabouts revealed. I thought of Lorraine.

I imagined how it could play out with the good doctor, tempted initially by a subtle approach: *"Say, I was just down at Eddie Winter's in Dorchester— do you know Eddie's?—well, anyway there I was munching on fried mozzarella sticks while waiting for my good friend Dorthea Caulley . . ."* Less entertaining but more Christian would be a simple call to repentance, warning that his ship was off course, and its compass needed repointing to true north.

Confrontation was the obvious thing to do—but I wasn't going to do it. One issue was control. Now, Dorthea had to be accounted for. There was still the annoying possibility that what I had here were two unrelated stories, one in which Larry Kooyman appeared and one in which he did not. The links between the various players were still tentative, ill-defined. And I couldn't keep bluffing forever; like a trial attorney I wanted to know the answers to at least *some* questions before I asked them. If a confrontation with the imposter produced a shrug of his shoulders, I'd be left with a wild story for the police and a suspect who had been tipped off. My investigation was all scattered parts and no assembly instructions.

The second issue was frankly a spiritual one. To what degree did my faith inform my decisions in a world of sharp corners, an all too business-as-usual domain through which atheists and agnostics traversed as profitably as believers? I had already rationalized a departure from the Sabbath and it had paid off. How much further did I want to push it? It was really quite simple: Did I have confidence that putting God first on the Sabbath, four thousand years after some stone tablets said I should, was the right thing to do, tangible payoff or no? Was I confident that what my Church taught—who God is, where we came from, why we're here, and where we go after death—accurately describes reality?

I did and I was.

I stopped by Lorraine's on the way home. I wanted to see Ronnie, of course, and was disappointed that her car was not in the driveway. Lorraine still seemed caught between two worlds. Her mind's vice-like grip on the phone call purportedly from her husband had had, at least, the effect of pulling her from a burning house of anxiety. Yet she was still within range of the heat. She had made a new truce with her home. Whereas before the shades had been pulled tight, then flung open, they now were pulled halfway across the windows, hope fighting skepticism with Lorraine, a soldier still wary of snipers; steering clear of the gaps.

She was in white that day, slacks and blouse, and seemed to have been graced with a night's sleep. Medication? Her round, pleasant face retained the smile, sincere if dutiful, with which her generation was expected to face the world, even as her mind stared off through different eyes in a different direction. I might have been looking at my mother.

We took our places at the kitchen table.

"How was church?" she asked.

"Fine. I saw Marjorie and her husband there, but I had to leave early. I don't normally work on Sunday, but I was looking for someone who had been in a restaurant last Sunday, and I realized that the weekend wait staff might not be the same crew that worked weekdays.

"Did you find them?"

"No, but I did get a hold of the right waitress, so I guess it was worth it. I was on my way home and thought I'd stop by to see Ronnie. I take it she's still gone."

"Yes. She got up this morning and left."

"Huh. When, about? Did you see her?"

"Oh, it was about nine-thirty. I saw her briefly. She said she was going out for a while."

She couldn't have gotten to bed much before 4 AM—why jump out of it a few hours later? Too early for shopping. And why shop, anyway?—she had dropped two grand the day before. A spa? Had the evening's drama necessitated massage? Or had she gone to confront Vyridiak? (Was he in the phonebook?)

"Did she take her cell phone?"

"I don't know; I suppose so. It was probably in her purse," she added helpfully.

If she had taken it, it wasn't turned on. I had immediately gotten voice mail, not ringing, when I called.

"How was she dressed?"

"Jeans and a blue blouse. She took a jacket, I think."

"I'd hope so. Well, she'll be back sometime. How are *you* doing?"

"Oh, I'm fine."

Of course.

"I hope we hear from Larry soon. You know I'm not going to close this case until he marches through the front door. Well, actually he can march through *any* door."

She smiled. "I'm sure he'll be back soon," she said.

Are you, Lorraine? Are you sure?

I said: "Well, tell Ronnie I stopped by. I'm sure Marjorie will be by later."

I returned with sadness the rocket car to its owner, thanking him and testifying of its restorative powers and potent influence on romance. I chugged home in my meek Buick (*a Buick!*) my life as gray as the car and the sky above. The earlier drizzle had hardened into a steady rain by the time I pulled in.

Rabbits and hors d'oeuvres were the only signs of interest under my roof. I took one of the spicier cracker confections from the fridge and placed it on the kitchen floor. By the time I returned from the bathroom it was gone. In its place squatted a plump but firm white bunny with fierce, pink eyes. She was grooming her ears by grabbing each one with her paws and dragging it to her mouth. I was not surprised to find her there, rather than Ficus. In matters of food, rabbits and humans are not so dissimilar. For both, there's the same spectrum. Ficus identifies food by whether or not it's wholesome; for Biscuit, by whether it fits in her mouth.

The quiet was welcome. Had this case been otherwise, one that slid without ceremony into the hands of the police, my sense of urgency would have been of the normal, professional sort with which I was familiar. But this time it was different, altogether darker, a tangle of disturbing clues that were suggestive but fragmented, refusing to fashion themselves into a coherent narrative. My mind had been in high gear for the better part of three days and the revelation about Dorthea and her Svengali was just one more stomp on the gas pedal.

Before retreating to my bedroom, I fanned out again the deck of What Goes With What? I added a new card, one depicting paradise with a bending palm tree and some squiggly lines for water. I left out the serpent, though I was sure it was hiding in there somewhere. I placed the card to my right. Soon, most of my *dramatis personae* had reported thither. First, naturally, Dorthea Caulley—a new card—and her Doctor Rogers, although I supposed I should allow for the possibility that he was only the procurer, and it had been another who had transported Dorthea to her destination. On the whole, I thought it unlikely, and had no compunction in pushing "Rogers" over to the Garden. Karl Roessner and his nurses followed and, therefore, so too did Vyridiak and his handler, Hector Ermiston. I realized that I needed yet another card, and I made one for the patient, if that's what she was, and set her on top of the Garden card. I didn't have a name for her. Finally, and reluctantly, Larry Kooyman made his way to join the others waiting for him. My cards were now congregated in two places, one bunch hovering in the heavens at the top of the table awaiting assignment below, and the others checked in at the G of E.

There wasn't any middle ground.

Leaving the cards on the table, I headed for the bedroom. What place would the Weaver at the Loom, who would select a thread for a sparrow's fall, find for me in this drama? It was time to ask.

I emerged from my bedroom around eight o'clock. The condo was dark, of course, the daylight drained away long before. I switched on a couple of lamps and looked around for bunnies. None in sight. They had the run of the place, though, and for them the several rooms with their furniture and obstacles was a Middle Earth in its variety and scope for exploration. I had turned off my cell phone and silenced the ringers on both the bedroom and kitchen phones and now I restored all of them to full voice. Messages had been left by Marjorie an hour before on both my cell and home phones.

Ronnie had not returned.

Nor was she answering her cell phone, Marjorie reported when I called her at the Kooyman's.

"She didn't answer earlier, either," I told her. "Needless to say, I don't like it."

"Where can she be?"

"Don't know," I replied. "but it's my new priority."

"Lorraine said you called and later dropped by."

"Yeah, I needed to know something about Larry. There's a whole new angle to this thing. Remember that nurse at Brigham and Women's Frank told us about who disappeared a few days before Larry? She's in play now."

"*What?* How can that be? *She's* connected to Larry?" Lorraine must have been elsewhere in the house.

"That's the theory *du jour*, but I'm still missing some of the connections." I related my visit to Eddie Winter's and laid out the new scenario.

"That's just weird, Del."

"Isn't it?"

"It's been thirty years—wouldn't he be a little rusty?"

"You'd think. They would have had to spring it on him at the last moment. That's if my theory is sound. It's still possible that in looking for Larry, I've stumbled into a separate drama. A lot of coincidences, though. Anything on the Garden of Eden?"

"Nothing that seems useful. There's a sort of theme park called the Garden of Eden in somebody's backyard in Kansas. The devil seems to be a concrete octopus representing banks and trusts."

And people go to Hawaii. I laughed. Genesis and the Grange. But it wasn't going to fly; Dorthea Caulley had reached her Garden and called Carmen within a couple of hours of leaving Dorchester.

"Let's hold off a little before I fly to Wichita." I changed directions. "Had a peek in Ronnie's room?"

"Funny you should ask . . ."

"Good girl."

"Her suitcase is still there and her clothes are still hanging up. There wasn't a note anywhere I could find. Nothing seemed odd."

"Okay. I'll see what I can figure out. How's Lorraine?"

"Oh, she's puttering around. She's quieter. She seems to be retreating inside herself. Before—you know, back before The Call—mood swings would knock her around, back and forth. You could actually get more out of her then. Maybe it's delayed shock or something. Anyway, it's sort of like she's *disappearing*."

"I understand." Marjorie had put it well; I realized I had been troubled by the same thing. Although her bodily mass could hardly have changed, Lorraine seemed now to take up less volume, to cast less of a presence as a person. It was unsettling.

"Do what you can to engage her," I suggested. "Don't let her disappear."

"I won't."

"I'd be surprised if the impostor Larry calls again, but look out for that as well."

"I will."

So where was Ronnie? I dismissed shopping and sport. A friend? But she never lived in Boston, and why would she turn her phone off? She must have known it would worry someone. Me, for instance. Would she tackle Vyridiak? If so, she surely would have been smart enough to leave a trail.

But I could think of one place to which she might have gone, a place where she wouldn't have thought she needed backup.

I dialed a number.

"Rex? How about I pick you up in twenty minutes?"

thirty

We arrived in Somerville shortly after nine. Streetlights and the glow from residence windows seemed modest through the steady rain that dropped out of the darkness above; we might have been living in a deep cave, high-tech Anasazi. With Schuyler's condo as the center point, Rex and I traced the grids of the neighborhood streets looking for Ronnie's car. As my course was set this was not strictly necessary, but the confirmation would be welcomed as a professional detail addressed, if nothing else. I limited our search to a square of the five blocks enclosing Schuyler.

We found her rental in ten minutes, three blocks away. The white Dodge was wedged in pretty well front and back, a punishment meted out by the proprietary residents for displacing one of their own. I hoped Ronnie had opted for the full insurance package. I got out to confirm the license plate number. I cupped my hands to the driver's side window and was unsurprised to find the empty, impersonal cabin of a rental car.

Rex, ever on top of his game, had shifted to the driver's seat of my car. He would slowly cruise the neighborhood, double parking as much as seemed prudent, staying within eyesight of the condo. Dressed in black and with his hair tucked up under a black stocking cap, he was begging for an audition in a police lineup. With his skepticism of institutional authority, he would probably enjoy it and try hard to look guilty. My *ensemble* was also appropriate to the task at hand, but consisted of more sociable black slacks, gray dress shirt with a black necktie beneath a charcoal sports coat, black rain coat, and black leather gloves. I was a gentleman bandit.

Part Two of reconnaissance was to check for Schuyler's Subaru. I would go in whether it was there or not, but I wanted to know. I strode down the driveway to the underground garage. His car was not there. He may have left in it with Ronnie, but I would soon find out.

I was losing count of the times I had dodged condo security by tapping out tunes on the buzzers and feared that the ruse would finally fail through the indifference or suspicion of the residents. But luck tipped my way once more as someone buzzed me in. Wouldn't they wonder when no acquaintance appeared? Maybe investigate, lean an ear into the hallway for unexpected, suggestive sounds? Had I hit different occupants on each occasion? Questions to which I would never have answers unless I polled the building unit by unit, which I was disinclined to do. And was it the hand of Providence, in its micro-provisional way, that had prevented (a cheap contractor? shipping problems in Shanghai?) speaker phones from being installed rather than buzzers?

Once inside, I bypassed the elevator for the stairwell, taking the steps two at a time in my black running shoes. There was a door at the roof in one of those little sheds that sits atop the modern urban dwelling. Would it be locked? You'd think so—if anyone wandered onto the roof and came to grief it would be a toss-up as to who would arrive first, an ambulance or a lawyer. I can pick ordinary doorknob locks, though I rarely have to. In Massachusetts, the possession of lock picks is tied to the intent to use them in the commission of a crime. I had no compunction about using them now; if the police wanted a piece of this I had a fallback plan—I would tell the truth. The only reason I was bypassing the local constabulary was that even if I could persuade them to meet me at Schuyler's, the most likely outcome was either no answer at the door or a Schuyler who would deny all—and I would be on the roof all the same but this time with my name tickling the back of some cop's brain.

The door was indeed the sort requiring a key for both outside and inside knobs, but this proved no special problem because it was unlocked. I stepped cautiously onto the roof, scanning the area with a narrow-beamed flashlight. A dozen or more flowerpots were scattered near the doorway, which may have accounted for the unlocked door. Most of the plants looked dead and a couple resembled a certain controlled substance.

I stepped lightly across the roof to the rear of the blacktop and lowered myself to hands and knees before approaching the edge. I looked down at the balcony below, the one directly above that of Schuyler's, feeling like I ought to be wearing an eye patch and holding a knife in my teeth. I leaned out over the edge to have an angle on the glass slider. It was curtained with light leaking around the edges. The balcony was wider than the slider, so I moved to a side where I could put my foot against brick. I crabbed over the edge and lowered myself until I was hanging by my hands, then dropped softly to the balcony three feet below. I quickly looked over the balcony railing and shone the light onto Schuyler's balcony; I didn't want to land on his barbecue. But Schuyler's porch was clear and no light could be seen through his slider. I swung over the railing, grabbed a wrought iron rail in each hand and slid down. I could almost touch Schuyler's railing with my feet, but swung my body inward and dropped onto the concrete balcony. From roof to here had not taken ten seconds.

It was my day for doors—Schuyler's was also unlocked. Why secure it when you're three stories up? I pulled the door open and stepped into the darkness. With my memory of the layout and my light, I negotiated this bachelor's obstacle course of matter unorganized. No one was in the front rooms and I heard nothing elsewhere. Better still, I *felt* no danger. I headed up the hall, pushing open each door in turn. The last one was to the master bedroom. I directed my light into the blackness. There was a long shape, like a rolled up carpet, lying diagonally on the bed. It was rocking slightly from side to side.

It was Ronnie Kooyman.

thirty-one

I had no reason to believe that my descent to the balcony and subsequent entry had been detected. I closed the bedroom door and flipped on the room light.

The room was as disheveled as the rest of the condo, but the air was even more stale and musky. Clothes everywhere, fossilized food as well, the dresser top like the deck of a mini-aircraft carrier whereon a squadron of flying junk had skidded to a stop. This room wouldn't be shown as the before picture on a home design network.

All this framed a grotesque rodeo. What scientist Schuyler had done was use the universal binder, duct tape, in conjunction with his rock climbing rope. Ronnie, in her blue blouse and jeans, was trussed up with the silvery tape around her ankles and again around her thighs, binding her legs tightly together. Her arms had been brought over her head and were bound at the wrists and around her forearms. The ropes kept her arms stretched toward the oaken bedpost, and he had tied her feet off at the post diagonally opposite. With difficulty she could rotate her body around the axis between the bedposts like a tormented calf. Her mouth had been gagged and taped. As a final touch to this torture, for torture is what it was, Schuyler had blindfolded her, although with a compassionate touch he had wrapped a green bath towel around her upper head before liberally taping that, too. The head wrap covered her ears as well but not her nose. I didn't get the blindfold. The gag, sure, but what was she going to see—dirty clothes and the alarm clock on his nightstand? And he had used more rope than was necessary as well; the whole thing smacked of the sloppy, exaggerated job a drunk would effect. She must have been initially stunned or had been subdued by a second person.

I moved quickly to the bed. I put a knee on the mattress and leaned toward her. She stiffened. I put my fingers under the head wrap near her ears and pried it up.

"It's Del," I said. "Hang on." I touched her cheek, the small patch that was available, with my finger tips. I peeled back pieces of the duct tape and wiggled off the entire head wrap. Ronnie blinked up at me with red and swollen eyes. She had been slapped or smacked with something on the left side of her head. The tears flowed.

Next was her mouth, but I hesitated. "We're getting out of here, *but don't scream, okay?* I had to break in. Nod your head if you understand."

She nodded.

As carefully as I could I peeled off the tape and pulled out the wash cloth used as a gag. Shouting out was not going to be an issue; her mouth was a dry socket and her voice a rasp.

"*Oh, Del!*" she sobbed. "*I hurt.*"

"I know, I know, babe. Hang on. I'll get you out of this."

I released her arms. It wasn't the Gordian Knot but it was a mess, the ropes a mass of serpentine confusion. I worked the wad of cords back and forth until the whole thing could be lifted over the bedpost. She cried out in agony, her frozen muscles and joints rebelling against what should have been routine movement.

"Relax your arms and move them very slowly," I instructed as I loosed the coils from her wrists.

Freeing her legs was a smoother affair; having been taped up in a more natural position the trauma was less severe than that to her arms. I quickly unwound the tape from around her jeans, untied the rope and she was free.

Ronnie slowly bent her arms at the elbows and brought them back to her torso and then pulled up her knees, curling into a fetal position. I touched her shoulder intending to massage it, but she jerked in reflex.

"Don't!" she croaked.

"Sorry. Look, we can't stay here. I can carry you out, but it would help if you could put your arms around my neck."

"Okay," she whispered, but I wasn't sure how tuned in to the moment she was. Part of her mind seemed to be rationally processing the current flow, but she was also fighting pain, confusion, and humiliation. How many people (at least as adults) *ever* get tied up as a prisoner?

"How did you get here?" she whispered.

"Over the roof," I said. She went blank, unable to make sense of this.

Ronnie had been twisting and flexing her shoulders and arms in small, undulating movements. The duct tape binding her wrists had at least prevented rope burn there, but she was still in pain. She looked down now at her hands, focusing on something I had seen when freeing her wrists—an engagement ring, a solitaire diamond of at least a carat and on the appropriate finger. I could guess what it meant and how it got there. She let out as much of a shriek as she was capable, twisted the jewel off her finger, and flung it away.

I moved to get off the bed.

"Don't leave me!"

"I won't—I'm not. I'm going to clear a way to carry you out of here. Don't worry, we're the only ones here."

For now.

I rushed down the hallway. Now I threw on every light switch en route. I followed a path with my eyes around the furniture and debris. I unbolted the front door and left it ajar. As I turned back my eye caught something familiar lying on a nearby table. My business card, the one I had left there the day before. I picked it up, pulled a pen from my inside coat pocket and wrote on the back of it. Another few steps and I spotted the refrigerator in the kitchen and had another thought. Along with the beer there were a few bottles of water; maybe he used them occasionally to flush out his liver. I grabbed one and slipped it into a coat pocket. Next stop: bathroom. Surely someone awakening to his head every morning would have laid up painkillers in the medicine chest. There was indeed a selection. Ibuprofen. Perfect.

At that moment, my cell phone vibrated.

No. Not now.

"Schuyler's back," Rex said calmly.

My heart leapt.

"His car just turned down the driveway."

Time enough. For a moment, I considered waiting it out. It would be quite a welcome for him when he opened his front door and got punched to the other end of the hall. Maybe I could duct tape him to the wall until the police came.

But Ronnie came first.

"Is he alone?"

"Couldn't tell; he came from the opposite direction."

I was sorry I wouldn't be there to see his face when he looked in the bedroom.

"We're coming out the front door," I said and hung up.

I ran back to the bedroom. Ronnie was still lying on the bedspread in the same position, quiet, her eyes closed. The ring had bounced off the dresser and lay on the carpet near the bed. I picked it up.

"We're outta here," I told her.

She rose up a little, eyes wide. *"Is he coming?"*

"Nope. Don't worry about anything."

I put my knee on the bed and leaned toward her. I pulled her towards me, getting her into a position where I could scoop her up. When she was near the edge I retrieved my card and tossed it and the ring to the wet spot in the middle of the bed. Reaching under my coat to the holster under my armpit, I pulled out my compact 9mm handgun and held it in my right hand. She didn't see it. I cradled her and stood up. She winced, but was just able to encircle my neck with her right arm.

"My pants . . ." she whispered.

"Not a problem."

Out and down the hall. Weaving to the front door. I toed it open and left it swinging into the condo, disappointed that Schuyler didn't have animals I could liberate. I strode down the hallway towards the stairwell; I was going to have to carry her down. A low-pitched drone told me the elevator was in motion. Surely I had beat it—but then a problem: I had to turn the doorknob to enter the stairwell and I had a gun in my hand. To use the other hand, I would have to bang Ronnie's head against the door. I let the trigger guard swing on my little finger and clutched at the knob.

The elevator stopped.

Plan B was to drop the weapon and then kick it into the stairwell, but I got the door on the third try. I stumbled in, the door closing slowly behind us.

We were barely down the first short flight of stairs to the intermediate landing when I heard the elevator door slide open.

Steps, a cry, and feet pounding down the hall.

I smiled as I turned the corner and continued the descent in a quick staccato. Ronnie seemed weightless in my arms.

A door slammed above us.

Had Schuyler been clever enough to feel the bed and find it still warm? Or was he driven by sheer frustration with no other outlet? Either way, he would be pursuing us as a madman.

My heart was pounding. Then before us was the vestibule door. No need to trick our way *out*; I pushed down on the handle with my elbow and again at the outer door and then there was cold air in our faces, and rain. Usually annoyances, they were now the heralds of freedom.

The car was there, double parked in front of the building. I stumbled but recovered. The door flew open behind us. Fortunately, Ronnie had sunken into herself and was responding to none of this. Rex had allowed enough room and had swung the back door fully open. I almost threw Ronnie in ahead of me and dove in behind her, pulling in my feet.

I looked back and extended my gun arm. Not five feet away was Schuyler, Ronnie's former fiancé, grasping after us. The gun froze him into a gargoyle's grimace. For two seconds that lasted much longer, we locked on to each other's eyes.

And then no one was there; Rex shot the car forward and we were away.

The door swung closed as we sped down the street. I holstered my gun. For several moments all I could see was life as revealed through the eyes of Steve Schuyler. Anger, frustration, despair—these were surely there but something else was washing over them, something unexpected.

What I saw in his eyes in that split second as the car jerked away was relief.

thirty-two

Ronnie began squirming on the back seat, searching for a comfortable position. She was moaning; the shock of rescue that had blunted some of the pain was withdrawing. She might require physical therapy, which raised an immediate concern. I twisted around on the car seat to face her.

"Ronnie, we've got a decision to make and we've got to make it now. Hospital and police or my place?"

These were choices with important implications. The one mandated official reports, the kind on paper, and the certain arrest of Steve Schuyler. But it would also require me to serve up my investigation to the police, the disadvantages of which seemed to me to outweigh the benefits at this point. But a delay in reporting the crime could mean unnecessary pain for Ronnie and loss of credibility with the authorities, while bypassing hospital and police altogether left Schuyler walking away from a felony.

Ronnie's brain either moved instantly through all these layers of calculation or, more likely, had bypassed them altogether, for her response was immediate:

"Your place. No police, no hospital." She added: "I'll be okay."

I wasn't sure how far "okay" could be stretched, but found no objections sufficient to overrule her decision. It was late and we could reconsider on Monday.

"That's what we'll do then." I knew Rex had followed this exchange and was charting a course accordingly.

I called Marjorie. "Grab a bunch of Ronnie's clothes and meet us at my place. We're heading there now. Um, undergarments, the full spectrum. And make up something plausible for Lorraine."

I returned to Ronnie. "Can you sit up?"

She grimaced again as I helped her. I ignored the seat belt. It was likely the first time she had been subjected to this degree of physical abuse and with it the overthrow of the predictability of life. The mugging of her dignity might well prove the deepest wound of all.

"Relax," I reassured her, "you're safe now. Ficus and Biscuit will take care of you."

She smiled wanly. "Rabbits."

I uncapped the bottle of water and held it at her mouth. "Take a sip of this and swish it around."

She spluttered, and we tried it again. And again.

She was able to take the bottle, and I twisted off the cap of the ibuprofen, held the bottle up so she could see it, and shook out four tablets into my palm.

"Down the hatch." She got them down in a few gulps and then laid her head back against the seat.

"I can't tell you how sorry I am," I said. Now removed from the immediate press of events, I was fighting a battle between my own tears and anger. "He's lucky he wasn't there—I don't know what I might have done. I mean it. I can't have . . ."

She moved her hand over to me. "I thought about you all the time. You were the only hope I had. And then you came."

"You're paying top dollar," I said.

Tears flowed again. "Oh, Del . . ."

She sobbed for a while, and I held her, my own face wet. I thanked God she was alive.

"He had Daddy's lunch box," she said after a while. She was still trying to shrug away the discomfort; the pills were only beginning to kick in.

"The one with Mickey Mouse?"

"Yes."

So it had been there after all, somewhere in all the junk or back in his bedroom.

"It doesn't surprise me," I said. "I'll tell you a story when we get to my place. I think I know what happened with your father, at least the general outline. I don't have an ending yet, but we'll get there."

I paused for a few seconds. "I think ole' Steve got into something over his head and is going down for the count. This isn't going to help him. I can't have anyone hitting you, Ronnie. I just—" I couldn't find the words through the anger. Turning the other cheek and doing good to those who despitefully use us seemed inadequate as I held her. Perhaps there could be a variance.

She became calmer. "It's weird," she said. "I thought I had been tied up forever, that each moment was unbearable, but now it seems like it was all over in a few minutes, in no time at all."

I didn't push for more, content to let the story come out at the pace she favored. I took it for granted that she had not learned where her father was.

"How did you know where I was?" she asked.

"Process of elimination. It had to be an errand worth losing Sunday sleep over. I broke into Schuyler's on spec, you might say. I was originally afraid that you had gone after Vyridiak."

"He's not in the white pages," she said.

"Lucky guy." So she had taken aim instead at an easier target, one from whom she expected cooperation—or capitulation.

The silences got longer between comments; not only were body and mind stretched and bruised, they were exhausted as well.

"Company," Rex said unexpectedly.

"Huh? You're kidding. Great." It didn't happen often, but occasionally someone got dramatic.

We were being followed.

"Uh . . . our boy?" I hated this clipped speech in front of Ronnie, but she had enough on her plate.

"No."

"Near?"

"No, a couple back. Blue BMW. It showed up just after our boy returned but continued down the street. I'm sure this is the same one."

"What are you talking about?" Ronnie asked.

"Oh, we had a lookout helping us," I lied. It seemed to make some sense to her, and she drifted off again.

So Schuyler had picked up a tail somewhere, either after leaving his condo or on the way back. Who and why? What did someone *else* need to know? And why follow us—had I been recognized?

Rex could almost certainly lose the tail, but first I wanted to know who it was. I peeked out the rear window and saw bright headlights close behind.

"Okay," I said. "Glove compartment." When was the last time anyone had stored gloves in one of these things—1929?

Rex leaned over and worked the latch. He found the scope, basically a shorter version of the one on a rifle, and handed it back.

"Okay," I said again.

Rex began the process of isolating the BMW. This involved taking rights and lefts at major intersections. If the car immediately behind us happened to be taking that same turn, unlucky us. We'd keep turning until our paths diverged. Eventually, the BMW would be exposed long enough so that I could get the license plate number.

This gambit worked at the first turn; a white Mercury continued on straight, as did the car behind it. The BMW hesitated but followed us around the corner. It hung back, maybe hoping another vehicle would intervene. Too late. I had the plate. Dancing reflections across the windshield prevented me from seeing who was behind the wheel.

"Okay, Rex, I got it. Let's go with Mr. Oblivious."

There are a number of strategies I can use to lose a tail. There's Live Free or Die, where I drive deep into New Hampshire until the other guy gives up. In Worm Ouroboros I plot a serpentine route until I am tailing the tail. It works more often than you'd think it would. Drag Racer is satisfying with its squealing tires and smoke, but it's dangerous and illegal. More fun is to be had in Dungeon and Draggin, which calls for high jinks deep within parking structures. At the extreme end, tempting but untried by me, are D-Derby and Will It Float?, wherein the tail's vehicle is rendered in a condition that encourages thoughtful reflection on further pursuit. The goal of Mr. Oblivious, my choice now, was to shake the tail in such a way that he believes he was never spotted and simply lost the target in contrary traffic.

Mr. O calls for finesse, and Rex, the jazz musician, is just the driver to effect it. In our present circumstance, late on a Sunday night and in an unfamiliar neighborhood, the solution proved to be timing our arrival at a stop light so as to hit the gas at the end of the yellow, as any driver might, and enter the intersection just as the light turned red. Our BMW escort was too far behind to make a convincing case for running the light. We returned to cruising speed and after a couple of blocks took a leisurely right—and then Rex punched it, making a quick left and right after that.

Marjorie was already at my place when we pulled in. She has her own keys; someone has to supervise the bunnies when I'm away or they'll rearrange the furniture as a practical joke. No doubt she had already laid out, as would an English lady's maid, Ronnie's change of clothes.

I carried Ronnie in from the car and down to the bedroom, laying her on an altogether more welcoming bed.

"Schuyler had her hog-tied," I told Marjorie as we entered. I looked her in the eye. "She may have been there eight hours or more."

"I understand."

"He had to knock her down to get her tied up, but otherwise she's mostly just sore. I'm not sure about pulled tendons or ligaments. We'll decide about doctors tomorrow."

I closed the bedroom door behind me on the way out. This left Rex on my hands. Having him take one of my cars was problematic because of the parking issue in his Back Bay neighborhood. Ronnie was in the caring hands of Marjorie and I expected nothing more from her until Monday afternoon; just as well drive Rex home now.

The late-night Second Saturday traffic was still disconcerting—why were people even out?—but had thinned enough to allow a round trip of under an hour. We talked about the case on the way there, and I bounced a few of my theories off him, some of which were pretty harebrained.

"As usual," I told him at the drop-off, "thanks for your help. You drive a mean getaway car. You're a good man, Rex." Our world, while long on criticism, is short on deserved, specific praise. I think it means as much to him as his paycheck.

On the return, my mind raced as fast as the car. I could hardly imagine Schuyler remaining home to await further developments—police, for example—but where would he go? His lab? To Vyridiak or Ermiston? Saskatchewan? Had I finally worn the guy down?

I called his cell phone, not expecting him to answer. He didn't. I left a message.

"Steve," I said, "Del Price here. It's time to stop this nonsense. I know about Doctor Rogers and Dorthea Caulley. My guess is she was replacing one of Karl Roessner's nurses. So here's the deal—call up and tell me where Larry is and in return I'll leave you alone—no more calls, no more visits, no more anything. It's a good deal, Steve, because after tonight you really don't want me to find you. Just give me Larry—and now Dorthea—and I'll cut you loose. Bye bye." I closed the phone and set it on the passenger seat.

It was leverage of a sort. All I really had was a story that could only enter a courtroom in a wheelchair. But Schuyler and his buddies had to wonder how I had any story at all. Of course, not being an officer of the court has its advantages. I don't care if my What Goes With What stories can be proved;

I care whether they describe reality and can help me find that which is lost. And maybe, at the end of the present story, whether the hero gets the girl.

Ronnie was out like a light when I got back. No surprise there. The woman had fallen from pinnacle to pit, from belle of the ball one night to gagged baggage the next, enduring a year's worth of grief on the way down. She'd want escape.

I looked in on her. Marjorie had left on one of the bedside lamps so she wouldn't awake in darkness; I found a 40-watt bulb to replace the brighter reading light. She was burrowed in snugly among the sheets and pillows wearing the white satin pajamas Marjorie had found in her suitcase, her hair damp and her tough-urchin face now girlish in sleep, peaceful at last. I thought of the black dress hanging in my closet. I closed the door part-way and joined Marjorie in the living room with a tray of last night's *hors d'oeuvres* (I was getting a lot of mileage out of them) and a bottle of sparking cider. It was near midnight.

"New Year's Eve has arrived early," I announced.

"Goody."

We munched without appetite. We didn't sing "Auld Land Syne."

"She was exhausted and sore but determined to shower," Marjorie said.

"I bet."

"She'll have a bruise on the side of her face, but her hair covers most of it. I put her clothes in the wash, but we should probably just dump them in the garbage."

"Yeah, I can't imagine her wearing any of them again. I'll see what she wants tomorrow. Did you call Ned?" Ned is Marjorie's husband.

"Yes."

"He's a good man. Sometimes I'm surprised he puts up with all this."

"We've been married for thirty years, and he's afraid of me."

"Of course." Only the first was true. I think.

"What happened to her, Del?"

"She went over to her ex-boyfriend's to shake the truth out of him; she figured she had an advantage she could press and on paper it looked like a plan. But Schuyler has been trying to drown a bad conscience while waiting for the other shoe to drop on his career. At some point, Ronnie found her father's lunch box, and he snapped. He had to go somewhere to do something or see someone and couldn't have Ronnie running around loose. He kind of went overboard in the restraint department. It's lucky he didn't run into me. Or maybe I'm lucky."

"What's the lunch box mean?"

I shrugged. "You know most of my theory. Even before Dorthea got dealt into this game I had thought of one way Larry could have been made to disappear. Suppose a friend calls him up around noon and says something like, 'Larry, I need a favor. I need you to meet me at such-and-such a place in ten minutes, but don't tell anyone where you're going. I'll explain everything to you, but it's got to be hush-hush until then. This is big.' Everyone has friends they'd do that for."

"If you're right about everything else, he could hardly explain on the phone why he needed Larry."

"It would be an impossible sell," I agreed, "even from a friend. I doubt that it was Schuyler that needed him, though. He was just the procurer."

"Do you think . . . something has happened to Larry?" Marjorie had lowered her voice, as though the words might float down the hall and sink into Ronnie's ear.

"Not necessarily. He may be held against his will until whatever this is blows over. Maybe something went wrong or they need to wait for something or someone. There's a foreign element that may be complicating things. Travel adjustments. I don't know."

We sat silently for a few moments.

I shook my head. "Hector Ermiston is going to sit tight, and I have no doubt he'll sew Vyridiak's mouth shut if he has to. If Schuyler doesn't come clean all we've got is this Garden of Eden. I'm just afraid it's a nick-name for some place rather than the actual name. Or worse, the code name for some project and not a place name at all. We can't seem to find anything."

"It's only been a few hours, Del. Something will happen."

"A lot of things are already happening. It's like standing in a river and trying to grab passing fish. Speaking of which . . ." I looked around for bunnies but saw none. Guarding Ronnie, I hoped with middling confidence.

I stood up. "It's late. You take the guest room, and I'll stay here. Do you have everything you need?"

"Of course."

"I ought to work for you, Marjorie."

"Who says you don't?"

Something was shaking or being shaken. I couldn't tell which. Hold it, it was me—I was being shaken. Then Marjorie was there; she was the one doing the shaking. I was asleep, or had been. It was still dark, but that told me nothing; during a Boston winter dark was a sixteen hour stretch.

"How's Ronnie?" I stammered, grasping for bearings.

"Still asleep. It's early." What would be early for Marjorie—3:00 AM? She was excited.

"We got a reply from the PIN!"

"Huh?"

"We found it! *The Garden of Eden, Del, the Garden of Eden!*"

thirty-three

"**A** motel? The Garden of Eden? You've got to be kidding."
It sounded ludicrous. I was now fully awake, though.
"Do you remember Brother Leavitt?"

I did. Fred Leavitt was a New England native who, in his seventies, had succumbed to the Gulf sun in Florida. He took with him a wealth of experience and wisdom that was still available to me through the PIN.

"He says that back in the fifties there used to be a motel on Route 2 called the Garden of Eden. It was somewhere between Concord and Acton. He thinks it was kaput by the early seventies. He says it was always kind of a second-rate place."

Only ten to fifteen miles west. Route 2, which fed traffic to and from Leominster and New Hampshire, ran past both Brother Leavitt's motel and my place. Spooky.

"Wouldn't it have been torn down by now? Don't tell me it's a biblical theme park (*in Massachusetts?*) or a historical site or something."

"I couldn't find anything on the Internet, but if it's that old, who knows?"

It didn't make much sense at first blush but it was kind of funny and I had to smile at the picture of professionals leaving behind the Alps for a flea-bag motel. Why? Wouldn't you get a better continental breakfast on *that* continent? I still thought the Garden of Eden made more sense as a nickname for something else, but it was intriguing and easy to investigate.

"What time is it?"

"Six-thirty."

Monday morning. It could have been worse.

"Okay. Tell Brother Leavitt thanks, we'll check it out. I'll drive there now since it's nearby. Maybe I can spot a fig tree. If not, I'll call on city hall in Concord and see what I can turn up. Somebody must know. Maybe a real estate agent." Any patch of ground in America that could be used to grow money would figure in someone's calculations.

"There's not much else I can do this early. I should be back before long, before noon in any event. We'll have to see what Ronnie wants to do and what we want to say to Lorraine. You and I are the only ones who know about this Garden of Eden. Let's keep it that way for a while."

It was nearer to Concord, on a slight rise a mile past the traffic circle and state prison. Our modern urban ice age, pushing glaciers of concrete ever outward, hasn't quite reached here, and I found myself in a pleasant region of trees and tilled earth. This far out, Route 2 is an uneasy hybrid of freeway and surface road where you race between traffic lights, hoping for green all the way. It now served me well, allowing me to pull off onto a narrow access road that led to the structure. I stopped and stared out the windshield through the dim Monday morning drizzle.

Any sign identifying this place as the traveler's paradise was long gone, but it clearly had been a motel of the mom-and-pop, post-WWII sort and, with the painted palm trees, placid herbivores, and flying birds fading into invisibility along its walls, was clearly my target.

Nor had Brother Leavitt's memory failed him in his assessment.

The Garden of Eden was a dump.

It was small, crouched timidly against its hill, the rooms laid out in a square "U" with the open end facing the highway. The courtyard was obscured, however, by another, unconnected building set in front of the motel and centered between the two arms, probably the office and innkeeper's residence. Perhaps the motel had once been painted green beneath its garden mural, but the color had been pummeled into a tired taupe. The flat roof, now fertile, would better grace a sod house. Trees around the perimeter drooped towards the rooms, too tired to either protect them or attack. The grounds were a uniform carpet of thistles, noxious weeds, wet leaves, and needles. Even in its day, with a lawn and motivated timber, I could see it only as a prom night motel, cheap, its façade a street siren in her garish makeup.

Adam and Eve hadn't been expelled from this Garden, they'd fled.

But there it was, still standing against the odds, surrounded now by a chain link fence with signs warning against trespass. The access road ran only to the motel; it was impossible to see where the property lines beyond the fence might be. I got out of my car and walked to the gate. It was locked with a new padlock. Within the gate, on either side of the road, were tire tracks running over each other. Good old mud, preserver of footprints from dinosaur to Dodge. One set belonged to a larger vehicle, surely a truck. I traced them back through the gap between the office and motel rooms until they disappeared into the courtyard. I pulled out my camera and took a few shots.

Was *this* the end of my journey? Was *this* the place from which Dorthea Caulley had phoned her garbled cry to Carmen? To which Larry had been lured to practice ancient skills? Was *this* the endpoint of a Swiss exodus, the best someone could come up with wherein to transact their business? Hard to see Prime Meridian herding investors here.

I looked toward the highway with its steady rush hour flow, a continual audience. I walked along the fence away from my car, the weeds at least providing a choppy pathway over the mud. I turned the corner and walked until I was behind the motel and hidden from view, pulled on leather gloves and scaled the fence, which fortunately was not crowned with barbed wire. The problem now was that there was no entrance to the courtyard from here; the rows of rooms formed an unbroken block along all sides of the "U." As the west side offered more in the way of tree and brush cover, I slid along it, close to the wall, not breaking stride as I rounded the corner and continued through the gap between the rooms and office building and so into the courtyard.

As befitting paradise there had been a pool, an unimaginative, un-para-disiacal rectangle, but it had long ago been filled in with dirt and was now a giant planter for weeds. The cement poolside separated those weeds from friends and relations that had strangled the lawn in the rest of the courtyard. A couple of large cement pots stood at the far end of the pool at either corner and allowed for elevated weeds. Had palm trees been witlessly attempted here, they had disappeared after the Fall.

And it was quiet, too quiet for being eighty yards from a busy highway, the traffic noise mysteriously muted to white noise that was soon lost. Even the light seemed quiet to me: solemn, no flickering, no excess, revealing objects without illuminating them. I was apprehensive, uneasy.

The courtyard was large enough to park and hide several vehicles. From the placing of the doors I could tell the rooms were miserly, just enough for bed and bathroom. A thin, creeping mould or lichen had composed a crude calligraphy across the walls. Most of the windows had been boarded up with plywood that showed its age, but along the east wing the boarding had been pulled off several rooms and the glass exposed. These windows were covered by white curtains or sheets, but one room was free of them and I walked over to it.

The room was empty of furniture or any other adornment, but disquietingly so—it was not simply empty but *clean*. The walls had been freshly painted an antiseptic white and the floor, carpetless, appeared dust-free. The room itself was of the type designed for motels, with interior butterfly doors, two thin doors fitted against each other in the same frame, which allowed access between rooms at the mutual desire of the occupants. One of these doorways stood open.

I tried the doorknob on this sterile nest, Room 17 according to the pitted tin digits nailed to the door, and found it locked. The knob was new, a standard, inexpensive hardware store device. I stepped back and looked up and down the row. Of the seven units from 15, in the corner, to 21 at the end, new knobs sprouted on Rooms 16 through 20. Of course—the original keys to the fifty-year old units were long gone or unavailable and new authority had been established. Each of the doors proved unyielding. I went back to 17, pulled out my set of lock picking tools and was soon able to push open one of the gates of Eden.

It was clean, all right. I pulled off my right glove, knelt and felt the floor with my fingers. No dust or plaster or grit of any kind, no scuffs or scrapes, its sheen coming from a recent coat of polyurethane. Even so, it seemed unnaturally spotless.

I rose and looked around at the walls. Hospital white, white like the buildings on Greek islands—no creamy designer elements in this treatment. Sloppy job, though—the walls had been hastily prepared and so were not smooth; they had the texture of a landscape as seen from an airliner. No care had been taken to tape off the window or wall moldings and so the paint had inevitably slopped over onto them. Nor, interestingly, had the ceiling been painted; water damaged, moldy, and malevolent, it hung there, a filthy, undulating cottage cheese.

The light switch was near the door, which was now revealed to have been fitted on the inside with a hasp and staple for a missing padlock. Was this to keep someone out—or in? I tried the light switch and a small dome on the ceiling responded with a hundred-watt glow. New bulbs, surely. But how was it that the electricity was on in a property abandoned decades before? There would be a bill and a name. Ditto for water and probably a plumber: a new set of fixtures—toilet, sink, and shower—had been installed. All were clean as a whistle. No replacement mirror had been installed over the vanity counter, though—clearly a man had been in charge of this refurbishing.

It was tough in the tiny room to get a decent photograph showing perspective and I snapped only a couple of perfunctory shots of the floor, walls, and door. I walked to the door opening into Room 16.

Except for the absence of plumbing, it was a mirror image of Room 17, clean, empty, and white with the same dirty, disintegrating canopy. Same padlock set-up on this door too, again without the lock. I hesitated. I wanted a basis of comparison, an appreciation of the effort given to transform this shoddy sleep-over into an apparent field hospital. Room 15 had not been fitted with a new outside doorknob, so I went to the butterfly door connecting it with Room 16. The lock on it was tarnished and sooty bronze, clearly the original. It was bolted and looked as though it hadn't been opened recently, if it ever had been. I walked back to the doors into Room 17. These locks were the originals as well but had been opened by either key or pick; no violence was evident to the bolt or door frame. Had they gotten their hands on a fifty-year old key after all? Or had there been a locksmith? If so, another trail to follow.

The doors connecting Rooms 17 and 18 were closed, but unbolted. With the door flush in its frame I had to squat down and pull it open with a car key wedged between door and floor. I drew it back fully and pushed its twin into Room 18.

Room 18 was somewhat different than its neighbors.

Room 18 had bullet holes.

thirty-four

With bullets there sometimes comes blood, but there was none to see here. It was unsettling, though, to discover that two of the walls had been scoured with bristles hard enough to leave swirling patterns across the arctic whiteness. The scrubbing had also left behind a faint but unmistakable odor of chlorine. No bathroom facilities here, either.

As for the bullets, two glowing eyes of daylight left convincing evidence of where a pair of them had punched through the back wall where the mirror had once been. The holes were near each other, about four feet from the floor, and I squatted to peer through them at the great outdoors. A third slug had buried itself in a stud in the wall between Rooms 18 and 17. The dry wall had been smashed out around the wood and the bullet roughly dug out, maybe with a screwdriver, the chewed stud nearly severed.

Any other shots fired in this room hadn't reached a wall.

I was sure of something else now, as well. The floors in at least these three rooms must have been covered with a painter's tarp, probably a thick plastic one. When it had been time for the Big Skedaddle, any large stuff had been muscled out into the truck. (A rental? Yet another trail. Follow the money, Woodward and Bernstein had been told. Good counsel.) Whatever remained could be wrapped up in a big plastic envelope and dragged out to complete the task.

Room 18 also sported the padlock setup at the entry, but this time a padlock was closed around the steel loop, securing the room from within. I walked to the window. The curtain was indeed a white bed sheet, queen, and still creased from its packaging. It had been nailed into the wall above the window. This one was the flat top sheet—had its bottom companion, the fitted one with stretchy corners, been used in another room? There were other holes as well, recent and spaced around the window frame so as to bore into studs. More substantial than nail holes, they had been shafts for hefty wood screws. Something else had been secured over the window. I pulled back the fabric slowly but it was unnecessary; the courtyard of the Garden of Eden was, as it must have been for decades, still and forlorn.

The door to Room 19 was unlocked and slightly ajar. I prised it toward me with my finger tips and pushed open its counterpart. No bullet holes in here, at least. But there was another round of scrubbings, this time more vigorous and wide-ranging as the swirls moved like tumbleweeds across much of the wall between Rooms 19 and 18.

Why all the cleaning? Blood had already come to mind, of course, but I was dealing with the white coats of research here and so the lineup of suspects could include other miscreants as well: Some chemical that had splashed out of bounds? A virus? Aggressive DNA? Science fiction has given the contemporary mind plenty to work with. And why in two rooms? A paranoid *and* sloppy gang.

The room was otherwise the same as its fellows, emptied and swept clean.

Almost.

Where the back wall met the floor lay a shard of glass. Had it fallen between the wall and the curling edge of the plastic tarp and so was missed during the mop up? It seemed an odd place for it to have fallen. About the size of my thumbnail, it was the thickness of a tumbler, crystal clear with a couple white lines across its tightly curved arc; the vessel couldn't have been more than an inch in diameter. Lab glass, surely, from one of those tall, thin cylinders you got to fool around with in high school chemistry. I pulled from my jacket pocket a zippered plastic sandwich bag and dropped in the fragment.

After four days I finally had one piece of physical evidence. How Marjorie would beam at me. Maybe I could put it on my refrigerator, down low for Ficus and Biscuit to admire.

Evidence of what, though?

That was it for Room 19. Tally: Two rooms clean and empty, one scrubbed clean and with bullet holes and this fourth one, scrubbed but with an overlooked piece of broken lab glass. And, I now noted with satisfaction, a fitted sheet for its curtain. They had needed to buy three sets of sheets, a purchase difficult but not impossible to trace unless some Einstein of crime had purchased each set at a different store. I took another look outside and felt again as I had when parked near Eddie Winter's the day before: alone, like a Dickens orphan, sojourning in a world miserly of spirit, intent on confounding every generous intent.

Room 20. Only the butterfly door on my side was open, its complement locked. Unable to pick the lock from this side, I used another specialty tool I had brought along. With a distressing crack the door sprung open and I lowered my foot to the floor, regretting that Ronnie and Marjorie weren't here to applaud. That final room revealed the Garden of Eden in its true spirit—dark, musty, the cement floor gritty. Except for the sheet draping the window, embarrassingly white in this setting, the space had all the cheer of a damp, barren cell in a warehouse basement. The original wall and ceiling color was long gone, smothered by a sooty, smeary film of mold that moved if you looked at it long enough.

I flicked on the switch but the light was ineffective here, pushed back toward the ceiling fixture by the oppressive room. There were more signs of activity in Room 20, though, tracks of scraping and shuffling recorded on the sandy floor, and bites taken out of the wall by the hard corners of equipment or furniture. A storage room, it seemed, unworthy of remodel.

"Where are you, Dorthea?" I asked aloud. "Larry?"

Silence. The room sucked up my words like a sponge; I wasn't sure I had even spoken them, so quickly were they gone.

There was nothing more for me to see, but I was certain the Garden of Eden would keep a police crime lab profitably employed. After checking the courtyard yet again from the window, I opened the door and stepped outside. It said something about the dreary motel that it made a soggy Massachusetts winter morning seem refreshing. I checked the ground along the front of the rooms, kicking through the soggy clumps of weeds and dead grasses.

It was under the window of Room 18 that I found it.

Exhibit B.

I thumbed it on and soon outwitted the menu, looking for the last call. It was a number I recognized because I had called it the day before. An apartment in Dorchester.

I was holding Dorthea Caulley's cell phone.

She had had the time to turn it off, saving the battery, before dropping it out the window. It had fallen through the ground cover and my foot had kicked it free. She had violated the strict charge given to her, a black woman with plenty of experience being cautious, and that transgression had been enough to bring me here.

I made a final call on it.

"Steve," I said at the beep, "we're here at the Garden of Eden. I'm calling you on Dorthea Caulley's cell phone, which I just found outside of Room 18.

"Why are we here?"

thirty-five

I made my next call to Frank. He didn't answer, but this time I left a concise, detailed message, chaining together Schuyler, Dorthea, Ronnie, her father's lunch box, and the motel. I told him not to lower the boom yet on Schuyler, desiring to postpone the conjunction of him and an attorney, who would promptly advise his client to dry out and clam up.

What would Stevie Boy do when he got my message—pass along the panic? Would someone hightail it to the Garden to touch up the cleaning, this time with gasoline and a match?

To forestall the latter, I had purposely thrown in a "we" in my message to Schuyler. Hadn't Queen Victoria referred to herself in the plural, and wasn't every man a king of his own castle? Maybe I had multiple personalities. If the "we" suggested a crime lab with tweezers and ultraviolet lights, who was I to quash the imagination?

In fact, I was reluctant to call in the local cops. I'd have to tell them a story with all the substance of a UFO sighting. Bullet holes? *Some kids coulda done that, Mister; kids have been messin' around at the ole G of E since it shut down.* Really, officer—know any youth who've recently discovered the thrill of painting four rooms and resurfacing the floors? *Well, maybe new owners did that.* I could see nothing but potholes down that road and too many questions I couldn't or didn't want to answer. And keeping an eye on the place would have to involve Rex or sub-contracting out to another agency. Neither option was attractive. For now, I would just have to rely on their apprehension to keep the bad guys away.

I retraced my path back out of the motel and then stood self-consciously at the car picking burrs and nettles from my slacks. I was only half successful. I gave a final look at the Garden of Eden, this sad, half-hearted little perversion. It had been perfect for their needs—isolated, fenced off, the courtyard protected from passing eyes. Who had found it, and how? Somebody owned the property; perhaps the answer lay there. Another challenge for Super Marjorie. Sated with questions, bullet holes, and gloom, I headed home.

I found Ronnie awake and sitting up in bed, finishing off eggs, ham, potatoes, toast and jam, and orange juice, the kind of breakfast no one has time to fix or eat anymore. That Marjorie had found all the fixin's in my kitchen confounded me.

Ronnie looked tired and a little frowzy, but markedly improved from the night before. A healthy specimen, she would not be defeated by the physical trauma. I'd seen teenagers in much worse shape, victims of vampires you'd think, who'd come through. Emotionally, though, she may well have been treading water, working hard to keep afloat. I sat down on the edge of the bed, gratified to spot Ficus keeping vigil from under a nearby chair.

"How's the survivor?"

"All right."

Sure, just like her step-mother. Her face darkened. "What about Steve?"

"You first."

"I'm stiff and sore but not as bad as I expected. It's really just my arms and shoulders." She rotated the latter in little circles to demonstrate. "I don't even have a headache."

"I'm glad. You have a bruise on the side of your head, but that'll go away. No bones were broken or anything pulled too far out of place; you were just stuck in the same, awkward position for several hours. We can go to a doctor if you want. I can probably get someone to make a house call, even in this, the twenty-first century."

"I don't doubt it," Ronnie said, "but, no, I don't think that'll be necessary."

Marjorie thought of something crucial that required her attention elsewhere and left.

Ronnie held out her hand and I took it and then carefully gathered her in my arms.

"My hero," she said softly.

We sat there clutched together for a while. You hear about those moments where nothing needs to be said, and one was actually here, in my life.

I let her fall back against the pillows. "I should have figured out sooner where you had gone," I said.

She shook her head. "Only you would apologize. I should have let someone know. I didn't think he'd flip out like that."

"He's not himself. He's got guilty knowledge that's like a tumor inside him. That's why he's drinking. He intends it to be medicinal, but his problem is spiritual so it isn't working."

"You sound like you're sorry for him."

"I'd say his future looks rather bleak."

Yes, I felt sorry for him. Choices have consequences. He had slid his tray along the cafeteria line and was about to reach the cashier. If nothing else, crossing my path again would test the Harvard dental plan.

"He's on the run now, I suppose," I added.

"You think so?"

"Well, I'm reasonably sure he's not waiting around to be arrested for battery and kidnapping." I didn't know whether bondage was a subset of kidnapping or a crime in itself. "Which brings us to law enforcement. Do you know what you want to do yet?"

No, she didn't. It was six of one, half a dozen of the other. Sure, her old beau deserved to be brought to account, but she wondered what it would cost her as well: in medical verification, in the grinding out of the trial process, and in the probing of her prior relationship with him. I would come under scrutiny as well. And, as I had, she wondered how shutting him down now would affect her father.

"Well, if you want to make a police report, sooner is better than later. You know I'm with you all the way."

She nodded. "I know."

"There were some developments yesterday. Remember the nurse that Frank told us about Friday night? She was another missing person who had worked at Longwood. Well, she had some contact with Steve before she vanished."

Ronnie rose up in the bed. "What's going *on*? Is he some kind of *serial killer*?" It was difficult for her to keep processing shock.

"No. Remember Vyridiak at the reception—something else is going on. I don't think it can go on for much longer."

"Del . . . ?"

"Yes?"

"Did you . . . take any photographs of me . . ."

I shook my head. "Wouldn't think of it."

"Thank you."

Marjorie reappeared, knocking lightly on the bedroom door, which was standing open.

"Who is it?"

"Me, of course. Del, there's a message for you on the office phone. You're going to have to figure it out."

The office? Oh, yeah. I had an office. People called it? Maybe this is why I had one—it was a really expensive way to have another phone jack.

"Okay. I'll be back," I said to Ronnie. "Ficus will keep an eye on you."

She peered around. "Where is he—or she?"

"He." I pointed him out. "He keeps a low profile."

"Bring in a massage therapist," I told Marjorie as we walked down the hall. "The table, oils, candles, ethereal music, the whole bit. Preferably a woman."

"Okay. I think the message is from Steve Schuyler."

Adrenaline.

"You're going to have to figure it out, though," she added.

"Cryptic?"

"Very."

I called the office from the kitchen punched in the requisite codes. Perhaps Marjorie had already cleaned out the queue, for Schuyler's was the only message. It was scratchy, competing with generic urban background noise. He sounded lucid but tired, rationing out his words.

"You're a clever guy, Mr. Price. I don't know how you did it. The others think it's me. You've put me in a difficult situation. But you're wrong about something. You haven't seen too much of Switzerland." There was a pause. "Tell Ronnie I'm sorry. There's no excuse. I'm sorry about Larry. About everything." A final pause. "It seems like a dream. How I wish it was just a dream. This shouldn't have happened."

That was it. I listened to it several times trying to locate its origin, but no voice in the background announced an airline boarding time. I was annoyed. Why the ambiguity? Invest five minutes for crying out loud. Was the bout between Confession vs. Concealment still slugging it out in the late rounds? Had Larry and Dorthea been spirited off to Europe, or was I being lured out of the way? Interesting phrasing, too—*enough of*—just as I had put it to him. What was the point?

Then I saw one.

A hiding place. He had thought of a hiding place for something.

"I need to go out," I told Marjorie.

"Were you able to make sense of it?" She brightened. "Are we going to Switzerland?"

I shook my head. "Don't pack your bags just yet, Heidi. This trip is strictly metaphorical. Just tell Ronnie I had to run an errand. I shouldn't be gone too long."

The quickest way to Harvard was the Mass Pike to Allston. I took the Honda, the smallest car in the Price fleet and the easiest to park. I wedged it into a spot near the Kennedy School of Government and jogged up the street to the Square and beyond to the Bio Lab Building. I nodded to Bessie and Victoria, who I was certain remembered me.

The planets had lined up in the heavens. The preternaturally beautiful Janelle was once more at the desk in the office down the hall from Schuyler's lab.

"Hi, Janelle!" I said. "Remember me? Please say yes."

She smiled. "Sure. The private eye. Nick Price?"

Close enough and a better name for a detective anyway.

"Del," I corrected, "but I'm impressed. How much would I have to pay you to sit behind my desk? I feel it would be good for business."

She smiled.

"Look, you remember I was looking for Steve Schuyler? Well, I found him. And it turns out that one of the reasons I was looking for him has to do with that tree trunk of chocolate." It was still there, keeping the filing cabinet from floating away.

"Oh!"

"So, I need to borrow it for a while. If anyone asks, tell them I have it. No, wait—tell them Nick Price has it."

She laughed and the auburn cascade rippled. What would Janelle think—what would any of Schuyler's colleagues think—if they could see Ronnie hog-tied on his bed? Harvard Schuyler vs. Somerville Steve. That's just *one* life out of balance. Multiply it by a few billion. And we don't need a Savior?

I couldn't get my hand all the way around the cardboard prism and it was too heavy and unwieldy to do anything but carry it with two hands. I strode purposefully down the hall, acknowledging the appreciative stares, holding it like it was a piece of the True Cross. I expected people to fall in line behind me.

I spotted a men's room—perfect.

Entering a stall, I laid the bar across my knees. It looked untouched, but when I started fiddling around with the end caps I saw that one had been loosened and taped. I pulled it open like a door on a hinge. The chocolate, wrapped in shiny foil, seemed solid. I placed the end on the floor and holding the package vertically, pulled the cardboard up and off the candy, leaving a standing column like a core sample taken from the earth. Unstable, though—it crumpled in the center and collapsed. It wasn't chocolate all the way through. A middle piece had been broken out, removed and something substituted in its place.

A cassette from a camcorder.

thirty-six

I was sitting on a toilet seat in a men's room at Harvard with a video tape and a three-foot candy bar. When you think of how your life might turn out, this isn't one of the pictures you see. I slid the cassette tape into my inside coat pocket and coaxed the chocolate prism back into its box. I could return it to Janelle's office but I didn't want to cede control of it. Better to lug it around.

How to view the tape? I had a camcorder back at the office but no video tape player or TV there. I'd have to watch it, initially, through the viewfinder. Was my camcorder compatible with the tape? Probably, but why chance it? I was annoyed at myself for not keeping current with technology and vowed to revisit our office electronic inventory.

The Harvard Coop, a miniature department store, stood between me and the car. I found the electronics area, held up the cassette, and asked after compatible cameras. There were three choices and I bought the middle one in terms of price. I had the clerk give me their biggest bag, large enough for both my purchase and to angle in the chocolate girder.

The last thing I was going to do was return home and screen a tape of unknown content with Ronnie nearby. I took Memorial Drive to the BU Bridge and was at my office in twenty minutes. I was anxious, breathing fast and yet I sat at my desk hesitating. Clarity and peace were fast giving way to apprehension, even fear. What was the sticker price for this knowledge?

I unpacked the camcorder and its wall outlet adapter. A contrary adapter cord wouldn't reach my desk. I moved to the moderately comfortable leather sofa, plugged into the socket there, inserted the cassette and fiddled with the controls. It didn't occur to me to consult the instructions.

I put the viewer to my eye.

And returned to the Garden of Eden.

I couldn't tell which room it was, but things were different—this one was furnished with a crowded layout of hospital and lab equipment. The camera had been mounted on a tripod and set back to capture the widest view in the small room. The central focus was on a hospital bed or table, roughly parallel to an interior wall with the connecting butterfly doors visible behind. The one on this side was closed.

A young woman with short blond hair lay on the bed, draped in white sheets and weakly conscious, moving her head and trying to arch her back. Her face was drenched in sweat and she was moaning. Her feet were elevated in stirrups. The setting became clear: She was about to give birth.

Three men and a woman, all in hospital scrubs and surgical masks stood around like awkward shepherds at the Nativity. They must have been choreographed so as to not obstruct the camera. The nurse was slender and white, clearly not Dorthea Caulley. She stood next to a tall man with a distinguished mane. Karol Vyridiak. He was standing at the head of the table, a spectator expected to stay rooted to his spot. Maybe there was an "X" on the tarp under his feet. To his right, with the bed between him and the camera was Hector Ermiston, not doing much himself but allowed to move up and down along the table.

I also recognized the final man, in profile at the foot of the bed and point of delivery. There he was with his balding pate and fringe, everyone's favorite doc, the straight shooter, a grandpa to all, staring intently down at the target.

Larry Kooyman.

I had found him.

It was fitting that Lorraine, after viewing a thousand miles of imaginary Larry movies, would find that a real one had been made.

The camcorder captured the sound, but as the tape began only the mother contributed. It was unpleasant listening to her distress while none gave comfort. Larry couldn't have been easy himself, hoodwinked to be a substitute for the late Ulrich Roessner. *Doctor* Lawrence Kooyman—MD then, PhD later—had given up his OB/GYN credentials when he jumped from medicine to research. It was his first delivery in thirty years. I still couldn't make much sense of it. Who was the mother—the daughter of a drug lord? But those guys were zillionaires who could *buy* a hospital. How had this poor woman wound up giving birth in a hastily refurbished sad sack motel?

Larry became more animated. He gave some instruction I couldn't catch because of the mask.

Ermiston's stentorian tone was easier to make out. "How are we doing, doctor?" he asked.

"*I'm not a doctor!*" Larry hissed.

And now the moment had arrived. Larry told the mother to push, but it was hard to know whether, in her hazy state, she had complied or even could. I couldn't see anything that looked like a response, but moments later something had occurred, concealed from the camera's eye by the mother's leg and the draped sheets. The shot moved slightly to the left and began to zoom in. There was an operator behind the tripod.

Of course. The fourth man.

Larry had his hands at the crucial spot, and then gasped and moved back.

"*What in the name of . . .* !" he cried.

At that moment, Hector Ermiston reached over and in, snatched the infant and held it up, this most recent arrival to planet Earth.

"*SUCCESS!*" he cried out. "*SUCCESS!* Look at it, Karol, look at it!"

And it screamed.

A thin, sharp, howling screech of chalk on the blackboard, a sound of uncomprehending, visceral pain that felt like a thick metal file being pulled across the edges of my teeth.

That it could make any sound at all was remarkable given its peculiar anatomy.

The baby had no head.

thirty-seven

I t wasn't a straight shot across the shoulders; there was a plum-sized hump that passed for a cranium. But it had a mouth and, evidently, lungs.

"What was that?" Karol Vyridiak finally exclaimed.

Ermiston had recovered the quickest and was beaming.

"I guess we'll have to call it a birthing pain," he said, chuckling. "Technically, there's no reason for a mouth at all, or the limbs," he continued as he swiveled and admired his little creation and its umbilicus, "but you can't get everything right on the first pop."

The proud father held up his mangled little creation for the camera. It couldn't have weighed more than four pounds and was the color of corned beef. There was one blinking, milky white eye on the hump but off centered, near two slits that must have been nostrils. An irregular lipless gash further below was the source of that keening cry of agony. The body was triangular, sloping inward from the tiny shoulders. Two crooked legs of different lengths hung limply from the point at the bottom. It had one stick arm that jerked around spasmodically.

Whether it was a child in any meaningful sense was open to argument. Surely its blueprints called for the dicing and splicing of genes early on in its creation—or production? What the poor woman had given birth to, if that was even the right word, was a human handbag, repulsive in its mockery of life.

And Ermiston had been ecstatic.

I suppose it depends on your definition of success.

213

I had just become a member of a highly select group, one of a half dozen witnesses to the dawn of a new genetic millennium, wherein people would be seen as stacks of Legos.

I paused the tape.

I could piece together the main points of this melodrama. Hector Ermiston's research of late had been directed at halting the body's rejection of transplanted organs. Maybe the reward was too slow in coming, the drip-drip-drip of accumulated scientific progress frustrating, unlikely to pay off in his lifetime. No Nobel Prize. No limelight. Insufficient glory for one such as him. But Ermiston was in thick with Karol Vyridiak, the head of a booming biotech firm that was beefing up its anti-rejection offerings and flush with cash. Of course, an obvious way around rejection would be the production of organs that wouldn't be rejected. Clones. Pieces of yourself kept on a shelf somewhere, out of sight, like auto parts.

An incubator would be best, impersonal and efficient, but as far as I knew machines of the sort described in *Brave New World* were still out of sight. What would be the next best thing to experiment with? An animal, perhaps, but you'd still have to overcome the rejection problem so better still would be human hosts, preferably insensate and disposable ones. A living torso would suit, with just enough brain to keep the organs moist and fresh. No rights issues. No pension plans. No back talk.

Gene manipulation of that sort didn't seem to be where Ermiston's research was tending, but maybe he was burning the midnight oil or maybe that was Ulrich Roessner's specialty. What the Higher Mind had managed to engineer was a headless human, the prototype of a line of portable organ banks: Sausage people—human casings stuffed with goodies.

The whole endeavor had been socked away in Switzerland somewhere. Perhaps a herd of Ermiston's designer piglets were used to practice on, but eventually a woman was selected as the new Eve. How much had she been told? What sort of drug regimen had been necessary to keep her from rejecting the mutant?

But something had gone wrong. Exposure of the experiment must have been imminent. How else to explain a transatlantic flight to a dead motel in Massachusetts, a stone's throw away, ironically, from a latter-day Athens of research universities? They had their own staff—an obstetrician and nurses—until a car wreck took out three of them. Helpfully, there is no shortage of nurses in the Boston area, and Dorthea Caulley had been dragooned. Finding an obstetrician to replace Roessner must have been tougher.

But then Steve Schuyler remembered something.

Something about his mentor and would-be father-in-law, Larry Kooyman. Something about his past.

"Bring your lunch with you," he had said to Larry.

So unto us a child was given. It didn't have to last long, just enough to demonstrate that a live birth could result from such extreme genetic tinkering. I couldn't fathom how so much of our birthright could be suppressed, but here was proof that it could, fresh from the womb. Perhaps the procedures used in the experiment could be doled out stealthily, piecemeal, into legitimate research. Ermiston wouldn't get his Nobel and acclaim would be delayed. But he got his drama.

Fine. Success. But what of the other actors in this play? What happens in Act Two? My hand shook as I released the pause on the camcorder, for I already knew something about the Garden of Eden.

About Room 18.

Not everyone was as ebullient as Ermiston. The mother, for one. She had managed an exhausted sigh and sunk into welcomed unconsciousness. And Larry Kooyman, for another. He tore off his mask and began immediately to remonstrate with Ermiston, who was torn between admiring his handiwork and mollifying the long-ago doctor.

"What do you mean by this?" Larry stammered. His head was bobbing back and forth between Ermiston and his patient, to whom he was still attending. The afterbirth, I figured. Larry clearly wanted to say more but was having trouble forming the words; the manifold objections to this project seemed so obvious that it was proving difficult to articulate an argument that shouldn't have to be made. Words like *criminal* and *inhuman* were eventually brought forth. He was getting wound up and soon would be wind-milling his outrage. And why not?

"Say, Larry, some fellows and I are in a jam . . . Oh, didn't I mention that

we need you to deliver the Next Big Thing at an abandoned motel? Well, as long as you're here . . ."

While Larry was demanding answers, the nurse (Swiss, or a recruit like Dorothy?) heretofore a mannequin, came to life and moved to the table. With her thumb she slid back the eyelid of the exhausted mother and puttered around doing the sorts of ineffectual things done for someone who's unconscious. Then, she turned and opened the door into the adjoining room. She disappeared but immediately returned pulling an empty wheeled bed behind her. She motioned to Vyridiak, who snapped to and helped transfer the mother to the mobile bed, which the nurse then pushed back into the neighboring room. Vyridiak shut the door behind them.

Back to center stage. It was difficult to catch the entire dialog on that first viewing, but Ermiston was losing patience. Yet what had he expected? Was it hoped that after the final revelation Larry would be quickly converted to the Ermiston world view? *Hey, it's okay—it's science!* Perhaps a generous research grant was to be dangled. Or was Larry to fold like a lawn chair to this: *"Look, we're clearing out of here pronto; the mother will be taken care of, the little Shape of the Future will be hustled off for analysis and the Garden of Eden will be swept clean—who are you going to tell? What evidence will you have? Be content with your part in history."*

Larry wasn't content. And as for evidence, he pointed straight at the camera and addressed its operator. Maybe he expected an ally.

"Steve! What have you got me into? How can you be a part of this?" His round face, the face of a genial gardener, the face ever before Lorraine's eyes, was screwed into a visage of anger and betrayal. It was this rebuke, I thought, that paralyzed Schuyler behind the camcorder; he needed something, anything, between him and Larry, something defining a separate physical and psychological boundary he could hide behind, avoiding confrontation and judgment.

And now Karol Vyridiak, the purveyor of hail-and-well-met, the seducer of investors and Hector Ermiston's tag-team partner, waded in.

"Be reasonable!" he demanded.

Of course. *There* was the solution—why hadn't anyone thought of it? It had been reason, after all, that had brought them to this place. Thanks, Karol.

"Reasonable?" Larry retorted. "You call *this* reasonable?"

"Certainly," Ermiston said. He was still wearing his surgical mask. For sanitary reasons? Because the camera was still running? Perhaps the latter, for he motioned to Schuyler.

"Steve, you can turn that thing off."

But Steve didn't turn that thing off and Ermiston continued to wave his hand at the camera while attending to Larry.

"No one has been hurt," he asserted, the travails of the mother of no moment to him.

"*That creature . . .*" Larry began.

"*That creature* has no higher brain function, Dr. Kooyman. It's not suffering in any meaningful sense of the term. One day it will *prevent* suffering, doctor."

At one time some Germans had a phrase. *Lebensunwertes Leben.* Life unworthy of Life. It had been applied to *untermenschen*, an ever expanding category of those who had been born with something they didn't deserve. And now we had a new, pre-emptive angle. Life unaware of Life.

"We can talk of this later," Ermiston said dismissively. He was getting antsy about his little wonder, which had fallen silent after its initial screaming protest.

I wasn't going to find out how this would have played out (Larry restrained until cleanup was complete?) because at that moment the door into the adjoining room was thrown open and an earlier cast member reappeared. Formerly horizontal, she was now vertical, or nearly so.

It was the mother.

She had awakened and must have found herself unsupervised. Fighting a medicated haze, she heaved herself off the bed of agony—sallow, stringy-haired, and sweaty—and confronted her tormentors, who stood frozen.

And thawed too slowly.

Ermiston had turned to face her unexpected entrance, the birthing table now between them, presenting to her the fruit of her womb.

"Brigitte?" he asked quizzically.

She screamed and grabbed the nearest object, a thin glass cylinder, maybe an inch in diameter, which stood on a cart of lab equipment. She smashed off the base against the table edge, barroom brawl fashion, sending shards flying. Then she swung her jagged spike in a violent arc at the closest target, who reacted by jerking his arms up to his face.

Too high.

She buried it in Larry Kooyman's throat.

thirty-eight

"*WHAT!*" I screamed out into the silent office. "*NO! NO!*"

I was too stunned to do much else. It was clear to me how this was going to end. I had enough facts for my mind to connect the dots and it did, well ahead of my ability to comprehend the events, or feel anything about them.

The glass tube in Larry's neck was a perfect pipeline to drain away his life's blood. It gushed freely, a dark, rich stream, the first pulse splashing across the table on which he had just brought forth a twisted life that would now cost him his. He tried to pull it out, but his fingers slid down the wet cylinder and off the end. He stood there for a moment, apparently in little pain, a look of incredulity on his face. *What was happening? How? Why?* You sit down at your desk, the one you've been at for years, to your wife's chicken salad sandwich and butterscotch cookies, and an hour later you're a standing dead man in a decrepit motel.

No time for good-byes, no time to put your affairs in order, no time for Lorraine or Ronnie, no time for anything. The end of sixty-five years of life. *Bam.* Right here and right now, without ceremony. Within a few seconds his eyes fluttered, and he sank to the floor. He was unconscious by the time he hit the fortuitously placed tarp and dead moments later.

Dead—as his wife was at home folding clothes for charity, hours before his tardiness would begin to bore into her mind.

Dead—the day before I had first heard the man's name.

Steve Schuyler finally bestirred himself. The camera wobbled as he came out from behind it, calling Larry's name. He moved around the table and

218

knelt out of sight behind it.

A face appeared at the open doorway, a round, black one. My first and last sight of her as well. Dorthea Caulley.

Ermiston, spared by the width of a table, responded now. His brain had connected the dots, too. "Here—take this," he ordered Vyridiak as he thrust his dying creation into his partner's hands. He grabbed the mother, now blank and shivering, her passion spent, and shoved her roughly into Dorthea and then propelled them both back into what I knew now was Room 18. There was noise, yelling.

"Calm down!" he was shouting ineffectually. *"Pipe down!"*

Then there was the snapping of firecrackers, a lot of them, a whole string, it seemed.

Gunshots, all but three finding a target.

Vyridiak, persuasive as a performance artist posed as a statue, continued standing there holding the limp little mass at arms length. Schuyler then reappeared, looking into the lens of the camcorder, his eyes wet. He was pulling something out of the pocket of his clinic coat, his hands covered with blood. It looked like a camcorder cassette. He had heard the gunfire. With perhaps the last lucid thought granted him in this horror, the ray of sunshine that punches through the cloud cover, he knew what he had to do. I stretched out my arm into my office, trying to reach him, but he disappeared out of the frame and my viewfinder went blank.

The end.

There were no credits.

thirty-nine

It took me several minutes to sort out the two realities fighting before my eyes; if anything, my office was more the fiction. I sat there for a while shaking and weeping. Clinically, I must have been in shock.

How are our Father's purposes fulfilled in *this?* What are the limits of freedom? Since no one dies, really, every one of us leaving mortality en route to eternal worlds prepared, justice though postponed is inevitable. Moral agency, the God-given right to choose between good and evil, cannot exist unless the consequences of bad choices are real and permitted. Justice is important, but freedom comes first. But how *much* is permitted? When is enough, enough?

It is said to be the darkest before dawn. Lorraine—how would I tell her?

I was relieved that this could be, had to be, postponed. For now, the tape was everything. Schuyler should and may have made copies but I didn't know and in any event couldn't count on retrieving any. I probably had the original; it had to go to Frank and I would be jumpy until it was in his hands.

It was mid-afternoon by now. I trotted back to my car, looking over my shoulder. I headed up Beacon. There is a small electronics store off Coolidge Corner that caters to the plentiful market of college students. The staff today was a thin, older man in frameless glasses and silver hair, likely the owner, and a student or at least someone of that age. He had dark, unruly hair and an intelligent face. I targeted him as the one more likely to be flexible. A plastic name plate, pinned on his shirt so casually that it was almost vertical, identified him.

"Hi, Heath," I said. I held up the cassette. "I need to make copies of this as fast as possible. They're for an important court case. Cost is no object. I don't have time to mess with a professional film studio. One: how could I go about making copies? And two: do you have the equipment to do it?"

They did. He explained that there were tape decks expressly designed for making fast copies but that there wasn't enough demand for the store to carry them. The simplest solution was to connect the camcorder directly to a VCR. The film would be copied onto the larger VHS cassette.

"I'll buy the tape deck and blank tapes," I said, "but I've got to make the copies here. It's only a fifteen or twenty minute recording. I'll pay you a hundred bucks."

"You don't need to do that," Heath said, obviously a liberal arts major. "Just come down here where I can plug in everything." We moved to the end of a glass counter. I suspected that the owner had been following this exchange, but seeing that he'd made a sale and that my request was not outrageous, had seen no need to intrude. I slipped the tape back into the camcorder and rewound it. The clerk broke out the VCR from its box and set it up.

"Do you want to see it on a TV screen as well?"

Goodness.

"Uh, no."

I would monitor progress through the viewfinder. We skipped the step of setting the current time on the recorder, the most important function for my mother, who had used our VCR at home as a four hundred dollar clock.

Cords soon united camera and tape deck. "Start the camcorder and then press this button here. You'll have to copy the tape in real time."

"I understand."

It took over an hour to make the four tapes, and it was torture. Life flowed by, eddying around me as customers came and went, but in my world a shrieking abomination was delivered and then returned to the womb to come forth again and again and again, Larry took it in the neck and then reported back for more of the same, dumbfounded each time, and Hector Ermiston kept reloading his gun.

I thanked the clerk and tried to replace the VCR in its box, but as with most repackaging of this sort the fit was only approximate. I put the original cassette back in my jacket pocket, dumped the copies and camcorder in a bag, tucked the new video deck under my arm and hustled back to my car, where I locked in the trunk everything but the copied tapes.

The next stop was the Post Office, around the corner on Beacon. On the way I stopped and bought a *Globe* from a vending machine. I packaged three of the tapes, using newspaper as padding, and mailed one to my home and a second to my Post Office box. The third went to Frank's home address. Just in case. For his package, I ripped off the blank last page of the VCR instructions and on it wrote a synopsis of this dark drama including all the cast members I could identify. I kept the fourth tape with me.

Outside, I leaned against the brick wall. I was relieved but had a final errand. I drove further up Beacon to Washington and then crawled down it to the police station in Brighton near St. Elizabeth's hospital. Frank wasn't there, so I gave the desk officer the original cassette and my card, explaining that it was evidence and that Lt. Kilcannon was expecting it.

At last a burden was lifted that had increased in weight moment by moment on that interminable day. I felt materially lighter, buoyant even. Funny how a four-ounce hunk of plastic had become a twenty pound brick of uranium.

How badly had I been burned?

forty

My office door was ajar, the wood around both locks gouged out, leaving a pile of splinters on the floor. My keen detective skills told me that someone had broken in.

I listened but heard nothing. I had locked my shoulder holster and gun in the car during my errands and was now, in fact, carrying them in my hand. Setting the holster on the floor I used the barrel to push open the door until I could see that the door to my private office also stood slightly open. I had closed it two hours before. I peeked behind the hallway door, through the gap between the hinges. No one.

I stepped lightly into the outer office. It seemed untouched. Now there was shuffling around in my inner sanctum and I moved toward it. As I moved past Marjorie's desk something caught my eye, something the monitor had obscured. Something that shouldn't have been left there. One more housekeeping chore. The sounds of violent shaking now came from the inner office. I stepped up to the door and slammed it open.

Hector Ermiston was wrestling with my filing cabinet. At the moment it was upright but the way he was going at it, that could soon change. He couldn't know it, but the cabinet was there as a design element, not as a secure repository—why keep sensitive documents in a piece of furniture susceptible to just the kind of treatment Ermiston was dishing out? I used it as a catch all for the kinds of stuff you later wonder how you got and why you kept. It's true that there are files in the top drawer, files of great cases like *The Giant Rat of Sumatra,* and *Rodan vs. the Smog Monster.* On slow days I might add a couple more. But Ermiston didn't have x-ray vision and so there he was with his arms around it, doing a rough rumba with the thing. He started, of course, at my entrance. He had a crowbar on top of the cabinet and now grabbed it and glared at me. He could see my gun.

"This isn't going to look good on your annual appraisal," I said.

He was battling with self-control. Like Schuyler, he was being pushed to the limit. But having seen the tape, I knew that drink wouldn't be his coping mechanism.

"You meddled in my affairs so I'm returning the favor."

He was wearing expensive designer jeans and flannel shirt. They weren't him, exactly, but they did bespeak the self-assurance of the urban Marlboro man. His aristocratic face, though, broadcast the opposite—the high forehead now red, the straight, full brows pulled in tight, and the mouth pursed in frustration and anger.

"Yes," I replied. "I certainly owe you an apology. Imagine a woman wanting to find her missing husband. I took the case for the sheer novelty of it. My first guess, of course, was that he was in Canada with key government officials."

"You don't understand the importance of my work!" He was trying not to fly apart. "You have to put things in perspective."

"Thanks. That's how I'll explain it to Mrs. Kooyman. Her husband's death was for the Greater Glory Of. She'll understand. While we're mulling the big issues, here's another one: I've got a gun and you don't."

I wiggled the pistol a little. He was at least twelve feet away. Perhaps he could have thrown the crowbar like Davy Crockett and impaled me, but I doubted that this was a skill he had picked up along life's highway. After a couple of seconds the bar dropped to the carpet. Much of the emotion fell with it.

"I thought you people were against violence," he said.

What did he know about me?

"If you mean my church, you've got us confused with the gentleman on the oatmeal box. Self-defense passes muster. Don't worry, though; I'm a fair shot and won't shoot to kill. There needs to be enough of you left for trial."

He snorted. "You don't know *what's* going to happen, Mr. Price, believe me."

"I *don't* believe you. And what I *do* know is that you won't be reporting tomorrow to your office with the big desk and lovely stained glass shrine as though nothing had happened. Nor will your pal Vyridiak."

I glanced quickly towards the other half of the office. The chocolate box was torn apart atop my desk.

"Why would you think I would lock up so important a tape in a stupid filing cabinet?"

He didn't need to respond. It had been desperation.

"You don't know where the film was shot." Had Schuyler not told him? Was he the one now fishing?

"The Garden of Eden Motel," I said. "I was there this morning."

He seemed truly surprised. "I don't believe you."

"Room 18. Two bullet holes through the back wall and one you dug out of a stud. I had you pictured as more of a five-star kind of guy."

He stared at me for several seconds. "Schuyler's family owns it," he finally said. "An estate still in dispute. I agree that it's squalid, but we only needed it for a few days. I knew he was feeding you information. You couldn't have found the motel without that stinking drunk."

It was no use trying to argue this and I didn't. I'd had trouble enough getting anyone to buy my stock.

"He was smart enough to switch the tape in the camcorder with a blank."

"Yes. His insurance, he called it. The moron. I should have taken care of him there."

"The police have the tape now. The original. Copies are on the way to their destinations, and neither rain nor sleet nor snow will stop them. I have an extra copy, though, if you want it. You know, something to share with the guys in Cell Block C."

"I thought you were coming to see me first. We could have made an arrangement. You could have named your own price—you still can. What exactly do you think the tape will prove, Mr. Price?"

"Everyone is going to see it," I countered. "You tell me what they're going to think."

And that was it, the sticking point. He was right—who knew what the legal status of the tape was? Exhibit A or inadmissible? But it would be shown, and he knew it. Everyone in the global scientific community would see the latest episode of Nazi Doctor.

His silence was his answer.

"I don't know what to tell you, Hec. Some days you're the dog and some days you're the hydrant."

He didn't respond.

"I'm curious—do you even care about the women you shot?"

"What women?" And he smiled. A V-shaped, no-lipped, reptilian smirk. A smile straight out of hell. I didn't know facial muscles could deform a face so. It scared me.

"Fine," I finally said. "Police time. You know what? I think I'll put you in the bathroom where I know you'll be safe. No windows." It was off the reception office. I motioned with the gun. "Through the door. Walk backwards through it."

His eyes flashed for a moment.

I backed him out the door, closer to him but still several feet away. On the way to the little bathroom, we had to pass by Marjorie's desk. He moved over to brush by it, grabbed the 9mm pistol he had left there by the monitor and fired from the hip. He was quick and smooth and would certainly have hit me had there been any bullets in the gun—which there weren't because I had removed the clip and ejected the chambered cartridge. He looked down at the gun and turned it sideways, as though expecting it to speak up and apologize. Then he looked up at me, his face empty.

I was generous.

"No bullets? Here, I'll share."

I pulled the trigger, twice.

My gun gave no apology.

forty-one

Frank pointed his chin toward Ermiston. I had called the police station in Brighton and told them to send some uniforms over and to notify Frank as well. He had arrived about five minutes after the first cops. A couple of them were now holding the slouching and wheezing Dr. Mengele under the armpits, preparing to frog march him out.

"He's probably deaf," I said. "I fired a round past either side of his head. He ran into my fist, too. I've sort of had it with him," I confessed.

The shots had utterly discombobulated the guy. *Spitting fire! Screaming muzzle!* The world an exploding kaleidoscope, surely death had come. He had pulled his head down between his shoulders, grimacing. I stepped in, tossed the gun from my right hand to my left, and let him have it just below the rib cage, a hard knuckled fist with plenty of shoulder and leg behind it. He had crumpled in on himself and then down to the floor, his red face a silent scream.

Frank nodded. "I appreciate the restraint."

"It's new carpet," I said.

He nodded again. "Where did the slugs go?"

"Into the sofa."

I had actually considered the trajectory and aimed low over his shoulders; I couldn't count on hitting studs twice, and sending hot lead through the walls didn't seem neighborly. I hoped the unusually comfortable sofa could be healed without leaving scars.

"And he was between you and the door with an empty gun," Frank said flatly, as flat as his face as he looked at me. It's tough to get anything past Frank.

"I have to draw the line at being whacked in my own office. It's unpro-
fessional."

He nodded. "So then, it's off to the hoosegow with him," he observed as
we watched the two officers haul off Ermiston.

I smiled. Sometimes, if you wait long enough . . .

The remaining pair of cops was huddled together. It would soon be
Statement Time. I'd thought about that, too.

"Larry?" Frank finally asked, looking off to the side.

I shook my head. His gaze dropped to the floor.

"Not in Canada?"

"No. Concord."

"Let's go into your office."

We walked in but left the door open. I described to him the finished
puzzle, What Went With What. The experiment in Switzerland that had to
be relocated at the last minute. How Steve Schuyler had a hiding place on
some vacant family property. How, soon after, the souls of Karl Roessner and
two of his assistants had been required of them. How Larry, briefly an OB/
GYN in an earlier life, had been beguiled into helping a friend, what it produced, and what it had cost him. And finally how Ermiston, facing trouble
enough at persuading the bit players to silence, had realized at Larry's death
that a permanent solution was required. He gave life; he could take it, too.

Frank worked another stick of gum into his mouth.

"Mary, and Joseph, and all the Saints," he said. This was wild even for
him.

"Well put," I said. I had saved the kicker. "It was all filmed."

He stopped chewing and looked at me.

"They had a camcorder set up. The shootings occur off camera, but
still . . . The original tape is at the station waiting for you. I mailed a copy to
your house as well."

"Schuyler finally spilled his guts?"

"He's letting the video speak for him. I have no idea where he is now."

Steve Schuyler had been hoping that all the unpleasantness would somehow disappear, the vice crushing his conscience would relax, and he could
awaken to a new day, full of fresh resolve to do good works, and so atone.

But then, out of the blue, I had arrived—and kept showing up like
clockwork to give the handle another half-twist. When I found the motel,
that was it.

"How did you piece all this together?"

"The power of chocolate, Frank."

It came together because Estelle Westerbad had run into a Harvard acquaintance who was only at Longwood that day because of a baby shower. Because of a pair of skis. Because out of fifteen hospitals a missing nurse had worked at Longwood and so caught Frank's eye. Because she had made a last call to a live-wire roommate. Because God knew what Hector Ermiston was going to do long before Hector did and had made small, but crucial, provisions.

"I need a favor," I said.

"What?"

"I want you to leave me out of this as much as possible. You can take the credit, or the police, whatever."

He was incredulous. His mouth actually fell open and his gum dropped out.

"You've got to be *kidding!* There isn't even a case yet for us to clear! Until five minutes ago we didn't even have a crime!"

He stopped and backed off a little. "Del, you figured this whole thing out in—what—five days? I haven't had time to *begin* getting the phone records. I still have the missing persons report! You barely talked to any of these guys. You ought to get some kind of award. No one else could have done what you did. No one."

I continued patiently. "Lorraine hired me to poke around. I did. I contacted several family friends. One was Schuyler. I left my card. Later, he called me and in a fit of remorse told me where a tape was and I turned it over to the police. Ermiston thought I had it and confronted me here and filled in some of the blanks. The police made the arrest and the DA will file charges."

"Looking at it that way, you hardly did anything!"

"Let's look at it that way."

"You're crazy."

"What do you want me to do, Frank—ride this to glory? What message does that send to Lorraine? This story is going primetime—genetic voodoo, a dark motel, headless babies—it's a screenwriter's jackpot. Maybe something good will come of it, but Lorraine is going to have to go into hiding for awhile. Can you imagine reporters sticking microphones and cameras in her face and asking her how she *feels?*"

Such is the poverty and callousness of contemporary culture that the emotional distress and embarrassment of others count as entertainment.

Frank shook his head again but was beginning to see how it could work out. Schuyler was the only one who could contradict me, but how motivated would he be? He wouldn't want Ronnie brought up and so might tone it down. We'd see. I couldn't control everything. I remembered his message left on my office phone and hoped it wouldn't be accidentally erased in all the confusion.

"I want to make a statement later," I said. "I need to see Lorraine and Ronnie first."

"Sure. That I can understand." He went out to work it out with the officers.

I called Marjorie. "There have been developments. Bring Ronnie over to Lorraine's as soon as you can."

It was a dark journey. On a few occasions I had been the one to bring word to parents of the death of their child, and this was just as heartbreaking. Another dreary afternoon had shrunk away into dusk. I pulled in at the Mall at Chestnut Hill so Marjorie would arrive before me. I sat there for a half hour in the parking lot looking through the windshield, splotched with rain, at bare spindly trees, harsh unfriendly lights, and the sheen of wet asphalt.

Our world.

They were there waiting for me at the oak kitchen table, Lorraine in a bright green blouse, Ronnie in a black one, and Marjorie in white. No matter how I would have walked in, no matter what mask I could have worn, the news would still have clung to me like the smell of smoke.

"Larry's dead, isn't he?" Lorraine said.

It wasn't even a question; she wasn't looking for contradiction. No longer nervous or furtive, she was the calmest one in the room, as though a storm had passed and now the damage must be faced. Where had this strength come from?

"Yes."

Ronnie gasped. She was not calm. I realized how little I knew of her, of her storms. The past few days for her had been one punch after another with a kiss in between. She burst into tears, sobbing. It was now Lorraine who reached out to her and pulled her in.

She looked straight at me. "He died that Wednesday, didn't he?"

"Yes, he did."

"I always knew it," she said.

forty-two

So Hector Ermiston did the Perp Walk.

As I left for Lorraine's, Frank had had the Waltham police pick up Vyridiak at Prime Meridian as a person of interest. His pal Ermiston hadn't tipped him off. Hector was desperate, thinking only to deal with me and the tape, and couldn't spare a thought for the CEO. Part of the Darwinian struggle, I guess. A shaken Vyridiak was waiting for Frank who, after viewing the tape, came calling for him. Steve Schuyler was sought as well.

Bail was set for Ermiston on burglary and assault charges. The DA's office, hoping to get his passport, attempted to persuade the judge that with a probable murder charge hanging over him, the Alps would be beckoning. No go, but the respected scientist was admonished not to leave the state. Ermiston gave assurances and posted bond.

And promptly disappeared.

When Harvard authorities came looking for him at his office, they found an explosion of shattered stained glass. A pair of skis lay among the ruin.

I wasn't surprised by his flight and was of course concerned; I thought it possible he bore me a grudge. But what was I to do—live in fear? I took the obvious precautions and warned Marjorie. Locks, watchfulness, and prayer were put into effect. Of the three, clearly the last was most important. A God could defeat the armies of Pharaoh could probably frustrate the likes of Hector Ermiston.

The story was fleshed out over time. Karl Roessner turned out to be something of a rogue researcher, like Ermiston willing to cut corners en route to the future. As with Larry, it had been medicine first and then genetics, but Roessner had not retreated from his practice. He had indeed been briefly associated with Schliemann-Schmidt but had been turned out for "irregular practices." Where the Project had been staged prior to its fruition at the Garden of Eden remained unknown, as did whatever or whoever had flushed them out of Europe. No one came forward, nor could any documentation of the Project be found; it was surmised that there must be confederates in hiding.

With Roessner dead and Ermiston gone, their partnership had proved difficult to explore. Ermiston had made many flights to Geneva during the preceding three years, but his movements while there were tougher to trace. He always rented a car. The Swiss police tried to make something from the mileage driven but really, what could they do? He stayed at hotels and ate in restaurants. So what?

The mother's name was Brigitte Brolet and she had been a graduate student in genetics and a part-timer at Schliemann-Schmidt. Perhaps she had been part of the reason why the firm began looking askance at Roessner, but the biotech had picked a lane and stuck to it, marginalizing the pair as former peripheral associates and offering nothing else.

The investigation into the death of Larry Kooyman and presumed deaths of Dorthea Caulley, Brigitte Brolet, and the third Swiss nurse, Geli Markel, was now in the hands of the police, and it proceeded fitfully. They had the tape and the Garden of Eden and they had me, but this trio did not persuade the District Attorney to prosecution. Vyridiak had clammed up after denying all and declaring the tape a hoax—whatever was on it. But he was a walking nervous meltdown and prosecutors could smell a plea bargain. I stuck by my story as a minor cog, a mere conduit between players and police. It was an easy sell. They didn't seem to view me as much of an investigator either, and this time I was content. Who they wanted was Steve Schuyler, without whom there would likely be no accounting to justice, at least in this life. Almost the entire weight of this fiasco had been shrugged off onto his shoulders.

He couldn't take it.

A week after Ermiston took a powder, Steve Schuyler walked into the police station in Billings, Montana, making sure to look directly into every ceiling surveillance camera. He plopped down two video tapes and a lengthy written confession, complete with all the confirmation he could muster—truck rental records, some hardware store receipts, an account at Prime Meridian from which money may have hemorrhaged, and a few Swiss papers relating to Roessner.

One tape was a VHS copy of the original he had given me. With the video equipment in his apartment he had made copies in the same way as I had done. The second tape was a later Schuyler production, this one featuring the filmmaker seated in front of yet another camcorder with a blank wall behind him. He had shaved and combed his hair but couldn't hide the face of a sailor coming off a bender. He looked fifty. The statement started off a ramble, a blend of narrative, regret, and apology, but it managed to cohere into a useful declaration. He had been brought on board belatedly because of his access to the Garden of Eden (did they have a good laugh at that?) and he described his seduction by Ermiston into So Great A Cause. Vyridiak came off as a puppet, a homunculus, his soul a wholly owned subsidiary of Hector Ermiston. They had apparently grown up together. Schuyler became more agitated as he related his recruitment of Larry by cell phone that noon on Wednesday. The confession confirmed nearly everything I had surmised, providing a small, grim satisfaction.

A favor. Larry Kooyman died because of a favor.

He described both the outfitting of the field hospital at the Garden of Eden and the frantic clean up. Everything, including the bodies, had been dragged from the rooms and dumped into a rental truck. Ermiston had driven off with the whole of the carnage but not before fishing Larry's keys out of his pants pocket. Steve was instructed to retrieve Larry's car in the dead of night. The idea was to leave the impression that Larry had driven off to parts unknown. Schuyler actually made a couple of late night passes by Larry's house in the Honda, but couldn't face Lorraine. Ermiston picked up the car on Saturday and disposed of it. It hadn't occurred to me to look for it in Schuyler's neighborhood Thursday or Friday, and I felt a sting of anger. Dumb, dumb.

He authenticated the videotape he had filmed that day at the motel, detailed how he had switched out the original with a blank tape before Ermiston had grabbed the camera, and how he had hidden it and tipped me off. It was my only appearance in the documentary. Whether he sought to deny me credit or was giving me an out, I could not know. Ronnie was not mentioned at all. I was grateful now that we had not reported her ordeal to the police, another graphic tabloid tale forestalled. Ronnie's humiliation would have been broadly enjoyed, and I would have come off as Tarzan. Finally, Steve apologized to his colleagues, to his mother, and to Lorraine. He hoped that science would be well served by this cautionary tale of the capabilities of genetic engineering and that the evidence offered would be sufficient to serve justice.

It would have to be. After dropping off his package—the tape and papers pushed snugly into a black vinyl lunch box with a cartoon mouse on the lid—Steven James Schuyler, M.S. Boston College, PhD Harvard, a man walking on wet cobblestones in new shoes, returned to his room in a cheap motel outside Billings and hung himself. He could not shed his millstone and knew of no other shoulders on which to roll it.

I did know of shoulders that could have borne it. Could I have convinced him?

A worker in the Billings Sheriff's office whose business instincts trumped his ethics made a copy of both tapes and sold them to a network. They were aired just before formal criminal proceedings had commenced. Larry's death was edited out by a kindly media. From there both tapes took up residence on the Internet, fully intact. I turned over my copy of the tape to my attorney, who issued a brief statement on my behalf describing my humble, limited role as messenger boy. You'd think my ambition was fulfilled in getting out of bed each day. I was largely ignored but closed up the office for a while anyway. It was hardly a sacrifice, although Frank continued to view this self-effacement as akin to mastering a difficult violin piece only to then lay down the instrument.

And where had Brigitte been laid to rest, her distraught parents wanted to know? It was the same question smothering the minds Geli Markel's family, as well as Lorraine, Ronnie, and Carmen Rosario. Lorraine had assumed her husband's body would be recovered—why wouldn't it be? It was one more blow then, almost as cruel as her husband's death, to learn that Ermiston had retained sole responsibility for this morbid task and had revealed his mind to no one.

The fate of the creature was likewise unknown, but it couldn't have survived. Perhaps its corpse had been frozen for future admiration.

I had sat down with Lorraine and Ronnie, of course, and told them the story of their husband's and father's death, carefully but truthfully. Lorraine had listened quietly, her head lowered. Ronnie withdrew into a shell.

"There are no words for my sorrow," I told her.

She raised her head. "You've done a remarkable job, Mr. Price. I'd rather know the truth, and I don't think I would have had it without you. I think you've downplayed your role. It sounds like all any of them had to do was keep quiet. I'm sure God was guiding you."

She was right about the help, certainly, but it had still been a rocky path for each of us, Ronnie, Marjorie, and me. But the darkest path had been trodden by Lorraine; half of her soul had simply disappeared one afternoon while she was folding clothes.

Ecclesiastes: *Who gathers knowledge, gathers pain.* Knowledge is a burden; it makes demands, confers responsibility. It's what Adam and Eve opted for, rejecting perpetual doe-eyed innocence. Had it been worth it to them? To us?

Before the drama had begun to unfold in its lurid and inaccurate retelling I had found an attorney for Lorraine. He prepared a statement affirming her and Larry's complete ignorance of the Project and encouraging public and media sensitivity to her loss.

My estimation of media sensitivity was such that I hustled Lorraine out of sight as fast as a submarine dives at the arrival of an enemy destroyer. The shades were drawn tight once again at Fortress Kooyman and yellow police tape encircled the house, lacking only a bow at the front door. Lorraine moved in with Marjorie and Ned.

I wanted to give the news in person to Jared Timmerman, Estelle Westerbad, and Carmen Rosario. To the first two I gave the more detailed explanation; I wasn't sure whether Carmen could even process such information. Timmerman recoiled at the horror delivered at the Garden of Eden and was shaken by the circumstances of his old friend's death; every feature of his face dropped and he buried his face in his hands. He asked no questions and at the end asked me to leave.

"Thank you, Mr. Price, for your consideration. It was decent of you. I'm sure we're in for nothing but distortions hereafter. Allow me to help Lorraine in any way that I can." He shut his office door behind me.

I visited Estelle at her home in Quincy. An appreciator of straight-shooters, she got the best aim I could muster. She too was shaken but a lifetime of self-possession did not desert her.

"How could Steve do that?" she wondered in indignation.

"I'm sure he was as shocked as anyone." It was about as much as I could allow.

I left it with her to tell the lab members and warned her to expect zealous reporters and well-aimed cameras.

I took Marjorie with me to comfort Carmen, who got the *Reader's Digest* version. Incapable of masking any emotion or calculating the liabilities of revealing her every thought, Dorthea's roommate burst into howling tears.

"Dorthea dead! No! No! No"

Dealing with Carmen at the best of times was delightful but demanding; in *extremis* it was like being trampled by wild horses.

"I'm afraid so. She died trying to help a woman who was giving birth." I left it at that. "You were right—the man at Eddie's was not a good man. Something went wrong at the . . .clinic and the witnesses were shot. What the men were doing was wrong.

"Having a baby was wrong? Was it an *abortion?*"

We were wading into quicksand. I got her to call her sister and a friend, and we waited until the latter arrived. I had already decided to bankroll Carmen's foray into fashion design but would have to wait to tell her. I thought she had a shot at it. The Lord has a way of watching over the earnest Carmens of this world.

With Lorraine safely ensconced at Marjorie's, Ronnie returned to New York. For her it had been two weeks of buffeting across the board—physical, emotional, psychological, even spiritual.

She didn't know what to do with me.

"I'm not really religious," she said. "I mean, I believe in God and all that, but I've never been very comfortable at church. And now here you are, a Mormon. You're not even someone I'd normally be interested in. Yet here you are, the greatest guy. I still say you're too good for me. I'm afraid I'd disappoint you."

Then don't, I thought.

"I can see I'm going to have to make good on the felony plan," I responded.

"No. You wouldn't be you anymore. I'm confused," she concluded.

So was I, but less than I had been. I'd known her all of three days, but it was one of those relationships that seems timeless, an association resumed rather than initiated. But I wasn't, after all, going to chuck everything in the throes of love. I wouldn't marry Ronnie on spec. There was still a big tug there, though, and the future was opaque. Who knew? Maybe she'd miss me in New York. Maybe I had ruined her for other men. I was, after all, an A minus.

"I'll come visit you," I said. "You can show me the big city. Maybe we can get mugged together."

She brightened. "Of course! I'd like that. Maybe I can convert you to a heathen. Just kidding."

"Take your best shot. You'd be saving me ten percent of my income."

I'd give it a while. It would take time for her to sort through the deaths of her father and former fiancé. She held neither against me, certainly, but I was bundled up with them in a package deal that had to be carefully separated over time. For now, an amicable parting was going to have to do.

I have little doubt that the extended Schuyler clan would have preferred to quickly settle their legal feud to the extent that the Garden of Eden could be obliterated from the surface of the earth. I'm sure they would have torn it down themselves with their bare hands—and could have gotten plenty of help from the equally mortified trustees of Harvard. As it was, the embarrassing structure, now the butt of jokes as the new Bates Motel, was instead put under an international media siege. It had to be guarded day and night. A second chain link fence was put up around the first. It was higher and crowned with razor wire. Instead of a flaming sword, there were guard dogs and the sentinels were hardly cherubic.

forty-three

No, it had not ended well at all. Good thing he had prepared for every outcome.

"Sure," he had told the court through his attorney, "you can count on me. I'm not going anywhere, your Honor. I'm a respected scientist and have been the victim of an extortion plot by a sleazy private detective. I intend to fight these charges."

With that, he had walked out of the courthouse, gone straight to his apartment, and patiently fed a serious stack of documents into the fireplace. He packed a few things—he would buy a new life at the other end—secured three false passports in a pouch around his neck and drove off in his blue BMW.

He stopped briefly at his office to retrieve and dispose of a few incriminating items. He left no instructions for the lab. He cared nothing for it. His life's work—interminable, all that effort so he could toss, without glory, a few grains into the silo of knowledge. Genetics hadn't paid off after all, except for a brief moment in a broken-down motel. (Well, that and the cash cow that was Prime Meridian, a portion of whose assets now rested comfortably in several off-shore accounts he had created under aliases.) He took none of the photos. Before he left his office for the last time, he slaked his anger against the luminous Gemini glass. He would not leave it behind for others to enjoy.

At JFK in New York he found himself telling the ticket agent that, yes, he intended to enjoy his trip to Montevideo. Did they speak Spanish there or Portuguese, he wondered? He was surprised and a little amused that he didn't know.

No matter. His five-star stay there would be brief before he moved on under another identity.

There was plenty of time on the flight to reflect.

If Ulrich hadn't imperiled the Project and forced its flight into the wilderness. If a truck driver had controlled his rig. If Brigitte hadn't freaked out. If a Hungarian family had moved to Akron rather than Cleveland or had just stayed put and waited out Hitler.

But to speculate along those lines was fruitless. Who knows where anything begins? More concretely, it had been Schuyler, of course, who had been the weak knee. The convenience and serendipity of the ancient motel had blinded him to his colleague's accompanying liabilities. Conscience and booze were never a good pairing. But Schuyler would have held up without that meddling Mormon gumshoe, long enough, at least, for Hector to plan a propitious dispatch for the sodden loser. Maybe a drug overdose or a fall over his balcony. There just hadn't been enough time. Why, oh why, hadn't he killed Schuyler with the others? Had he just assumed the young scientist would behave reasonably, appropriate to the new reality? Or had he simply needed the third set of hands to empty the Garden of Eden? When he had grabbed the camcorder (dragging with it the tripod it was attached to) it hadn't occurred to him that the cassette might have been switched out. Sometimes people surprised you.

He could see how Price had done it, using Schuyler's own weakness against him. Freshen up your drink there, Steve? *It had been* in vino veritas *all the way. What other possibility was there? Maybe Price had found the cassette after Schuyler had passed out, clawing through all those piles of junk in his condo.*

Like any rational person he detested religion and, even more so, personal devotion. Mormons and their golden book. New and improved revelation from a long dead Jesus, no less. Was there no end to gullibility? Wobbling at the edge of a non-descript, outlying galaxy, the earth was a mediocre little marble that God Himself couldn't find again if He wanted to! It was hardly a coincidence that Mormon and moron differed by only a letter. And they were just like all other religionists, hypocrites to the core. Weren't they against alcohol? And yet Price had had no compunction in plying Schuyler with the poison. That's what you got with that type.

And money. Churches were all about the money. You couldn't be saved unless you ponied up. Price was rumored to be independently wealthy, yet clearly he had gotten a good sniff of the green at the reception and wanted more, more than he had already fleeced from Kooyman's wife, and had hinted that the shakedown would take place that Monday at the lab. Instead, they had found themselves in the detective's office and then it had been he, not Price, who had jingled the coin. And had been rejected. Curious. Perhaps Price had switched targets to Karol, a more obvious Midas, and would use the arrest as leverage, offering Karol his freedom for a fee. That must have been it.

And what of that drama Sunday night? He had been tailing Schuyler but then had run into the detective hauling the Kooyman daughter out of the condo. Why was she there? Had she been doing a Mata Hari on poor old Steve, part of a tag team with the detective? Perhaps she had been sent in to snout out the tape and found herself in need of rescue from he-man Price. Too bad he'd lost the getaway car after a red light. Had Schuyler been a brute to the girl? He grinned at the thought.

Well, Steve had already choked on his just desserts—would that he had tightened the noose sooner! A little more rope there, Stevie Boy? He would have been only too glad to have helped.

He pushed back his first class seat, swirled the ice cubes in his bar glass, and sighed.

No clues and no leads, yet here he was forced into exile by a parasite with his inherited ease playing Sherlock Holmes as an amusement. The memory of being duped and then gut-slugged by the creep burned with a white heat. And then to be hauled about like a sack of laundry, photographed front and side like the common scum of criminal. So many putting hands on him that day. Well, he would soon repay Mr. Del Price with a one-way ticket back to his God. These things could be arranged from anywhere.

And good luck finding the bodies. He'd had to hustle that Wednesday afternoon. The cleanup had been onerous—muscling equipment around, dragging bulky plastic cocoons across the floor, keeping Vyridiak and Schuyler on task, scrubbing away the blood—eased only because neat packing in the rental truck was no longer necessary. He had had to return to the rental agency for a rig to tow his car behind the truck. Then a quick trip to Rhode Island for explosives. He bought topographic maps and located an abandoned quarry in Maine, parked the truck fifty yards into a cave in the wee hours of Thursday and set off the dynamite. The proof of his guilt was now buried deep in the earth.

On Friday he had shipped his little genetic plaything, packed in dry ice, to an address in Austria.

Karol—well, alas. He had been Karol's spine for forty years. Enough. Let the Hungarian sock puppet stand on his own now, face the consequences if he *could of his so-called life. Hector wouldn't be there to support him for this final exam.*

He looked out the window of the plane. Blue skies, bright sunshine and a fluffy white comforter beneath. It was good to get out of dreary Boston.

Brazil, he was certain, was Portuguese. For some reason, he thought they spoke Spanish in Uruguay.

forty-four

So I baptized the babe.

Lorraine, that is. Ronnie wasn't having any of it.

Mormonism—the twenty-first century!

She came up for the service, though, and paid attention. She liked seeing me dressed in white.

"It suits you," she said.

"There's another place where you can see me in white," I told her.

"Where's that?"

"Maybe you'll find out someday."

She looked confused, but figured it must be something churchy. "Maybe," she said doubtfully.

What Lorraine wanted was to feel whole again, whole with her husband. A welcomed member of the universe instead of a sad little accident. The restored gospel gave her that and more hope besides.

Absent Ermiston and Schuyler there was only one person left to stand trial and he wasn't up to it. His attorney thought he would skate away from a conviction, but Karol Vyridiak wasn't going to be ground zero for public and press scrutiny no matter how problematic the evidence. He, too, knew what was on the tape from the Garden of Eden and, perhaps, faced as well one of the keenest of human fears—that of being found out, that others will discover we aren't what we seem. He pled out to a conspiracy charge and fiscal malfeasance and received a three-year sentence. He was expected to serve nine months.

Before taking the plea, the astigmatic visionary had stepped down as

CEO of Prime Meridian "for the good of the company." He had had little choice—the other option, vigorously argued for by several directors who, with clearer views, could see the immediate future of the company, was to be thrown through the plate glass window of his seventh-story suite. I thought it a sound alternative.

The bodies of those ushered into the spirit world at the Garden of Eden hadn't been found; neither, indeed could the rental truck be located. Police were still investigating self-serve storage places by the rental date of their units. Had the bodies been removed first and buried elsewhere? Speculation along this line could be maddening, but with her baptism Lorraine had given away that burden along with many others, a different kind of package deal. On the other side, Larry's thoughts and prayers were doubtless inclined toward his wife, as hers were to him here. They would be reunited.

A year later I made a Saturday excursion to two temples. Two different visions of this world. I stopped first at Prime Meridian and stood again at the foot of the huge crystal globe representing life and the planet. Vyridiak had already been released from a minimum security prison and had missed the first appointment with his parole officer. He could not be located. Was he hiding in some exotic land where he could stretch a buck? Or, terrified at facing life with only his own empty internal resources, had he hooked up again with Hector Ermiston? Would the latter even take him back?

Surprisingly, Leigh, the Teutonic beauty, was still there as the Saturday flack. She had re-choreographed her hair from swoosh to sensible. It hung straight to her shoulders and swayed when she moved her head.

"Can't you get another job?" I asked.

"This suits for now," she replied.

"Remember me?"

"Sure. The detective. You were here just before the police came for Dr. Vyridiak. Did you have anything to do with that?"

"I brought him down single-handed."

She smirked. "I bet." Another fan.

"How's the company?"

"It took quite a hit, but it looks like we'll make it. Reporters were here all the time looking for hidden laboratories." She laughed. "One of our guys wanted to dress up in a Frankenstein outfit and lurch around the lobby."

I laughed as well. "I love it. A man after my own heart."

"Well, not everyone *here* loved it." She continued. "Dr. Vyridiak told everyone that PM had nothing to do with any of it."

"Except for stacks of PM money."

"Well, yeah, except for that. He meant the research; we weren't doing, you know, weird stuff. The reporters didn't seem to believe it."

"They didn't want to. That wasn't the truth they were looking for."

I marveled one last time at the cellular components represented within the glowing sphere. The essence of life is its ability to increase and reproduce, giving variety and interest to the face of the earth. There are over 10,000 species of ants—wouldn't a couple of dozen do? From amoeba to man, God is preaching a sermon: His work is about life and variety and its eternal continuation.

To which end I reported to the other temple, a white granite one set on a hill in Belmont overlooking Route 2. Marjorie and Ned had come. There I was baptized as proxy for and in behalf of Lawrence Kooyman. It was then up to him to accept it or not, as free on the other side as on this to hearken or not to the gospel message. A little later I joined hands with Lorraine Kooyman across an altar as a proxy again for her husband and they were sealed as husband and wife, no more to be parted. Larry could decide if he wanted to accept that, too. We all rather felt he did.

A story of ancient lineage is told of a boy dropped into a pit by his brothers and then bound up for slavery in a foreign land. For good measure he was then unjustly thrown into prison. A series of events unlikely to engender much confidence in Higher Powers. But Joseph was a different sort of fellow and a funny thing happened. From the pit he became Prime Minister of Egypt. And, years later, during a famine, his brothers made their own way to Egypt and knelt before him, their little brother, not recognizing him.

Joseph had several options at that point. He might have dug a nice deep hole for the supplicants. We can imagine him standing near the edge peering into its depths.

"Ring any bells, guys?"

That's one thing he might have done, but it wasn't what he did.

He forgave them. He had seen the design on the Weaver's loom.

"You thought evil against me," he told them, "but God meant it for good."

✍

We were standing outside on the brightly flowered temple grounds, but I was apart from the others. Intending to gaze at the western horizon, instead I found myself looking again into the eyes of Steve Schuyler that last time at Ronnie's rescue.

Behind them was a Pandora's box of emotions, but I had not seen hope.

What had he seen in mine?

But his fall wouldn't mar this happy day and the memory receded. The sun threw its beneficence across all of New England and shadows fled. Birdsong added sparkle and it was warm, there, on a green hill overlooking the rest of the world.

Marjorie found me and walked over.

"You're all smiles."

"Blue skies," I said.

discussion questions

1. What is the significance of the novel's title?
2. How are the two quotations introducing the book relevant to the story?
3. What are the recurring themes in *Shadows of Eden*?
4. The detective, Del Price, is concerned with maintaining his integrity as a Latter-day Saint. What challenges does he face? What moral dilemmas does he acknowledge? Is he consistent in his conduct? What are his strengths and weaknesses?
5. How is the contrast between coincidence and divine design developed in the novel?
6. What characters do you identify with?
7. Did you like the author's writing style? Why or why not? Where is it effective?
8. How is the role of religion in the modern world commented on in the novel?
9. What do you think the novel is about?
10. Do you think that genetic engineering is as dangerous as the author seems to think it is?

about the author

Tim Bone was born and raised in Spokane, Washington. He has degrees in history and religious studies from Brigham Young University and Boston University. He currently works for the Federal government and lives with his family in the Seattle area. *Shadows of Eden* is his first novel.